TERMINAL

ELLIE JORDAN, GHOST TRAPPER, BOOK FOUR

by

J.L. Bryan

Published 2015
JLBryanbooks.com

Terminal by J.L. Bryan
Copyright 2015 J.L. Bryan
All rights reserved.

This book or any portion thereof may not be reproduced or used in any manner whatsoever without the express written permission of the publisher except for the use of brief quotations in a book review.

All characters appearing in this work are fictitious. Any resemblance to real persons, living or dead, is purely coincidental.

ISBN-10: 1511691611
ISBN-13: 978-1511691611

Acknowledgments

I appreciate everyone who has helped with this book. My beta readers include authors Daniel Arenson and Robert Duperre, as well as Isalys Blackwell from the blog Book Soulmates. The final proofing was done by Thelia Kelly. The cover is by PhatPuppy Art. Most of all, I appreciate the book bloggers and readers who keep coming back for more! The book bloggers who've supported me over the years include Danny, Heather, and Heather from Bewitched Bookworks; Mandy from I Read Indie; Michelle from Much Loved Books; Shirley from Creative Deeds; Katie and Krisha from Inkk Reviews; Lori from Contagious Reads; Heather from Buried in Books; Kristina from Ladybug Storytime; Chandra from Unabridged Bookshelf; Kelly from Reading the Paranormal; AimeeKay from Reviews from My First Reads Shelf and Melissa from Books and Things; Kristin from Blood, Sweat, and Books; Aeicha from Word Spelunking; Lauren from Lose Time Reading; Kat from Aussie Zombie; Andra from Unabridged Andralyn; Jennifer from A Tale of Many Reviews; Giselle from Xpresso Reads; Ash from Smash Attack Reads; Ashley from Bookish Brunette; Loretta from Between the Pages; Ashley from Bibliophile's Corner; Lili from Lili Lost in a Book; Line from Moonstar's Fantasy World; Lindsay from The Violet Hour; Rebecca from Bending the Spine; Holly from Geek Glitter; Louise from Nerdette Reviews; Isalys from Book Soulmates; Jennifer from The Feminist Fairy; Heidi from Rainy Day Ramblings; Kristilyn from Reading in Winter; Kelsey from Kelsey's Cluttered Bookshelf; Lizzy from Lizzy's Dark Fiction; Shanon from Escaping with Fiction; Savannah from Books with Bite; Tara from Basically Books; Toni from My Book Addiction; Abbi from Book Obsession; Lake from Lake's Reads; Jenny from Jenny on the Book; and anyone else I missed!

Also by J.L. Bryan:

The Ellie Jordan, Ghost Trapper series
Ellie Jordan, Ghost Trapper
Cold Shadows
The Crawling Darkness
Terminal

The fifth Ellie Jordan, Ghost Trapper book will be available in August/September 2015

The Jenny Pox series (supernatural/horror)
Jenny Pox
Tommy Nightmare
Alexander Death
Jenny Plague-Bringer

Urban Fantasy/Horror
Inferno Park
The Unseen

Science Fiction Novels
Nomad
Helix

The Songs of Magic Series (YA/Fantasy)
Fairy Metal Thunder
Fairy Blues
Fairystruck
Fairyland
Fairyvision
Fairy Luck

For Johnny

Chapter One

"So explain to me about the three types of banshees," Stacey said over my headset.

I was down in our new clients' basement, exploring with my Mel-Meter while Stacey sat in the van, watching our array of thermal and night vision cameras over the monitors. It was about two-thirty in the morning, and all was quiet for the moment, though Stacey had picked up some cold spots in the basement earlier that night.

"Three basic types, but they may all be different evolutionary stages of the same kind of ghost." I kept my voice low as I explored the shadowy rooms. The basement was unfinished, lots of bare studs and concrete, empty except for a heap of U-Haul boxes in one corner. Our clients hadn't lived here long. The basement was mostly aboveground, sharing the bottom level of the house with the garage.

"Okay," Stacey said. "First there's just a sad ghost, right?"

"A ghost whose primary emotional tone is grief," I whispered. "Usually encountered as an auditory apparition. Weeping, sobbing, moaning, screaming..."

"Like what the Kozlows were talking about." Stacey was referring to our clients, a married couple in their late twenties. The wife, Ember, was expecting their first baby within the month. She and her husband had both heard a female voice weeping softly in their house, always late at night, usually down in the basement. They'd never been able to find the source of it.

"We'd call that a first-stage banshee," I said. "A ghost with uncontrollable grieving issues. Often suicides, or people who suffered deep emotional pain in life. They won't let go of their pain, and it ties them to this world."

"Then the second type is the really dangerous kind?"

"In a sense." I walked to the basement door and looked out through its glass panes. The Kozlows' back yard was like something from a home and garden catalog, a lush carpet of vibrant grass dotted with hopeful young magnolia and peach trees. A stone birdbath stood near the center, and an actual white picket fence enclosed the yard.

Beyond the back fence, I could see the next street in the neighborhood—a couple of skeletal, half-built houses and many acres of raw red earth, the area looking as dead as a Martian landscape under the moonlight.

"The second type of banshee has learned to feed on the grief of the living," I said. "That's when they become real problems. That's the banshee you usually hear about in legends. It becomes a fully visible apparition, so solid it can be mistaken for a living person. People say when you see them it's a warning that you or one of your family members is about to die."

"But that's not true?" Stacey asked.

"The banshee doesn't show up just to be a pal and let you know about impending doom." I checked and adjusted the night vision camera in one of the unfinished basement rooms, walled only with bare wooden studs that made me feel as if I stood in a cage. "It shows up at the scene of an approaching death for the same reason vultures and crows gather around a dying animal. The household is about to be flooded with grief, and then it's feeding time for the banshee."

"But how do they know the future?"

"I'm not sure, but that's what draws them, like sharks to blood." I sat down on one of the unpainted wooden steps that led up to the kitchen on the first floor.

"They say my great-grandmother's yard was full of vultures the day before she died," Stacey said. "They hardly ever showed up on the farm before or since."

"Certain animals have a sixth sense about death, too," I said.

"So what happens when a banshee feeds on you?"

"Prolonged grief, incurable depression, eventually suicidal urges," I said. "It's like a dark emotional cloud that never leaves your mind."

"Sounds about as pleasant as an alien face parasite. And what's the third type?"

"The one who's figured out how to cut out the middleman. Instead of sniffing around, trying to find grief, it goes ahead and creates it. It will kill you with its own hands to sow grief and misery in your household. It might look like a household accident, a heart attack, or a sudden illness. Ghosts don't exactly leave fingerprints or DNA samples all over their crime scenes."

"So how many people do you think ghosts kill every year?"

"No way to tell," I said. "One favorite method, like you said, is pushing people down stairs. Falling down is the second-largest cause of accidental death after car crashes. Half a million people a year around the world die from falls."

"So there could be tons of murderous ghosts out there," Stacey said.

"It's possible." I turned on the high-sensitivity portable microphone I'd brought. "I guess we'll try the EVP approach. If this is just a first-stage banshee, we might be able to convince her to move on."

"You're the boss, boss."

"Are you recording?"

"Receiving and recording, yep."

I took a couple of deep breaths as I began to walk through the basement again. Working in Savannah, I usually found myself in moldering old mansions thick with layers of history and tragedy, but this house was only four years old and had only been occupied for a few months. Much of the neighborhood hadn't even been built yet.

The neighborhood was actually a planned community called Town Village, with a dozen streets converging like the spokes of a wagon wheel onto the park at the center. On the developer's website, an artist's representation showed a golf course, tennis courts, and a large, grassy park with a baseball diamond, playground, and swimming pool.

In person, I'd noticed that the "park" was actually a wilderness of churned earth, weeds, and dense scrub pines a little taller than me. It was supposedly still under construction, but according to our clients, there had been no signs of new construction in the neighborhood since they'd moved into the house four months earlier.

"Hello? Is someone down here?" I asked, holding out my microphone like an intrepid reporter interviewing an invisible witness. "My name is Ellie Jordan. I'm here to help you." *Unless you threaten my clients*, I thought. "Can you tell me your name?"

I walked through the gloomy basement. The lights were off, but there was some illumination from the back porch light seeping in through the basement door.

"People say they hear you crying," I said. "Why are you sad? Can you tell my why you're here?"

I didn't hear anything, but later we'd review the audio captured by the microphone. It was surprising what could turn up.

I continued around the basement, asking the same basic questions. *Who are you? What do you want?*

"Ellie," Stacey whispered over my headset. "Under the stairs."

I looked into the shadowy area beneath the unpainted wooden stairs. I could feel a cold spot, and my Mel Meter confirmed that the temperature was nine degrees colder than the rest of the basement, with a noticeable rise in electromagnetic energy.

"Are you there?" I whispered.

A voice responded, or at least a thin echo of a voice. The sound was almost too quiet to hear, but I thought it might be a girl sobbing.

I pulled my thermal goggles down over my eyes.

She was hard to discern, a cluster of pale greenish-blue shapes that, taken together, seemed to suggest the figure of a small girl sitting under the lowest steps, her knees drawn up to her chin.

"I can see you there." I spoke as softly and gently as I could. "Do you need help?"

A moaning sound rose around me, like a low wind. Then the

crying really began.

"I can hear you," I said. "I can see you. What do you want to talk about?"

She cried louder, the sound interrupted by hitching sobs, as if I were just upsetting her more. I knew it could grow even louder than that. My clients had heard the crying all the way up in their bedroom, two stories above the basement.

"Can you tell me where you're crying?" I asked again.

Crying turned to wailing, so loud my ears began to ache.

"Don't be afraid." I squatted near the space occupied by the ghost. She sounded so full of pain and sorrow. My heart went out to her. I wondered what could have inflicted such grief on someone so young, and how she had died.

"Ellie, behind you!" Stacey barked over my headset, making me jump.

I felt it before I even turned around—a deep freeze washing over me, as though someone had just opened a door and stepped into the basement from deep in the icy steppes of Siberia, bringing a severe wind with them.

Something else was in the room, watching me, and it felt powerful. My Mel Meter went crazy with the dropping temperature and surging energy.

My heart was already thumping much too fast as I turned around, drawing the three-thousand-lumen tactical flashlight from my belt. What I saw through my thermal goggles almost bumped it up to an actual heart attack.

The shape was enormous, a purple-black cloudy mass swelling toward me from the door to the back yard, sucking all the heat from the room. It looked like a storm cloud moving just above the ground.

I planted my feet, ready to click on my flashlight, but it distended around me. It was moving toward the girl-ghost, who'd gone silent under the stairs. As it approached her, she began sobbing again, then screamed so loud my ears rang.

It looked like the big dark mass was here to collect the girl ghost, not to bother me.

Maybe I should have just backed off. My clients were paying me to get the weeping girl out of their house, and this other entity might be doing my job for me. There was no telling where it would take her or what it would do to her, but the easiest and safest thing would be to sit back and do nothing.

I couldn't, though. I couldn't stand by while the larger entity dragged her away screaming.

"Stop!" I shouted, blasting my flashlight toward the cold mass. It stopped its approach and contracted a bit. Through my thermals, I could see the bright beam of my light slicing past the purple layers of cold, right to the black heart of the entity.

"Ellie, do you need me?" Stacey asked over my headset.

"Wait there."

The dark cloud shifted, refocusing its energy toward me. Tension swelled in the freezing air, and I felt it was about to attack.

I blasted Vivaldi's *Juditha triumphans* over the speaker on my belt, a powerful and upbeat oratorio about an Israelite woman who killed an Assyrian king to protect her city, accompanied by trumpets and drum.

"Leave this house!" I shouted at the big, dark entity, hoping to sound threatening. "On behalf of all that live here, I command you to leave."

The darkness contracted more, taking the general shape of a man but solid black with cold. He appeared eight feet tall, like he wanted to be intimidating.

"Go!" I stepped closer, expanding the iris of my flashlight to try and engulf the dark figure.

The entity hesitated a moment, then barreled away from me, passing out through the door like a mass of steam.

I pursued. I wanted to see where it went in case we needed to track it later.

Since I wasn't a ghost, I had to pause to unlock and open the basement door. By the time I emerged, it was already across the lawn, passing through the slats of the picket fence like a patch of fog accelerated by swift wind.

I ran after it, turning down the volume on my music and keeping my flashlight pointed at the ground. Now that it was on the move, I didn't want it to chase it away too quickly. I was already having trouble keeping up.

The picket fence was not my friend. By the time I reached it, the dark fog was halfway across the raw red earth of the empty lot behind my clients' home. I had to clamber over the flimsy lightweight fence, which shuddered like it would collapse beneath me. I jumped to the earth, landing with the grace of a drunken hippopotamus.

I stumbled, regained my balance, and looked up.

The dark entity had resumed the shape of a man. It stood on the road ahead. There were a couple of half-built houses on that street, but most of the lots were completely empty, inhabited only by dirt and weeds. The street itself had been paved and completely built out with curbs, storm drains, sidewalks, fire hydrants, and unlit iron-post street lamps, all the amenities ready to support the houses that had never been erected.

The man-shape was not moving. It appeared to be facing me, watching and waiting.

I approached slowly, feeling a little more frightened with every step. It wasn't moving at all, like a predator lying in wait for its prey to foolishly approach.

"Ellie, I can't see you," Stacey said. "What are you doing out there?"

"Sh." I took a risk and lifted the thermal goggles off my face, wondering if I could see the ghost with my own eyes. The thermal images showed me where it was and how cold it was, but would never give me any real identifying details.

I blinked while my eyes adjusted.

Then I saw it.

The figure was still dark and shadowy, though no longer supernaturally large. I had the impression of a man in a brimmed hat and heavy coat, but nothing clear enough to give me a hint of the clothing's era. It could have been anything from a bowler hat and overcoat from the nineteenth century to a trenchcoat and fedora from the early twentieth. A pale cloth concealed his face, so he looked almost like a sheet ghost with a hat and a coat.

"Who are you?" I asked him.

He reached a hand toward his hat brim, as though he intended to tip his hat in the old-fashioned manner.

Then he vanished.

I checked through my thermals again, but there was nothing to see. The thing had hit the road without a trace.

"Ellie?" Stacey asked. "What's up?"

"What are you seeing over the monitors?" I asked her.

"Baby banshee is screaming, and the client's on the way down to the basement. Where are you?"

"The next street over."

"Town Terrace Way? Or Terrace Town Court?"

"Whatever, the one right behind the house." I reached the empty street and stood where the apparition had been. There wasn't even a trace of the cold spot left, just a warm early-September breeze on a summery night.

I pointed my flashlight toward the empty cul-de-sac at one end. Then I looked the other way, where the street terminated at the big roundabout at the center of the community. All the central neighborhood streets connected there. It seemed like the community was originally designed to include a few hundred homes, but only about forty houses had been completed, most of them on the streets near the impressive, columned front entrance.

"You said the clients are up?" I asked.

"If I had to guess, I'd say it's related to the screaming in the basement," Stacey said.

"She's still screaming?"

"She's gone quiet. Client is in the basement, looking at your gear, probably wondering where you are...he's walking out the door now..."

"All right. There's no telling where the Big Bad Wolf went. He could be anywhere." The planned community sat on hundreds of acres, much of it still scrub and piney woods on the undeveloped northern half, which was adjacent to a federally protected wilderness area.

"Did you get a look at it?" Stacey asked.

"Just a shadow guy so far. He wants to look big and impressive. He was almost as tall as the basement ceiling the first time I saw him." I jogged back across the red dirt of the vacant lot. Our client stood at the fence in his yard, wearing striped pajamas and thick glasses. "Hi, Tom."

"What happened?" Tom Kozlow asked. He was lanky, twenty-seven years old, junior partner in a suburban dental practice. "It was screaming bloody murder down there. Woke up both of us."

"Tom, what's happening?" a woman's voice asked, startling me.

Tom raised a cell phone. It was his wife, Ember.

"I'm trying to find out." Tom looked at me expectantly.

"I encountered a second entity." I spoke loud enough that Ember could hopefully hear me over the phone. I imagined her up in her bed, heavy with advanced pregnancy, listening to unexplained screams in her basement. "I pursued it back to the next street."

"You mean there's another ghost in our house?" Tom asked.

"I mean there *was* another ghost, but I don't think it's necessarily rooted to your house," I said. "We need to figure out the history of this place and what was here before this development. Then we might be able to put together who these people are."

"Did you see the one in the basement?" Ember asked over the phone.

"We picked up some thermal impressions of her." I looked at Tom. "Would you mind opening the gate for me? I don't know if your fence will survive me trying to climb over again."

We returned to the basement, where the small girl ghost had vanished from her dark nook under the stairs. While Tom returned to his wife, I searched the basement again, finding a few electromagnetic residual traces, but nothing more. If the ghost was still there, she'd hidden herself extremely well.

I stayed in the basement for the rest of the night, but I didn't hear her again.

Chapter Two

Sometimes, you get lucky and clients want to provide breakfast after you've been up all night watching for ghosts in their house.

Ember Kozlow didn't move like a woman who expected to launch out a baby only days from now. She bounced on her feet as she moved around the kitchen, letting Stacey and me help only with those things she couldn't do, like reach the griddle in a low cabinet. Ember whisked together eggs and flour, mumbling Cyndi Lauper's "She Bop" half under her breath, as though not entirely aware she was singing out loud at all.

"I hope you kids like crepes," she said, while rinsing blueberries. "Tom tries to keep me off my feet these days, but I'm going crazy. I miss working. I'm going back as soon as the boy's born." Ember was part owner, along with a couple of her college friends, of Seaside Treats, a small bakery and candy shop on River Street. She was pudgy and glowing with her advanced pregnancy.

"These look awesome," Stacey said, accepting the first plate of blueberry crepes. "So you make candy and your husband's a dentist. It's like you're in cahoots."

"It's a cavity conspiracy," Ember said, with a smile and a tone that told me this was a well-worn joke in their marriage.

"Thank you," I told Ember as she slid me some of the ultra-thin pancakes. They were delicious, doughy and sweet.

"I'm just glad to be doing *something*," Ember said.

"So how did you get into the candy-slinging business, anyway?" Stacey asked.

"My mother," Ember said. "She's kind of a...hippie poet type. She teaches community college theater in North Carolina. How do you think I got stuck with a name like 'Ember'?"

"I think it's pretty," Stacey said.

"My older brother Wolf got the worst of it," Ember said, and I accidentally, very impolitely snorted a laugh, almost dropping a bit of partially chewed crepe out of my mouth. I covered my lips.

"Sorry," I said.

"I *know*. He goes by Wally," Ember said. "Anyway, my mom was always making little candies and brownies. I learned from her. Later, some of my college friends wanted to start a shop where we'd make chocolate and sweets from scratch right on-site, with me in charge of the kitchen."

"Sounds like a dream job," Stacey said. "Chocolate everywhere."

"Packed with millions of calories." Ember smiled. "More crepes?"

"I'm trying to keep it under a million calories today," I said. "Thanks, though. They were really good."

"I know, I'm scared to try your actual desserts," Stacey said.

"What are you doing?" Tom entered the room dressed in a crisp white shirt and a muted tie. He approached Ember, who'd moved on to preparing a smoothie in the blender. "Dr. Patel said you need to rest this week."

"We tried to help," Stacey told him.

"I can't just lie around all day," Ember said. "Haven't you ever read 'The Yellow Wallpaper'?"

"I'll take care of this. Go and eat." Tom nudged her out of the way, taking control of the banana and grapes she was feeding into the blender.

Ember sighed and sat down with us, bringing her own plate of crepes with her.

"How soon can you get rid of the thing in our basement?"

Tom asked me.

"We're going to research the history of the land," I said. "If we can identify these ghosts, then we'll know how to bait the traps and catch them. I'm guessing there must have been a farm on the land before, although this far north of the city, it might have been just raw woods before the developers built your neighborhood. Do you have any idea why the developer stopped building?"

"They ran out of money." Tom ran the blender briefly, then poured a tall smoothie and served it to his wife, kissing her on the cheek. "They had all these plans at the beginning, you know, an old-fashioned front-porch community, sidewalks, common areas. Neighborhood softball team on the baseball field they never built, over by the picnic pavilion that doesn't exist. Did you see the retail strip near the entrance?"

"It looks like a ghost town," I said.

"It was supposed to be like our little downtown, with restaurants and shopping in walking distance of your home. It never opened. Now they've got it blocked off with traffic cones. You should see the old brochures." Tom laughed and shook his head.

"I'd really like that," I said.

"They're upstairs in the office--" Ember began to stand, but Tom stopped her.

"Stay. I'll get them." Tom hurried past her toward the front stairs.

"Did you just tell me to 'stay' like a dog?" she called after him.

"That's a good girl!" he called back, and she scowled, tightening her grip on her fork.

Tom returned with three full-color brochures, which I unfolded and spread out on the kitchen table. The spacious room had big windows admitting more and more sunlight as the day broke around us. Outside, I could see a pleasant suburban street, the ornate lamps spaced along the sidewalks fading as the neighbors climbed into their trucks and SUVs for their morning commute. The lawns were bright green and landscaped with young trees and flowering shrubs, the two-story houses essentially carbon copies of each other, with just the gables and porches rearranged for a little variety.

This was the kind of street advertised in the brochure, which consisted of more artists' renditions than photographs. The developers seemed to imagine a small-town atmosphere, populated by blond Abercrombie & Fitch models who liked to wave at each other while walking dogs and blond children past each other's front porches.

Step into an earlier, simpler time, one brochure said. *An old-fashioned community, built on traditional values. The neighborhood barbecue. Christmas carols. Fireworks on the Fourth of July. Softball and swim teams for the kids. Shopping and dining. Town Village: Convenience. Comfort. Community.*

Another brochure showed the "retail village" area, designed to look like the brick storefronts of any small American town circa 1951. The fictional businesses catering to the Ambercrombie models included a beauty salon, barbershop (with spiral pole, naturally), and a corner drugstore where cheerful kids drank malts at the counter, dressed in their Norman Rockwell Sunday best.

Town Village Park, the big circle of piney woods at the center of the community, was illustrated with a nature trail running through a botanical garden, as well as a bandstand, a duck pond, a large playground and baseball diamond complete with dugouts and a concession stand, and other features that clearly did not exist.

"So you don't think any of this will ever be built?" I asked Tom.

"If it ever happened, I'd go into severe shock." He buttoned his shirt cuff.

"But you bought the house anyway."

"Oh, yeah. For a hundred and twenty-five thousand less than the original asking price." He winked at Ember. "Now I have to go stare into some dirty yellow mouths all day to pay for it. Do you need anything before I go?"

"Just one thing," she said with a smile, and he bent down to kiss her.

Stacey gave me an *aww* look, and I rolled my eyes a little.

"Good luck with the ghosts," Tom said, glancing at Stacey and me on his way out.

"We'd better get going, too," I said. "We'll figure out our plan of attack and return this evening. By then, we should have a better idea of who these ghosts are. Ember, do you know whether any of your neighbors have experienced unusual activity in their homes?"

"I guess I could ask a couple of people." Ember didn't seem thrilled with the idea.

"These ghosts might be wandering freely across the neighborhood," I said.

"Well, they need to wander a little farther from my house. There are plenty of empty houses around here. Why do they need mine?"

"One possibility is that the little girl ghost might be drawn to you," I said. "If she feels lost and scared, she might see you as a mother figure."

"Oh." Ember glanced down at her swollen belly. "That kind of makes me sad."

"We'll find out more as soon as we can." I stood up. Stacey and I rinsed our plates in her sink before she could stop us and insist on doing it herself. "It's best if you avoid the ghost. It might feed on your energy. If you hear it crying, stay away from it. Don't try to interact with it."

"Hurry back," Ember said. "I'm not thrilled about sitting around this house alone, even in the daytime. I just keep expecting to hear her scream."

Stacey and I left our gear set up in the house. We pulled out of the driveway, both of us ready to head home and nap for the morning.

"So what do you think we're dealing with here?" Stacey asked, looking out the window as we drove southward down Town Village Boulevard, flanked by cheerful white houses and green lawns. It was the central road of the community, taking us past the ghost town of the two-story, never-opened retail village, identified by a hand-carved wooden sign as "Town Village Main Street."

We reached the front of the development, embellished with three-story brick towers featuring fluted columns and inaccessible decorative balconies. It was a pretty fancy facade for a community that largely consisted of dirt, weeds, and broken promises.

"I'm guessing an old farm," I said. "A large male who used to abuse and terrify a little girl. That's the general pattern we're looking for."

"Should we call in Jacob?"

"Not until we know where to look. Town Village covers hundreds of acres. That could take him days of wandering around, unless we can figure out where any old houses used to stand."

"To the library!" Stacey said, doing her best to sound enthusiastic. She hated digging into old tax records, land titles and all the exciting lost paperwork of history.

"I'd rather you spend some time going through our recordings. See if Moaning Myrtle answered any of my questions."

"That could take hours..."

"I'll go to the library while you do that."

"Woo-hoo!" Stacey said. "I mean, uh, shucks. No library dust for me today." She gave a mock frown.

We drove south—our clients lived in the Port Wentworth area, about fifteen miles north of downtown.

I dropped Stacey off, then headed home, which for me is a narrow brick loft in an old glass factory. There are some very fancy converted-loft communities for wealthy young professionals around the city. Mine isn't one of them.

I fed my cat, Bandit, and took a few hours to rest. Then I hopped into my old black Camaro, which I'd inherited from my dad after my parents died, and drove to the city archives. I spent a few hours there, and then a few more at the Bull Street library.

When the library closed for the afternoon, I went to meet Stacey at the Eckhart Investigations office, located in an ugly cinderblock building next to a car wrecker place. But, hey, the rent's cheap.

In the big workshop in the back, Stacey's face glowed in the blue light of three monitors arrayed around her at the video editing station. Calvin, our semiretired boss, sat behind her, his loyal bloodhound Hunter puddled on the floor beside him, lazily flicking his tail and looking bored.

"Ellie, you have to hear this," Stacey said.

"Did we pick up some anomalies?" I climbed onto the very uncomfortable wooden stool beside her.

"Maybe it's just static, but I want to hear your opinion." On the screen, a greenish video version of me walked through our clients' basement, looking like a weird apparition myself on the night vision while I questioned the crying ghost.

"Here." Stacey gestured to another screen, full of squiggly digital graphs of sound waves recorded by the high-powered microphone. She indicated a big spike near the middle. "Listen close and tell me if you hear anything."

The video skipped ahead, showing me from a fairly unflattering angle while I talked to a corner of the basement.

"Why are you here?" the video-recorded me asked.

The voice that answered was like a cold hiss of air, raising bumps all along my back: *"They died."*

I almost fell off the stool.

"That was *not* static, Stacey," I said.

"I didn't want to raise your expectations too high," she said. "I thought it would be a nice surprise."

Yeah, like finding your cat left a dead chipmunk on your doorstep. "I'm glad you found something. Is there more?"

"Just one more thing." Stacey selected another audio clip, and the video jumped to a moment when I was passing by the stairs.

"What do you want?" I asked. "What are you doing in this house?"

"Hiding." A single word, clear as a rattlesnake on a quiet night.

"Wish I could've asked follow-up questions," I said. "What else?"

"Some visuals." Stacey showed me the thermal video of the huge, dark mass filling the basement from floor to ceiling around the door. A night vision frame showed a suggestive outline of someone standing there—just a shoulder and arm shape, and a line where the brim of a hat would have been.

"That's the guy I followed outside," I said.

"Any leads on his identity?" Calvin asked.

"Just a heap of information," I said. "The land was originally part of a grant to a man named Joseph Thorburn. Scottish guy. He focused on the area along the river, though, growing mulberries and trying to cultivate silkworms—it was called Silkgrove Plantation."

"The ruins are still there," Calvin said, nodding. "Just north of the lumber-processing plant."

"The Town Village development is a little back from the river. It was pretty much wilderness until the..." I opened a thick folder of photocopies and print-outs from the library. "Until 1809, when it was sold to the Whalen family, who had a farm on the place where Town Village is now."

"So who got murdered?" Stacey said. I gave her a puzzled look, and she shrugged. "That's how these things usually go, right?"

"The Whalens lived there for a few generations," I said. "A number of children died young, which was normal for the nineteenth century. I did find a woman who died at the age of twenty-two, after having three children—Rose Whalen—and her husband re-married."

"But we're looking for a little girl, right?" Stacey asked.

"It could be an adult woman who was small. I do have the names of several girls who died of illness or accidents," I said. "There's something else interesting. The old maps show a rail line running through that property, on the wooded north side. I dug into that and found it was built by the Georgia Canal and Railroad Company in 1851, the first line to connect Savannah with Charleston."

"Georgia Canal and Railroad sounds really familiar..." Stacey said.

"The Paulding case," Calvin said.

"Isaiah Ridley," Stacey said. "The ghost with the belt from hell who used to beat his kids."

"He went bankrupt investing in GC&R," I said.

"Right, right, and we baited him with the little promotional train-toy thingy that was all rusty and spiky and probably full of tetanus," Stacey said.

I nodded, thinking of our clients. Toolie, who loved her job at the mattress store, and her husband Gord, who'd suffered severe emphysema until we'd eradicated the ghosts of drowning victims from his house. Crane, the eight-year-old whose imaginary friends had encouraged him to kill himself so he could join them. His sister Juniper, thirteen, who'd been fascinated by our work and ultimately helped us defeat the centuries-old poltergeist in her house. I wondered how she was doing.

"So do you think Isaiah's ghost could be involved here?" Stacey asked. "Because I really wouldn't want to be alone in a dark room with him again."

"I doubt it," I said. "I just thought it was interesting. Anyway, the rail line's gone now, but it used to bridge over the river and across the marsh islands. The crossing was right there at Silkgrove Plantation, next to the docks. The modern rail bridge is a couple of miles north of there, so I guess the marsh islands turned out to be a bad place for the bridge supports..."

"Did a train crash there or something?" Stacey asked.

"I didn't have time to dig into that yet," I said. "I just looked at a few rail maps over the years. I was mostly trying to figure out who lived here and when. I have a few families to investigate. Right now, I think we need to do a very broad sweep of Town Village and see if we can pinpoint where the ghosts are coming from."

"So we should call Jacob?" Stacey glanced at the time. "It's kind of late in the day to ask him..."

"For that wide an area, it might be better to bring Hunter," I said.

The bloodhound lifted his head and cocked his ears at the sound of his name.

"That's a good idea," Calvin said.

"Are you going to help us sniff out the ghosts? Yes you are! Yes you are!" Stacey leaned over to scratch behind his big, floppy red ears. Hunter shoved himself to his feet, his bunched-up jowls jiggling, tail wagging. He was a trained ghost hunter, from a family of police hounds and search and rescue dogs.

"We should get going before the sun sets," I said.

"Ellie, I'd like to speak to you for a moment." Calvin turned and rolled into his office, where we could talk privately. I followed.

"I'll just stay here with the dog," Stacey called after me. "We're going to have fun, aren't we, Hunter? Yes we are!" She rubbed the dog's back while he wagged his tail.

I stepped into Calvin's office and closed the door behind me, wondering what this little drama was about, and why it was worth keeping our clients waiting.

Chapter Three

"What's up, Calvin?" I asked. His office was beyond cluttered, full of bookshelves overflowing with everything from case files to old leather-bound books of occult and ghost lore.

"I have a security concern." He wheeled behind his desk.

"About Stacey?" I asked, surprised.

"No. I just didn't want to alarm her yet."

"Well, go ahead and alarm me." I dropped into the squeaky, worn rolling office chair to face him.

"The camera outside picked up something last night." Calvin turned his desktop monitor toward me.

In night vision green, the monitor displayed video of our parking lot from a hidden security camera. The parking lot is a shattered, uneven blacktop, having failed to withstand whatever heavy industry had occupied the building before us. Maybe a brick or cement factory, judging by the stress that had been placed on the pavement.

After a moment, a black Acura sedan pulled in from the road, stopped sideways in front of our office, and idled there.

"They triggered the outdoor motion detector, or I would never have known they were here," Calvin said.

The passenger-side window dropped, and a person inside snapped photographs of the building.

"Can we get a closer view of that face?" I asked.

"I've tried." Calvin maximized another window on the screen, showing enlarged still frames of a blurry, pixelated green blob.

"Great," I said. "What else did they do?"

"They just took pictures and drove away." Calvin replayed the video, pausing again to show me where he'd caught an image of the license plate. The numbers and letters were as blurry as the passenger's face had been, but the plate was encased in a frame with a cartoon duck wearing glasses in the lower corner.

"Honest Duck Rent-A-Car," I said. "That's something. Either they're from out of town or they're being very cautious. Why would anyone be spying on us? Who are they?"

"Coincidentally, I've been asking myself those questions all day," Calvin said. "I wanted to bring it to your attention before you left."

"So watch out for rental cars," I said. "Especially black Acuras. Gotcha." I was acting like it was no big deal, but it worried me. We don't usually deal with enemies who are still alive.

I wanted to ask Calvin something else, but I didn't. He'd recently mentioned retiring and leaving our little P.I. firm in my hands, a responsibility for which I didn't feel ready at all. Lately I'd seen him staring off into space, preoccupied.

"Is there anything else on your mind?" I asked, not for the first time in the past couple of weeks. "Aside from this spying situation?"

"Oh..." He shrugged, looking away from me. "Mortality. Meaning. The purpose of life."

"Any insights so far?"

He chuckled. "Nothing that hasn't already been reduced to cliches, platitudes, and bumper stickers. Here, take these." He opened his drawer and tossed me a foil bag with a cartoon dog wearing a crown on the front of the package.

"Dog treats?" I asked.

"Dried duck liver. His favorite."

"Thanks." Sensing I was dismissed, I stood up. Calvin turned to his computer. He was a little disheveled, his graying hair tangled, with three days' worth of black and gray beard stubble. Calvin was showing signs of depression, but I didn't know what was bothering him. I did know that he would deflect any questions that got too personal, and prying would just make him clam up tighter.

"Anything else?" I asked.

"Good luck," he said, not looking back at me.

"You know you can talk to me about anything that's on your mind, right?"

"You know the clients are already expecting you at their home, don't you?"

"Okay, we'll get going..." I hesitated a second, then walked out the door. "Try not to lose all your money playing online poker."

"I never play online," he said. "Where's the fun in that?"

Out in the workshop, I collected Stacey and Hunter and loaded them into the van, feeling weirdly like a soccer mom with a kid and a dog. Hunter wagged his tail, excited to be going on any kind of adventure. His tail slowed and his saggy, wrinkly face grew more saggy when he saw he'd be riding in his dog crate in the back. Calvin lets him free-range it inside the car, with his head out the window, but I planned to drive fast and didn't want to bang him around the van.

We skirted the edge of downtown and hopped onto the highway, traveling fast under the night sky.

I slowed as we entered Town Village, again passing the picturesque Main Street retail ghost town, followed by the lawns of white and brown McMansions lining the main drag, Town Village Boulevard. Side streets curved away in both directions. I kept my eyes out for any black Acuras, or other rentals with the Honest Duck logo, but didn't see any.

"What's up?" Stacey asked. "You're quiet tonight. Was it something Calvin said?"

"I'm just thinking over the case," I lied. "I think we should take Hunter toward the central park first. The Whalen farmhouse used to stand in that area."

"Okey-dokey. So you're keeping Calvin's thing secret."

"It wasn't a big deal," I said, pulling into the Kozlow driveway. "Somebody took pictures of our office late last night."

"That sounds like a big deal."

"It could just be somebody interested in buying the property," I said. "We have no idea."

"So what do we do?"

"Just be on guard, I guess. I'm going to speak to the Kozlows. Take Hunter out and walk him. His bladder's not as reliable as it used to be."

"Yeah, I think I smell dog pee, actually..." Stacey glanced back toward Hunter, who watched her from behind his bars.

"Then swab out his crate." I left the van as she wrinkled her nose at me.

I jogged up the long wooden staircase to the front porch on the second floor, above the garage, and rang the front door bell.

"Stay right there!" Tom Kozlow called over his shoulder while he opened the door. "I've got it."

"Is it them?" Ember shouted from somewhere inside the house.

"We thought you'd be here earlier," Tom said.

"Yeah, sorry," I said. "We found some interesting information on the history of the area, as well as some interesting EVPs--"

"What?"

"Electronic voice phenomena," I said. "Ghost voices. The female entity in your basement answered two questions--"

"Is it them?" Ember shouted from wherever she was. The living room in the back, maybe. "I want to talk to them!" Ember shouted.

"Should I come in?" I asked.

Tom sighed. "Just don't upset my wife. She's very delicate right now. I'd rather she didn't have to think about any of this at all."

"That's understandable," I said.

He led me into the house, a spacious place decorated with restored furniture, a few bright abstract paintings, and numerous pictures of friends and family. Ember sat in the living room on an overstuffed couch. A photograph of a crumbling general store with a big hand-painted Coca-Cola sign hung on the wall behind her.

She looked mopey, reading an *Organic Life* magazine, but gave me a smile as I entered the room.

"How are you?" I asked.

"Good. So what exciting things are we doing tonight?" Ember asked.

"You're going to be resting," Tom said, drawing a small scowl from her.

"We brought my boss's bloodhound, Hunter," I said. "We're going to walk him around the community tonight, see if he can zero in on a source for the hauntings. Unless you've had any trouble here?"

"She hasn't started crying yet," Ember said.

"You can just call my cell if anything happens." I gave her an extra copy of my business card. "If you leave the basement door unlocked, I won't have to bother you when I come back. You might be asleep."

"No problem!" Ember said.

"No, there *is* a problem," Tom said. "They've had a few break-ins around the neighborhood lately. I don't want to leave anything unlocked."

"Do you have an extra key?" I asked.

"Right here." Ember opened her purse and dug out her keychain.

"Just be sure we get it back in the morning," Tom said.

"Tom!" Ember said. "I'm sure she'll give it back."

"I definitely will," I said. I quickly caught them up on the case—what I'd gathered about the history of the land, and what the ghost had said when I asked why it was there.

"That's freaky," Ember said. "*Hiding. They died.* Can I hear the recording?"

"Sure, let me go grab my tablet--" I began.

"I think Ember's had enough stress for one night," Tom said.

This left me looking between them awkwardly, not sure what to do. They stared at each other, the tension uncomfortably heavy in the room.

"I'll just check on Stacey and Hunter..." I finally said, backing away slowly.

"I want to see the dog." Ember smiled, pushing herself up to a standing position. Tom dashed over to help her, or maybe to stop her.

"You don't need to go up and down all those stairs," he said.

"I would never have agreed to move into this house if I knew you'd use those stairs as an excuse to keep me prisoner."

"Nobody's keeping you prisoner! You could fall."

"I'm pregnant, not elderly." Ember strode past him, toward me and the front door behind me. "Let's go meet your ghost-sniffing dog."

I accompanied her outside, and her annoyed husband followed, and it was entirely unpleasant to find myself caught in the tension between them.

On the front porch, I stepped aside as Tom insisted on walking down the stairs in front of Ember, for her own safety. I'd first thought it sweet how he worried over his pregnant wife, but I could see how his concern probably felt domineering to her. I wouldn't want anyone telling me what to do from moment to moment like that. If I were her, I probably would have punched him in the nose by now.

Ember made it all the way down the stairs without falling, or having her water break, or any other five-alarm emergencies.

"She wants to see the dog," I told Stacey, who was letting Hunter sniff the fire hydrant. Stacey brought him over. Ember petted him and rubbed him behind his enormous, floppy ears, and his tail wagged.

"He can really find ghosts?" Ember asked me.

"My boss, Calvin, trained him from a puppy," I said. "Took him to haunted locations all over the city. Animals are usually more sensitive to ghosts, anyway. They don't have an elaborate rational mind trying to block them out."

"So you're saying the whole neighborhood is haunted? Is that it?" Tom asked.

"The ghost I saw was mobile," I said. "I think it's based somewhere else. There used to be a farmhouse in the area where the park is now."

"Yeah, the 'park,'" Tom said, making finger quotes for emphasis. "You should be careful out there. I was serious about those break-ins around the neighborhood."

"Don't worry about us," Stacey said. "We've got a dog."

Hunter rolled over on his back, paws in the air, exposing his rumpled belly to Ember so she could rub it.

"Can you point out which houses were broken into?" I asked.

"You'd have to ask Mr. Nobson. He's the neighborhood watch chief."

"I'll do that tomorrow." I looked up at the night sky. The moonlight was dim, and shadowy clouds gathered on the horizon, blotting out the stars. "We'd better get moving."

"Take care," Ember said, pushing herself to her feet while Tom hurried to assist her. "Call us if you get into trouble. I'll send Tom."

"Thanks so much," Tom replied.

Stacey and I grabbed gear from the van. I walked Hunter over to the sidewalk while Stacey carried a set of super-sharp lopping shears to help us cut through undergrowth. She carried her camera in her backpack, and both of us had utility belts loaded with our tactical flashlights and our usual array of ghost-hunting tools. I brought thermal and night vision goggles in my own backpack.

I nodded to Stacey, and we headed for the sidewalk, Hunter wagging his tail and ready to search. I glanced back to see Ember ascending the stairs again, Tom's hand pressed firmly on her back as if steering her.

"Cute couple," Stacey commented when we'd walked past a few houses. This street was well-lit, most of the houses inhabited and maintained, their yards groomed. The streets deeper into the neighborhood lay dark and empty.

"He seems a little overbearing to me," I said.

"Probably just nervous about the baby."

We reached the central hub of the community, the roundabout from which the main streets radiated. It enclosed an area that was meant to be fifty acres of parkland and amenities, but was instead filled with scrub pine and dense briers.

"This doesn't look like the safest set-up, does it?" Stacey asked as we crossed the two-lane roundabout to the sidewalk that encircled the undeveloped park. "All the kids have to cross the busiest road in the community to reach the park."

"Good thing there's no reason to come to the park," I said. We followed the curved sidewalk to a gap in the spindly trees and brush where the developers had managed to install a paved path just wide enough for a golf cart.

The lights of the inhabited streets had receded behind us, so we flipped on the small square LED lights clipped to our belts. They didn't have the same ghost-blasting oomph as the high-powered SWAT flashlights holstered at our hips, but they were hands-free.

The thicket of high, spindly pine trees seemed to swallow us up as we entered the park area. Stars glowed overhead, but the thin sliver of moon wasn't much help.

Hunter trotted along amiably enough, sniffing here and there but not fixating on anything.

"Hunter," I said, and he stopped and looked up at me, his dark eyes attentive from their nests deep in the red folds and flops of his face. "Find the ghosts."

He whined a little, but also wagged his tail and picked up the pace, his head higher now. Dog on the job.

We walked alongside a chicken wire fence. Beyond the crude, hastily constructed fence was a paved green area, obscured by years of pine needles and leaves. A light wind scattered more of the dried leaves, burying a few more inches of green pavement.

"I'm guessing these are the fantastic tennis courts we read about in the brochure," Stacey said.

"There's the playground." We slowed as we passed a shadowy area where red mulch covered the ground. Through the chicken wire, we could see the half-built equipment, including a couple of two-story castle towers connected by a plastic rope bridge and a pink spire with a slide coiled around it. Plastic horses, grinning gnomes, a big clown face, and baby swings decorated with cartoony plastic bugs lay strewn in the dirt like bodies on a battlefield, filthy with years of exposure to rain and debris.

"Looks like fairyland lost the war," Stacey said.

Hunter sniffed curiously at the fence, as if drawn to the playground ruins.

"What is it, boy?" I asked.

"Did Timmy fall down a well and find a ghost?" Stacey asked.

Hunter sniffed again at the fence, but then turned and kept walking.

"That's okay," Stacey whispered to me. "I didn't want to go in there."

Next came the tragedy of the community pool area, where partially-constructed tiki-style decks, gazebos, and cabanas surrounded a yawning Olympic-sized concrete hole filled with more leaves and debris.

"This place is starting to creep me out," Stacey whispered. "It's kind of post-apocalyptic, all the people gone..."

"Except nobody was ever here in the first place, except the construction crew. And they didn't finish."

"So, kind of pre-post-apocalyptic, then? Is that a thing?"

"Sure." We reached a very wide area of dirt and weeds, probably intended to be a big open lawn for Frisbees and such, as well as the promised community baseball field. A wooden concession stand squatted near one corner of the big clearing.

Hunter nosed among the weeds, and I let him lead the way. He took his time absorbing the scents.

"Let's talk about anything besides how weird this place is," Stacey said. "What's the news with Michael?"

"I told you all there is," I said. "We had a pretty good time."

"And that was a few *weeks* ago."

"We just have opposite schedules," I said. "I work all night hunting the dead. He's on the day shift, trying to keep people from turning into ghosts." Michael was a firefighter, and he'd been very helpful when we'd eradicated a fearfeeder from the mansion-turned-apartment-building where he lived. Particularly nice to me, especially when I'd had a face full of glass.

"You went out once, you had a good time...and...what?" Stacey asked. "Why are you so tight-lipped? Is he avoiding you?" She stopped walking.

"No, he's been out of town—wait, why do you assume *he's* avoiding *me*? If anybody's avoiding anybody?"

"Uh, no reason." Stacey suddenly looked very interested in a patch of wildflowers near the toe of her boot. "So you're avoiding him? Why?"

"Nobody's avoiding anybody. He was away for some ropes training for a while. Technical rescue stuff."

"He *was* away."

"I meant to call him back, but it's too late now. I'll do it tomorrow."

"You are avoiding him! Why? What dirty secret did you find out, Ellie? Is he a Michael Bolton fan or something?"

"Sh." I brought out my phone.

"Yeah, call him!"

"I compared the old property map of the Whalen farm to contemporary maps," I told her. "I did my best to come up with GPS coordinates for where the house was located. Come on, Hunter." I tugged the dog, following the digital map on my phone.

"So you're avoiding him and avoiding the subject of why you're avoiding him?" Stacey asked, strolling along beside me. "Do I have that right?"

"Keep prying into my love life and I'll start prying into yours. Have you told Jacob about The Country Barn yet?"

"I'm, uh...working up to it. Hey, I think all this talk is distracting the dog." It wasn't true, she'd just decided to end the conversation.

"There's not much here," I said.

"Except that."

I finally looked up from my phone and saw we stood only fifteen yards from the two-story concession building, painted white with red and blue stripes at the corners, the paint already weathered and peeling. The two big serving windows were closed and padlocked, sealed by panels of solid wood. Wooden stairs ran up along one side of the building, and the second floor had another big window, also sealed with a wooden panel. If it was like other such buildings I'd seen in the parks and high schools of America, the second floor was meant to house the controls for the scoreboard and the public address system.

Hunter sniffed a little louder and pulled me toward the closed-up building. After a few paces, he stopped and growled, staring at the concession stand.

"Uh-oh," Stacey whispered.

"Maybe that's where the farmhouse stood," I whispered.

"Don't forget the break-ins around the neighborhood."

Hunter growled and pulled harder.

We walked in a wide circle around the corner of the building, moving toward the piney woods behind it. Just past the foot of the exterior stairs, a door led into the first floor of the building.

The door stood ajar by an inch, giving us a view of solid darkness within the building. A long crack split the wood around the doorknob, exactly as if somebody had kicked in the door.

Stacey and I looked at each other. She raised her eyebrows, silently asking me what the plan would be.

I shrugged, put away my phone, and drew the tactical flashlight from my belt. I pointed it at the door. If we were dealing with a dangerous ghost, the high-powered light might help keep it at bay.

If it was a living person, the flashlight was designed to double as a solid metal club.

Beside me, Hunter continued his low, steady growl, his entire body oriented toward the broken door.

Stacey raised her lopping shears, ready to use them as a weapon.

I pointed my flashlight up the stairs at the door to the second floor. That one was padlocked from the outside, which I was happy to see. It meant nobody could sneak out that door and come around behind us while we were inside.

I gave Stacey a nod, then we charged the broken door. I kicked it open and swept my flashlight from corner to corner, revealing the dusty, cobwebbed interior of the concession stand, about the size of a one-room log cabin. Rusty nails, splintered wood, and broken glass littered the floor.

Built-in cabinets surrounded the shuttered serving windows, above and below a counter that ran the length of the room. Most of the cabinets had been smashed to pieces, as if someone had pounded them with a sledgehammer. Someone who really hated cabinets.

Another counter ran the back length of the room, with a big empty square cut out at the center. Through the shattered cabinet door below it, I could see a stainless steel sink and lengths of copper pipe, though it was impossible to say whether the sink had been vandalized or never really installed in the first place.

I didn't see anybody in there. A closet-sized room was built into one corner of the concession stand, and the door was shut tight.

"Hunter, stay. *Stay.*" I dropped his leash, leaving the bloodhound just outside the door so he wouldn't walk on the loose nails and broken glass. Hunter didn't argue. Bloodhounds might be the world's best tracking dogs, but they have little interest in fighting, confrontations, or anything that remotely resembles danger. They're more like Columbo: rumpled and amiable, but extremely perceptive. "Stacey, watch your step. It's the Land of Tetanus in here."

"Great." Stacey followed me inside, and together we approached the closet door.

"Police!" I said, banging the door as hard as I could with my flashlight. So it might be illegal to impersonate a police officer, but I figured that was more intimidating than the truth. "If you have any weapons, put them down now. Come out with your hands where I can see them."

We waited, tense, for some meth-crazed addict to leap out swinging a lead pipe at us. I held my breath, listening for any sound.

After a full minute, I gave Stacey another nod, then I flung open the door, ready to dent somebody's skull with my flashlight.

"You're kidding me," I whispered.

Stacey looked into the closet with me.

More broken glass and nails littered the floor, and cobwebs filled the corners, but it was otherwise empty. The bad news was the wooden strips nailed into the wall to form ladder rungs. These reached all the way to the ceiling, where a square panel offered access to the second floor.

"Light my way," I whispered, and then I began to climb the ladder.

"What?" Stacey whispered, shining her beam on the trap door. "Somebody might be up there, Ellie."

"That's why I'm up here." I reached the ceiling, braced my hand on the trap door, and motioned for Stacey to be quiet.

A loud thud broke the silence, followed by cracking wood and another banging sound, exactly as if somebody had kicked a locked door to the exterior stairs.

I heaved open the trap door and swept my light around the second story.

I'd emerged into another closet like the one below. The closet door stood open, so I could see out into the dusty room beyond. Its only feature was a bare, built-in table behind the closed window panel, the place where the scorekeeper would sit during baseball games, looking out over the field.

Past that, the door to the stairway landing outside had been bashed open, and still creaking back into place from its high-speed impact with the moonlit railing outside. I heard a single footstep on the stairs.

Outside, Hunter gave a few loud barks, then whined and fell silent.

I climbed down a few rungs and jumped off the ladder. Stacey and I ran back across the first floor and back outside.

"Hunter!" I shouted, swinging my light around. He wasn't in the spot where we'd left him, or any other spot I could see. I looked to the exterior stairs, but there was nobody there, either.

"Hunter!" Stacey shouted. We spread out, calling for the dog.

Something rustled in the scrubby pine woods behind the concession stand, like footsteps crunching pine needles.

I hurried toward it, widening the iris of my flashlight to illuminate as much of the woods as possible.

Something shadowy moved behind a dense curtain of thorny briers, and I circled it, jabbing my flashlight like a sword.

I heard him before I saw him. Hunter whined, shivering.

"Hunter, what happened?" I asked, as if he were going to recount whatever had startled him into the woods. I knelt and checked him over. Aside from a couple of scratches from the thorns he'd been hiding beneath, he was fine.

"Is he okay?" Stacey asked.

"I think so."

"Did you see anybody?"

"Nope." I pointed my light into the woods. "I didn't hear anybody, either."

I coaxed Hunter out of the briers and back into the clearing, while Stacey looked back and forth with her flashlight, trying to find any sign of what had scared the dog.

"Wait out here with him," I told her. "I'm going back in to take some readings. Let me know if you see anyone."

"Be careful."

On my way back to the building, I strapped on my annoyingly bulky thermal goggles, which felt like wearing a front-heavy hat made of solid rock. I left them propped on my forehead for the moment.

I returned into the shattered first floor of the concession stand and slowly paced around it, watching the Mel Meter ghost-detection device in my hand. The temperature dipped a degree or two here and there, but more significantly, it was giving me readings of two to three milligaus in a building that was well away from any live electrical wiring.

Peering through my thermals, I picked up pale blue cold smears scattered on the broken cabinets, as if a ghost had left greasy fingerprints behind. I saw nothing larger than that, no active presence in the room with me.

I checked the closet—a little colder, same electromagnetic frequency readings—then headed upstairs. The EMF readings were weak until I reached the closet, and they spiked around the trap door. It figures. Ghosts can obsess over doors, windows, mirrors, stairways, or anything that stands for crossing from one place to the next.

Still, I didn't see any active presence. If I waited around long enough, I might catch a residual haunting, or maybe something worse, like a roaming revenant with a destructive bent. If it could smash apart the fixtures in the concession stand, it could smash apart living people, too.

"There's nobody home right now," I said, stepping outside to join Stacey. "Something was in there, though. I found clear traces."

"You think a ghost did all that damage?" she asked, looking worried, which was the correct way to look under the circumstances.

"I'm pretty sure it wasn't a vagrant or drug addict committing a desperate burglary," I said. "They would have taken out the pipes to sell for scrap. So it's either teenage vandals or a ghost with strong psychokinetic abilities and a bad attitude."

"I'm hoping teenagers, then," Stacey said.

"We'll set up the works here tomorrow before sunset," I said, stashing my thermals back into my backpack. "Cameras, microphones, motion detectors. Let's head back. I think Hunter's been through enough tonight."

"Sounds great to me." We started back across the clearing to the paved road by the never-used recreation facilities. Then Stacey stopped abruptly.

"What is it?" I looked back to see Stacey half-turned away from me. Hunter was straining to walk in the opposite direction, toward the little thatch of thorns where he'd been hiding. "It's okay, boy. We're done for now."

Hunter whined and pulled harder against his leash.

"Is there something in the woods?" Stacey whispered.

I pointed my flashlight in that direction. "Nothing I can see. Okay, Hunter, show us what the big deal is."

I took his leash from Stacey. As soon I began to walk, Hunter broke into a little trot, his loose, floppy jowls jiggling, his nose to ground as he huffed excitedly.

He plunged us into the scrub pine and briers, pausing twice along the way while Stacey cut open a path with the shears.

We emerged onto a wide patch of red dirt and weeds. We'd reached the far end of the park. Across the roundabout lay the most undeveloped streets in the community, with a few skeletal house-frames and lots of bare red earth. Unlit streetlamps overlooked the empty lots and sidewalks.

Directly ahead lay a street that didn't even have street lamps, fire hydrants, or storm drains, just a flat black ribbon of pavement. While much of the land along the other streets had been cleared and flattened to make room for future houses, the land along both sides of this street was still full of old trees the developer had never cut down. The road ran out of sight into the deep shadows of the woods. It was the least developed area of the community, the back end of the enormous swatch of property, bordering the federal wilderness.

Hunter whined and pulled in that direction, and I let him lead us.

"Is it just me," Stacey whispered, "Or did the dog pick the scariest possible path?"

"This is actually as far as you can get from the entrance," I said, as we crossed the roundabout and started down the road into the woods. "Funny how it starts off strong with all the fancy columns out front, but by the time you reach the back, there's nothing here."

"Yeah. Pretty funny, I guess." Stacey shivered. "Is it colder back here?"

"Check your meter. I've got the dog."

While Stacey took temperature and EMF readings, I noticed that the chorus of night insects in the woods grew quieter as we followed the road deeper into the shadows. Hunter walked along the center of the street, never slowing.

The night grew colder as the dark woods swallowed us up, blotting out the sky above. I felt apprehensive, my stomach a tight knot. Something bad was waiting down the road for us.

Finally, when we were far from the lights of the inhabited portions of the community, and the woods were almost silent around us, we reached the end.

It was a dead end, appropriately enough, stopping abruptly and without fanfare, immediately giving way to dense old woods. There wasn't even a little barrier or any reflectors to try to prevent errant motorists from crashing into the thick oak trees.

"Okay," Stacey said. "So it looks like the develemergeoper ran out of money right about...here." She touched the end of the pavement with her boot.

"What do you say, Hunter?" I asked. "Are you satisfied? Should we go back now?" It was getting very late, and the woods were cold and silent.

Of course, Hunter was not satisfied. The bloodhound nosed into the tangle of vines and thorns blocking our access to the old woods.

"You're up, Stacey," I said. "Get lopping."

Stacey sighed and began carving a path through the dense growth. "There'd better be a whole pack of ghosts waiting in here."

"Careful what you wish for."

The bloodhound watched her impatiently, shifting from one paw to the next, clearly eager to pursue whatever it was he'd discovered.

I stayed on guard, keeping my flashlight in motion, watching for anything evil to emerge from the woods.

Chapter Four

After slicing through a number of thorny vines and thin branches, Stacey discovered a narrow break through the woods, leading straight ahead into darkness.

"Looks like an old deer path or something," she said, wiping sweat from her face.

"Interesting." I looked from the path to the road behind us. "It's like they paved over some older trail when they built this community."

"Why does that sound ominous somehow?" Stacey asked. "Are there such things as haunted trails in the woods?"

"What do you think?"

She sighed. "At least we can walk into the dark and scary woods a little faster now."

Hunter was eager to go, sniffing his way forward along the narrow trail. We still had to pause here and there for Stacey to clip away thorns and low limbs.

The night only grew darker and colder as we advanced, the old woods closing over our heads to form a canopy that blocked out the already scarce light from the moon and stars. The back of my neck prickled—the feeling you get when someone is watching you from behind, or from across a room, just before you turn and look at them. I didn't see anything when I turned, though. My flashlight found only scabby tree trunks and coiled poison ivy.

Stacey carved away another wall of thorns. As it dropped aside, cold air rolled out over us like a freezing wind from the north.

"I think we found a...tunnel?" Stacey whispered.

I poked through into an open space. The oak branches overhead had knitted together, sealed with layers of cascading Spanish moss, forming a long, cave-like environment in the woods. The canopy was just a few feet above my head. The brush thinned to knee-high weeds, making the area much more walkable than the woods around it.

"What is this place?" Stacey whispered.

I turned my flashlight down the tunnel in each direction, but I couldn't see where it began or ended. The darkness of the woods around us didn't exactly help with visibility, but it seemed to me that the gloomy tunnel of branches and long moss, hanging like witch's hair everywhere I looked, was absorbing the glow of my flashlight.

"It's cold," I said. "Take some readings."

"Forty degrees," Stacey said, after setting aside the shears and checking her Mel-Meter. "It was seventy-one before we entered the woods. This is not natural."

"EMF?"

"Just a low-level...wait." The lights flickered on her meter. "Three...five milligaus. Something's out here."

"What do you say, Hunter?" I asked. "Hunter, find the ghost."

Hunter waddled a few feet into the weeds, toward the center of the tunnel, then lay down and whined.

"What is it, boy?" Stacey asked.

I squatted by the dog and shined my light into the high weeds, flattening them with my hand for a better look.

A band of rusty iron lay on the ground in front of me. Two bands, it turned out, running in parallel, with the crumbling remains of wooden ties beneath them.

"The old train tracks," I said. They ran along the center of the mossy tunnel, obscured by the weeds.

Hunter sniffed at the track and gave another whine.

"Should we walk along it?" I tugged Hunter, but he wouldn't move. I touched the antique wrought-iron rail. It was as cold as a block of ice.

"Ellie," Stacey whispered. "What's that?" She pointed westward along the tracks.

It took a moment for me to discern what she was talking about. A smudge of red, glowing dully like hot metal, floated several yards away, just a few feet above the tracks. The longer I stared at it, the clearer it became. It was roughly spherical, a ball of low red light that seemed to bounce and shift as it drifted toward us.

I blinked, half-expecting it to vanish like a speck in my eye, but it remained in place, barely visible but gradually glowing brighter. It wasn't much, but it was clearly real and unnatural. The air turned freezing cold, making me shiver.

"Ellie?" Stacey whispered again.

"Lights off." I extinguished my flashlight and drew my thermal goggles down over my eyes.

On thermal, the red ball looked dark and purple, indicating it was actually very cold despite its glowing red color. Blue fragments floated on one side of it, roughly suggesting a human shape.

We'd found our ghost—or *a* ghost, anyway. I didn't know whether this was related to the banshee in our clients' basement, or the darker, colder thing that I'd chased across the yard, or the thing that had smashed up the concession stand. All I could say for sure was that we were dealing with two to four ghosts in the area.

"Are you recording this?" I whispered, keeping my eyes on the fragmentary apparition.

"Oops," Stacey whispered back. "I mean, yes. Hang on. Hunter, stay." The dog's leash made a crunching sound as it landed in the dry weeds. Stacey's backpack unzipped, and I heard her unfolding the camera.

I took a cautious step toward the ghost, feeling the usual signs of a supernatural encounter—gooseflesh all over my body,.a knot of dread in my stomach, a little voice at the back of my head screaming for me to get out of there right away and find a job doing anything else. Something less scary, like lion taming or working the night shift at an asylum for the criminally insane.

"Okay, totally recording now," Stacey said. "It's just a little red dot. What are you seeing?"

"One entity." I gestured for her to be quiet, then took another step forward along the old railroad track, from one crumbling old tie to another.

The ghost moved closer to me, the ball of extra-icy cold floating somewhere around hip level on the visible jigsaw pieces that suggested a human shape. The ball was about the size of a small pumpkin.

I kept my light in my hand, ready to blast the ghost with three thousand lumens if it turned hostile.

It didn't seem to react to us, though. It ambled forward along the tracks, neither slowing nor gaining speed as it approached me. Maybe it was a residual, reenacting a memory from when it was alive, virtually unaware of anything outside its own mind.

I stepped aside, off the tracks, deciding to observe rather than interfere.

The fragmentary ghost shuffled forward. I wondered how many years it had spent walking up and down these tracks, lost in some emotionally charged memory from life, some tragedy or death.

When it reached the spot where I'd stood, it paused. The icy ball rose up to the level of the ghost's head, then above it. I thought of someone holding up a light in order to see better, as if it were studying the railroad tie where I'd last been.

"What's it doing?" Stacey whispered.

"What are you seeing?"

"Just the little red light," she said. "It's...floating there. Rising up. It's creepy, Ellie..."

The thermal apparition grew completely still, the ball of light fixed in place, floating a foot or so above its head.

I heard a hissing, rustling sound from somewhere down the tracks. It was definitely approaching us, and fairly quickly.

My thermals showed nothing but the deep-blue air whirling toward us as a stiff wind approached.

"Ellie..." Stacey said. Hunter whined. The dog was a red shape hunkered on the ground by my feet, shaking hard.

I lifted the goggles away. With my own eyes, I could see the faint red ball of light hovering above the tracks.

The hissing and rustling approached, and now I saw that it was the wind itself, blowing along the tracks through the leafy tunnel, rustling the dry weeds and the long grassy tongues of moss hanging from the trees. Limbs brushed together.

The wind picked up, and it had an acrid taste, a hint of fire and smoke. It blew harder and faster, crashing the limbs together, the gnarled old oaks letting out the deep, disturbing groans of massive trees rubbing together, a sound I usually associate with a heavy storm blowing into town.

Hunter barked, then dashed away from the tracks, back up the trail from which we'd emerged, his leash trailing behind him like a racing snake in the weeds. Stacey chased after him, calling his name.

"Stay here and record!" I shouted to be heard over the rising, howling wind, which now tossed my hair back and forth across my face. Something cracked in the canopy above, and then a mossy limb as long as my whole body broke loose and fell into the weeds alongside the tracks. It splintered into chunks on impact, revealing years of rot within.

"But Hunter--" Stacey shouted back.

"He'll be okay! He's good at avoiding danger."

"Shouldn't we be avoiding danger, too?" Stacey asked.

"No. Get this on video."

"Get what on video?" She raised her camera toward the tracks. "The wind? I don't think--"

Whatever she said after that, I couldn't hear it, because the main brunt of the icy wind finally hit us, drowning out all sound with its own roar. The wind sent us both staggering, blasting us with hurricane speeds. I stumbled over another fallen branch and fell backwards, landing hard on the ground.

Stacey yelled something and I waved her away—I wanted her to keep recording. She held her camera out in front of herself, blindly, using her other arm to protect her eyes from the cloud of dust and leaves.

The roaring wind began to flag as the brunt of it blew onward down the tracks, leaving eddies of swirling breeze in its wake. The limbs, leaves, and moss continued brushing against each other for another minute, like a crowd of whispering voices, fading slowly into silence.

"Well, that was weird," Stacey said. She offered me a hand as I stood, but I shook my head.

The red light drifted onward down the tracks, trailing after the blast of wind, until it vanished out of sight.

"Is there such a thing as a ghost train?" Stacey asked.

"We'd better talk to Calvin. This calls for immediate research."

"Boring research sounds great right now. Especially in a well-lighted area with other people and hot chocolate. Can we please get out of here?" Stacey was shivering hard in the freezing air, and she looked frightened. I'm sure I looked the same way.

"Let's go find Hunter," I said.

As we started up the trail, I glanced back. The weeds had sprung up again, concealing the old railroad tracks. For a moment while the wind had blasted through, flattening all the weeds to the earth, I'd seen it laid bare, the two rails dark with decades of rust, the railroad ties pulverized by weather, time, and termites, lying crooked under the wrought-iron rails like the teeth in a crazy man's smile.

Chapter Five

We followed the trail back to the road, and my heartbeat finally slowed as we emerged from the cold woods into the warm night, flooded with the reassuring chirrups of swarms of crickets and katydids. We could see the lights of the inhabited streets ahead.

"Hunter!" I called. "Hunter!"

The dog didn't respond. We finally found him on the front porch of a half-built house on the next street. One exterior wall was completely missing, revealing two stories of square lumber caves within.

Hunter lay on his back at the top of the porch stairs, paws in the air, eyes closed. Drool leaked from his mouth, and he snored and chuffed. Fast asleep.

I poked him gently in the tummy, and he snorted, sniffing, and opened one eye. He took his time rolling over, pushing to his feet, and stretching.

"Okay, let's cut back through the park," I said. "It's faster than walking around."

"Are you crazy?" Stacey asked. "With the furniture-smashing ghost loose in there?"

"I'm kidding," I said. "Let's stick to sidewalks and streetlights.

I'd like to get back to the clients' house by midnight."

"Is it that late already?" Stacey glanced at her phone, then at a street with a few unoccupied houses and a number of empty red lots. "I don't like this place. With a haunted house, you can try to run outside and escape. Here, the ghosts are already outside, just wandering the streets."

"It's going to take a while to put together what's happening here," I said. We walked on the outer rim of the roundabout, following a curved sidewalk past streets that grew more and more developed, with white picket fences enclosing the weed-choked lawns of half-finished houses, until we reached the well-lit inhabited streets near the front of the community.

At the clients' house, Stacey and Hunter climbed into the van. The bloodhound slurped up more water from his portable water bowl, crunched some kibble and treats, then sprawled on the narrow drop-down bunk and resumed his snoring and drooling, while Stacey brought the array of small monitors to life. Our cameras and microphones had been recording the basement area while we were away.

Leaving Stacey in the van, I walked past the closed garage doors and around the side of the house, where I reached over the picket fence gate and slid open the deadbolt. As a security measure, the fence wasn't exactly the Great Wall of China.

"Headset check," I said.

"Check on that check," Stacey answered.

In the backyard, I approached the basement door and unlocked it with the key Ember had given me. Before stepping inside, I took a quick look around the yard and toward the street beyond, where the shadowy figure had vanished the night before. I didn't see anything, and my thermal goggles had nothing to add.

When I stepped into the cold basement, I immediately heard sobbing and crying. It sounded like the banshee was back, louder than ever.

Clicking on my flashlight, I approached the stairs where I'd found the banshee huddling the previous night. I didn't need any special ghost-detecting equipment, though, to see Ember sitting on the unpainted wooden steps. She was draped in a panda-print maternity nightgown, hunched forward as far as her belly would allow, her hands covering her face as she sobbed.

"Ember?" I approached her carefully, more or less the same way I'd approached the figure on the railroad tracks earlier. "What's wrong?"

She looked up at me, her eyes and face red, still gasping through her mouth as if she couldn't stop herself from sobbing.

"What happened?" I asked.

"My..." Her chest hitched. "My mother's dying. I'm going to be all alone."

"I'm so sorry." I climbed up the steps, but there wasn't room for me to sit beside her. I sort of stood there awkwardly and took her hand. Her fingers squeezed mine.

She was cold, like she'd just taken her hand out of the freezer.

"What am I going to do?" Ember whispered, rocking back and forth. "What am I going to do? I can't do anything! I don't know how to..." Her lip trembled, and she covered her eyes again, sobbing.

I eased my heavy, boxy thermal goggles down over my eyes.

A haze of cold blue surrounded Ember like a dense fog, rolling and swirling along her skin while she shuddered with her crying.

"Leave her alone," I said, doing my best tough-guy voice.

"What?" Ember asked, the red and green thermal image of her face turning up toward me.

"I think the ghost is feeding on you," I said. "Come on. We have to go upstairs and turn on all the lights."

"I like it down here," she whispered. "It's dark and sad."

"I'm serious." I took her arm to help her stand up.

"Don't make me."

I lifted the thermals off my eyes and looked at her. "I probably didn't explain this clearly enough, Ember. The ghost is surrounding you and feeding on your energy. That means it's feeding on your baby's energy, too."

Ember winced as if I'd slapped her, but then she nodded.

I helped her to her feet and stayed close behind her as she ascended the steps, feeling a bit like her overprotective husband.

"What's up in there?" Stacey asked over my headset.

"We're leaving the basement now," I said. "Let me know if you see anything unusual."

I turned on every light switch we passed. In the living room, I switched on all the lamps while she sank to the couch.

"Ember, I'm really sorry about your bad news." I sat down beside her and patted her shoulder. "You have to stay out of the basement."

She closed her eyes and slumped against me, still crying softly, her tears and nose juices soaking the denim sleeve of my jacket. I let her rest her head on my lap, feeling pretty uncomfortable with the whole situation.

"My mother," she whispered against my jeans.

"I'm so sorry. Did you just find out?"

"She was sick," Ember whispered. "Now she's gone and I'm all alone."

"You're not," I said. "You have..." I panicked for half a second before I remembered her husband's name again. "Tom. And the baby."

"Where am I going?" Ember asked, her eyes still closed. "What's going to happen to me?"

"You're going to be fine. Maybe I should go get Tom—"

"No." She grabbed my hand, gripping tight with her chilly fingers. "Don't leave me."

I drew the goggles down again. The nimbus of pale blue remained, though it had diminished up here with all the lights on.

"Ember, listen to me," I said. "The ghost is still with you. I wish I could just spray it with Ghost-Off, but that doesn't exist, so I'm going to need your help."

She let out a soft whimper and kept her eyes shut, resting her cheek on my leg, almost like a little kid.

"What do you do when you're sad?" I asked, while trying to think of an answer to that question myself. "What music makes you feel better?"

"Mother," she whispered.

I didn't think she was referencing either the John Lennon or the Pink Floyd song, or at least I couldn't imagine either one being comforting at this moment. What was it she'd been singing to herself the other morning, when she'd been happily cooking breakfast in the sunlight? Something by Cyndi Lauper?

I wrangled my phone from my pocket and typed the singer's name into my YouTube app. I picked a playlist, then set the phone down on my knee, next to Ember's ear, the volume low. She settled down and stopped sobbing part of the way through "Time After Time." By the time it reached "True Colors," she appeared to be asleep.

My thermals revealed that the entity had settled, too, but still clung to her like a filmy blue mist. The ghost was really obsessed with Ember. At least Ember was away and asleep now, less vulnerable to the spirit drawing out her misery in order to slurp it down.

I slipped out from beneath her softly snoring head, replacing my leg with a couch cushion to prop her up. I reclaimed my phone and killed the music.

"Keep watch on her, Stacey," I said. I found the nearest camera, a night vision on a tripod near the basement door, and moved it to the living room.

"Ten-four, good buddy," Stacey said.

Ember had left a distinct wet patch on my jeans legs, so my first stop was at the bathroom to clean off my client's snot of sadness.

Then I tiptoed upstairs, where I found the linen closet and took a couple of blankets. I glanced into the open door to the master bedroom to see Tom still asleep, ruler-straight on his side of the bed, blissfully unaware of his wife's distress.

I returned to the living room and laid the blankets over Ember. She murmured in her sleep and shifted on the couch. She seemed at peace.

A rattle echoed through the house. It fell silent for a few seconds, then it happened again, louder and more insistent. It sounded as if someone were at the front door, aggressively shaking the doorknob and trying to get inside.

"Stacey, who's at the front door?" I whispered.

"Front door? Let me climb up and look out the windshield..."

I stepped into the foyer, tactical flashlight in hand. The rattling had stopped for the moment, but I kept my eyes on the doorknob.

"Ellie, there's nobody there," Stacey said.

"Are you sure?" I looked out the window, but the front porch area was empty. So was the lawn below. Our blue van was in the driveway, pointed right at the front door. With the long flight of stairs from the elevated front porch to the ground, it would have been nearly impossible for anyone to slip away without Stacey or me noticing.

"Want me to hop out and look around?" Stacey asked.

"Not really," I said, thinking of the large, dangerous-looking entity I'd pursued the night before. "I'd rather you stay in the van. And lock the doors."

"Okay..." Over the headset, I heard the clunking of the van's locks falling into place.

"I'm going to stay with Ember. Keep an eye out for...anything." I made sure the front door was locked, then the back door, which led out to an elevated porch overlooking the back yard. "Watch the basement, especially," I added, while closing the door to the basement stairs. Unfortunately, it had no lock.

Ember lay on the couch, deep asleep now, not even stirring. I checked her with my thermals again. The layer of cold blue had vanished completely, as if the ghost had given up, or something had chased it away, leaving her in peace for the night.

Chapter Six

I tried to tiptoe out of the living room right at the break of dawn, but Ember woke up, groggy and blinking.

"How did I get down here?" she asked.

"Don't you remember last night?" I hesitated at the living room doorway.

"Ugh." Ember remained where she was, lying on the couch, looking up at the ceiling. "Last night. I...woke up. She was crying again, down in the basement. I could hear her all the way upstairs. The poor thing, I thought. What if it was my child, alone and in the dark like that, scared and sad like that? I wanted to go help her."

I'd warned her and Tom to avoid the ghost, not engage with it, but I didn't pick this moment to remind her of that. She'd already learned the hard way.

"So I...went down," she continued. "Down to the basement." She blinked.

"Then what?" I asked.

"That's it." Ember shook her head. "I had some bad dreams, something about a train at night, taking me somewhere I didn't want to go...and that's all I remember."

"Can you tell me about the dream?" I sat down in an armchair, facing her. I drew my notepad from my jacket pocket. It felt like the classic cartoon-psychiatric scenario, with her lying on the couch and me sitting nearby, asking questions and taking notes.

"It was dark," she said. "Like I was traveling at night. I just remember the train was hellish, all black iron and smoke, you could smell burning everywhere. I was scared and alone, walking through the train. Trying to escape. There was no way out. I had to escape, and then I had to pee. Really urgently. But I couldn't find a bathroom. Actually, I really do need to pee, right now." She pushed herself up to a sitting position, and I hurried over and helped her stand.

"Sorry." Ember gave me a tired smile. "I'm really not an invalid. I just feel drained right now."

"That's because the ghost was feeding on you."

Her mouth twisted downward in a look of horror. "What?"

"You don't remember that, either?"

"I'll be right back." She closed the bathroom door.

"Stacey?" I asked.

"What's the plan?" Stacey asked over my headset. "Do we take Hunter home now, then get breakfast? Or get breakfast somewhere outdoors so we can bring the dog? I vote eat outdoors, because I'm starving—"

"No breakfast yet," I said. "I have to speak with Ember for a minute."

"Well, Hunter's very disappointed to hear that. His face is all saggy and droopy."

"His face is always saggy and droopy."

"I promised him eggs and ham."

"You may have promised too much."

Ember stepped out of the bathroom. "Do you have time for breakfast?"

"That would be great! Thanks!" I replied.

"And I want to hear that recording of the ghost's voice," Ember said, leading the way to the kitchen. "Even if Tom doesn't."

"Can we leave Hunter in your back yard?" The sun was beginning to rise and I didn't want the dog overheating while he waited.

"Of course." She opened the refrigerator and sighed. "Do you mind handing me the milk? Sorry, I can't reach the bottom shelf anymore."

"Stacey, bring your tablet up here," I said. "Put Hunter in the fence."

"Sounds like it's going to take a while." She sighed. "My stomach is seriously rumbling, Ellie."

"Sorry." I muted my microphone and handed Ember ingredients as she requested them. By the time Stacey arrived, Ember was slicing cantaloupes while six little polka-dotted puddles that would soon be blueberry pancakes heated on the griddle.

"Breakfast!" Stacey said, her eyes wide. "Why didn't you tell me?"

"I thought you'd enjoy the surprise," I said. "Ember wants to hear the banshee."

"Anything for blueberry pancakes." Stacey sat down at the kitchen table and pulled up the files on her tablet.

"I hope you like them," Ember said.

"She likes everything," I told her. "Except craisins."

"Ugh, craisins." Stacey made a sour face, then played the audio of me asking the ghost why it was there, and the two answers it had given at different times:

"*Hiding.*"

"*They died.*"

The ghost's voice was a low, distant whisper, the intonation flat.

"That just made all my hair stand up," Ember said, staring at the tablet from where she stood at the counter. "It sounds like a woman talking."

"Can you remember anything else about your encounter last night?" I asked.

Ember shook her head. "I just remember feeling sad and alone."

"Did anything else happen on the train?" I asked, and Stacey's head perked up like a cat that just heard the can opener. "Was anyone else there?"

"The people didn't seem friendly. They gave me dirty looks or pretended I wasn't there at all."

"How were they dressed?"

"Oh, the women had these long, old-fashioned dresses, puffy lace around the sleeves...big hats with feathers and flowers. The men had those old bowler hats, dark suits, ties."

"It sounds like you were in another era," I said. By the description, I was thinking the Victorian years, somewhere around the border between the nineteenth and twentieth centuries.

"It was," she agreed. "Do you like maple syrup or honey? I'll just put both on the table."

"Ember!" Tom shouted, his feet banging their way down the stairs at high speed. "Ember, where are you?"

"I'm at Six Flags, riding all the roller coasters," Ember said as he walked into the room, dressed in gray pajamas. "Where do you think I am?"

"You weren't there when I woke up." He glanced at Stacey and me, seeming annoyed by our presence.

"Have some breakfast," she said. "There might be a pancake left."

"I'm going to be late for work. Did we get rid of the ghost yet?"

"We're still turning up lots of background information that should help us identify the entity," I said.

He shook his head and left the room. Sometimes people expect us to find, trap, and remove a ghost within a day or so. I wish we could. Dividing our fees by the number of actual hours I put into a case makes for a fairly sad wage. It wasn't as if I was hanging around just for the pancakes.

Then again, once I actually took a bite of mine, I thought the breakfast alone might be worth the long and difficult night. I could see why her friends had wanted to start a sweets shop with her.

"Wait a minute." Stacey looked at Ember. "Is that...brown sugar?"

"Just..." Ember pinched her fingers tightly together. "If you can taste it, it's too much."

"It's perfect," Stacey said. "These are like ten times better than...um..."

"Which fine establishment were you going to name?" I asked. "The Country Barn?"

"Maybe." Stacey narrowed her eyes just slightly at me. She didn't like me bringing up that particular ultra-kitschy chain of restaurants.

"Listen," Ember said, finally joining us at the table, her plate stacked with two big blueberry pancakes and half a cantaloupe. "I'd rather you didn't tell Tom what happened last night. He already worries over every second of my day anyway."

"As long as you promise me you'll avoid the ghost from now on," I said. "No more going down to the basement to comfort it. Remember, this thing uses sadness as a weapon. It can hook you in with pity. It's going to treat your compassion as a weakness."

"Okay," Ember nodded.

"You promise?"

"Sure. Of course."

"What are we promising?" Tom, having accomplished the bizarre male feat of showering and dressing in fifteen minutes, stepped into the kitchen for a slice of toast. He wore a black tie dotted with little cartoon teeth, each one of which had a big smile, wore a pair of sunglasses, and a carried a toothbrush in one hand.

"Hey, I love that tie," Stacey said, accompanying the comment with her most charming smile. "I like how the little tooth guys have teeth of their own."

"Ember bought me this." He looked down at it. "The Cherrier kid's coming in for three fillings this morning. If that kid's parents don't cut off his grape soda supply, his mouth's going to turn into a real gold mine. A sticky blue gold mine. I thought the kid would get a kick out of the tie."

"I bet he will!" Stacey said. "It must be such interesting work, being a dentist."

"It's not," Tom said. He kissed his wife. "Are you okay? Do you need anything?"

"I'm fine."

"You shouldn't be cooking. You need to rest."

"I'll just order pizza for breakfast from now on," she said.

"Sounds great. Make sure there's pepperoni." He walked out of the kitchen.

"Love you," she said, while the front door closed. The doorknob rattled as he locked it behind him, reminding me of the entity who'd tried to come inside last night.

"We have a lot to do," I said. "Ember, can you put us in touch with the neighborhood watch guy Tom mentioned?"

"Sure, Mr. Nobson. He's the watch chief, plus president and

treasurer of the neighborhood association, chair of the Adherence Committee...they thought a lot more people would be living here when they created the homeowner's association, so there are all these offices. Mr. Nobson's the only one who really wants them. He's retired."

"What's the Adherence Committee?" I asked.

"Making sure everyone's house and lawn conform to the association rules," Ember said. "No weeds, no boats parked in the driveway, only the approved colors if you paint your house. Mr. Nobson patrols in his golf cart for violations."

"Sounds like a fun guy," Stacey said.

"I'd also like to speak to the original developer," I said. "The people who printed those brochures. New Vision Properties."

"I think they went bankrupt," Ember said. "The bank owns the whole place now. But I'm sure Mr. Nobson can put you in touch. He's lived here since the beginning, when the buyers thought they were getting a lot more for their money. I think he's a little bitter about it."

"When do you think he could speak with us?"

"I'll call him, but if it's about official homeowner's association business, he'll probably be ready to meet anytime. The HOA is his life."

"Okay...It looks like we need to dig into the history of the railroad that ran through here, as well as the old farm." I quickly explained what we'd seen—the strange light by the tracks and the powerful gust of wind that blew along them. "We have a former client who was actually haunted by an owner of that railroad. She had some of his old paperwork in her attic. I'll give her a call."

"What about Jacob?" Stacey asked.

"That's our psychic consultant," I told Ember. "I'll bring him in eventually, once we have a better idea of what we're looking for. Stacey, let him know we're going to need him."

"And don't forget to call Michael," Stacey said.

"Why?"

"You forgot to call him back last night."

"Okay, I'll take care of that."

"You really should," Stacey said. She looked at Ember. "Ellie went on one date with this awesome cute fireman guy, and she can't find anything wrong with him, and she won't call him back--"

"Stacey!" I said. "We're not going to bother her with that."

"I'm just saying--"

"Why don't you call him?" Ember asked. "He sounds nice."

"Anyway, back to things that are actually relevant to the case," I said, with a quick glare for Stacey. She was really getting on my nerves with that subject. Why couldn't she let me deal with my issues myself? "After what we saw last night, we might be looking for a train wreck, something that would have led to a possible ghost train, if that's what we saw. The good news is that events like that should stick out in the historical records, so we should be able to find it pretty quickly. We also need to set up cameras at some of the active hauntspots we found last night."

"Well, it sounds like you know what you're doing," Ember said. "I just hope it's over quickly."

"I was sorry to hear about your mother," I said.

"What about my mom?" Ember looked alarmed.

"Last night, you said she'd passed away recently. That she'd been sick."

"Sick?" Ember snickered. "My mom's running a marathon in Indiana tomorrow. She's never sick. Her work even gave her an award for perfect attendance."

"Oh. Good. Did you have a bad dream about her or something?"

"Not that I remember. Maybe I should call and make sure she's okay."

We finished breakfast, and Ember insisted that we take some praline pecans she'd made. Stacey and I collected Hunter and returned to the van.

"I wish you hadn't done that," I said to Stacey as I drove away.

"Which part?"

"Trying to pressure me about Michael while the client was there. It's not professional, or appropriate, or anywhere close."

"Okay, you're right. I'll never do it again. In *front* of a client." Then she grabbed my phone from the dashboard charger.

"What are you doing?"

"There's no client here now." She gave me a wicked grin as she flipped through my contact list.

"Stacey!"

"M...where's M...wow, you don't have tons of contacts." Stacey held the phone to her ear, and I heard it ringing.

"Stop it! That's not funny."

"Hey, Mikey!" Stacey said into the phone. "Um, no, this is Stacey. Ellie's driving right now. But she wanted to call you and make dinner plans. Here you go." She held the phone up to my ear, waggling her eyebrows and giving me a thumbs up.

"Uh, hey," I said, snatching the phone from her fingers. I was so flustered I almost ran a stop sign, and I shouted a little as I slammed the brakes at the last second. An old man in a Chevy Nova blared his horn as he passed through the intersection, giving me a rude gesture.

"Sorry!" I shouted out the open window.

"Ellie?" Michael asked.

"Yeah, sorry, uh...what were you saying?" I asked.

"You called me," he said. "I mean your assistant did. How's Friday?"

"I have to work on this case every night," I said. "I don't know when I'll have a free one."

"So...why the invite?"

"I..." I couldn't think of a way to get out of it. I scowled at Stacey for forcing the situation. "I mean I eat my dinner at breakfast time, you know, so...want to have breakfast?"

"It's the most important meal of the day," he said. "I'm not working Saturday. Should we meet Saturday morning?"

"Sure, Saturday...Hey, and we'll have Stacey and Jacob along, too," I said.

Stacey furrowed her brow and shook her head.

"Jacob's the psychic guy, right?" Michael asked.

"Yep, Jacob the psychic," I said. "We'll all meet at The Country Barn."

Stacey gasped and punched me in the arm.

"Okay, interesting choice. Which one?"

"The one out on 516," I said. "Thanks, Michael. This will be...good." That sounded stupid. I was all mixed up from being pushed by Stacey but suddenly excited to see Michael again, despite my reservations about getting into any deep relationships at this point in my life.

"I'm going to kill you," Stacey said after I hung up.

"Never kill a ghost hunter. We make very dangerous ghosts. We know all the tricks."

"You're evil."

"We're both evil," I said, and then I called Jacob.

Chapter Seven

I dropped Stacey off and headed home to my narrow little brick loft. I fed my cat, Bandit, and then I was ready for sleep, but I had to make a couple of phone calls.

First I got in touch with my old client, Toolie Paulding, who was working her job as a manager for the Sir Sleepmore Mattresses outlet by the mall.

"Oh, Ellie!" Toolie said, after I identified myself. "How are you? And how's Stacey?"

"Everybody's fine," I told her. "How have things been with your family the last couple of months? Any disturbances?"

"Oh, no, no. Things are better than ever. Crane's back to his old self now that his invisible friends are gone. Gord's emphysema has dropped to levels where they can't even detect it. He's even working at his old company again."

"Is the house staying dry?"

"Oh, yes. Not a leak since you left. Even the back yard is staying dry." Toolie's house had been haunted by a few ghosts who had drowned, and they'd manifested themselves in ways that reflected it—including plumbing trouble, an unwanted pond in the backyard, and Gord's emphysema. "Are you just calling to follow up? Or are you in the market for a new mattress? Because I think you could really benefit from one of these pillow-top models."

"Thanks, but actually neither. I have a new case that involves the GC&R railroad company—the one that caused your ghost to go bankrupt just before he died—and I remember we found some paperwork and records in your attic. Would you mind if we stop by there and visit your attic again?"

"Goodness, no. You're lucky it's all still up there. I've been meaning to remove every trace of those awful ghosts from the house, but things have been so busy, with Gord working again and the new fall line-up of mattresses, and the kids going back to school--"

"I understand."

"Anyway, good thing we never put 'em in the trash. You're welcome to take as much as you want, because we're throwing out the rest."

"Would you mind donating them to the Savannah Historical Association?" I asked. "I'm sure they'd love anything related to one of Savannah's first railroads."

"Ellie, if you know somebody wants to come haul away all them papers, they can take it. His old desk, too. We don't want anything of his in our house."

"Would today be okay?"

"I don't know. Gord's at a fried-pie convention until Sunday—I think Pink Fairy cupcakes is looking into manufacturing them—and I'll be working until the store closes at nine, because it's all heating up for our big Oktoberfest sale. Can you come Sunday afternoon?"

"I was kind of hoping for much sooner. Like before the sun sets today, so I can get to my client's house before dark."

"Oh, that's a pickle. Tell you what, Junie should be home from school by four o'clock. I can text her and let her know to expect you. She's watching her brother until I get home, so she's stuck there anyway."

"I'd really appreciate it."

"Too bad I'm going to miss you," Toolie said. "You should come over and eat a fried chicken sometime. Maybe after Gord's back in town. He likes the dark meat, I like the white, that's why we get along so well."

"Thanks so much," I said.

"Is your new family in a lot of danger?" Toolie asked, her voice dropping to a hushed whisper.

"It's always a possibility."

"All right, I have to go. Oktoberfest decorations just arrived."

I was mildly curious to learn exactly how one decorated a mattress store for a Bavarian festival, but she hung up.

My next call was to Grant Patterson, semi-practicing attorney, skillful collector of art and gossip, and devoted Fellow of the Savannah Historical Association.

"The most exciting number in my entire contact list," Grant answered. "You're fortunate that I'm awake at this disturbingly bright hour of the morning."

"You told me you only sleep five or six hours a night."

"Five or six entire hours? I'd miss out on too much reading time. How are you? Eating well? Still dating the fireman?"

"I'm fine."

"And how's your family?" he asked.

"Still dead."

"Ah...I meant, of course, your *extended--*"

"I know, forget it. I have a problem with a haunted stretch of railroad track."

"I am instantly fascinated, dear. Which particular stretch?"

"It's an old Georgia Canal and Railroad line. Iron, not steel. It used to run through Silkgrove Plantation, those old ruins right on the river by the paper plant, about twelve miles north of--"

"I know all about it. That bit of rail must have been abandoned ages ago."

"It looks that way to me. We're trying to find any history of--"

"Tragedy and death," Grant said. "Suffering and murder. The usual?"

"The usual, thanks. Train crashes, especially. There was also a family farm in that area." I gave him what I knew about the Whalens, who'd lived there during the nineteenth century. I mentioned Rose Whalen, one of my suspects for the banshee, mainly because she'd been young and had something to grieve about since she'd left small children behind. It would be fairly convenient for me if she'd been a part of some tragedy on those tracks, or perhaps had witnessed some major event like a train wreck there.

Another possibility was one of her daughters. Ember, during or after her assault by the ghost, had dreamed of being alone on a train. She'd talked about her mother growing ill and dying. Maybe that had been the banshee's memory, seeping into Ember while the banshee oppressed her.

"All has been carefully noted," Grant said.

"I actually have something to offer in exchange," I said.

"Knowing that I've helped rid the city of its less pleasant ghosts is compensation enough."

"A former client is looking to offload a batch of paperwork surrounding the creation of the Georgia Canal and Railroad Company."

"Why didn't you tell me? What a treasure. I was, of course, referring to you, as much as I was speaking of that wonderful trove of old documents."

"If I knew you cared that much, I would've grabbed them sooner," I said. "The owner was about to throw them in the trash."

"That's as horrific as one of your ghost stories, Ellie. Is there anything else?"

"Haven't I given you enough homework?"

"I'm simply trying to earn my junior ghost hunter badge."

"You've earned it. Thanks, Grant."

"I will be in touch once I've assembled the most gruesome train stories in Savannah's history."

"I can't wait."

Finally, I could pull my blackout curtains tight, stretch out on my bed, and close my eyes. Not even my cat's relentless desire to use my face as a punching pillow could keep me awake.

In the afternoon, I woke up still unnerved from the night before. I made some strong truck-driver coffee and called Stacey.

"I want you to get on Google Earth and follow every inch of that old rail line you can see. Figure out where it begins and ends, and anything interesting along the way. Then comb through all the audio and video we took, see what you find."

"Good morning back at ya," Stacey replied with a yawn. "What will you be doing?"

"Kickboxing," I said. "Then I'll swing by the Paulding house to look through Isaiah Ridley's old papers about the railroad. Of course, if you'd rather do that while I analyze the audio and video--"

"Oh, gosh, thanks," Stacey said. "But I'll leave the dusty old papers to you. I know how much you like dust."

"I love it."

After I finished talking to Stacey, I got dressed and went to the gym a few blocks away, just in time for the kickboxing class. Forty-five minutes of punching and kicking later, my head felt clear and calm, my mood spiked up with fresh, sweet endorphins and serotonin.

I ran home for a quick shower, then over to the old Georgian mansion where the Paulding family lived. I parked the blue van out front and looked up at the half-circle balcony above the front door. A powerful old poltergeist, wearing the shape of the girl who'd created it more than a century and a half earlier, had nearly thrown me to my death from that balcony.

Following the brick walkway to the front door, I noticed that the front gardens seemed to have sprung back to life. They'd been half-dead before, from a malfunctioning sprinkler system that nobody seemed able to repair.

I rang the front doorbell. A pulsing crash of loud industrial music washed over me as Juniper opened the door, beaming. She startled me with a big ferocious hug.

"Ellie!" she shouted.

"Hi, Juniper." I recovered from the surprise and hugged her back. "How's my favorite poltergeist-smasher?"

"Pretty good. Except school." She made a face. Her dyed-black hair had grown out a little, revealing brown roots. A long braid hung in front of her face with a skull bead the size of my thumb at the end, swinging like a pendulum every time she moved her head. "Eighth grade. It's going to take *forever* to get to high school."

"It'll all blow by faster than you expect," I said. "The good and the bad."

"I wanted to start a paranormal investigation group at school, so we could hunt ghosts like you and Stacey, but they wouldn't let me." Juniper returned inside, and I followed her into the high but narrow entrance hall, cluttered with furniture on both sides, the three flights of the staircase rising in a squarish spiral near the back. "Do you think the high school would let me?"

"You have to be careful," I said. "Remember what we talked about?"

"No Ouija boards." We started up the stairs.

"Avoid all the occult stuff. You don't know what doors you might open."

"I *know*. I already kind of learned that the hard way. So I should just stick to video cameras and stuff, right?" She gave me an earnest look. She looked so innocent, I couldn't imagine her growing up just to get dragged into my world, the dark side.

"There are much better careers than this," I said.

"Like what?"

"Almost anything. It's better to do something where you help people."

"Don't you help people?" she asked. "You helped us. A lot."

"It's dangerous and the pay is pretty bad," I said.

"Then why do you do it?"

"Maybe I'm thinking about changing careers." This wasn't true at all. I'd still do this even if there were no pay, because I hate the ghosts who terrorize and harm the living. It's personal. I didn't want to get into that. I just didn't want to steer her down the wrong course in life.

"Seriously? What else would you do?" Juniper asked.

"Something where I don't get thrown out of windows and down stairs every day. I don't know. Maybe be a nurse?"

"That sounds way less fun." Juniper sighed and opened the door to the attic. "So what are you looking for?"

As we climbed the steep stairs up to the enormous, badly cluttered attic, I told her about the haunted railroad track.

"Oh, awesome! Can I help?"

"You can help right now." I clicked on my flashlight. The attic was dim as ever, lit only by three bare bulbs spaced very widely from each other along the ceiling. "Where's your brother?"

"Playing *Minecraft* in his room." Juniper spoke in a much lower voice in the attic, as though quieted by the memories of the spirits who'd once dwelled here. She activated the flashlight she'd brought with her. "He didn't want you here. I mean, not *you*, but he didn't want to think about...you know, all that."

"Right. How's he doing?"

"He's okay. He misses his imaginary friends sometimes."

"Even though they tried to talk him into killing himself?"

"Some friends are bad influences, I guess," Juniper said. "That's what Mom always says about Dayton."

"Are you still seeing him?"

"Some. He's okay but he's getting annoying." Juniper shrugged as we approached the antique bureau, full of dusty cubbyholes, the leather writing panel built into the top long since cracked and crumbled. "Mom said you wanted some of Isaiah's stuff?"

"I'm taking all of it," I said. "But first, you can help me look through it..."

We sat on the warped old floorboards and spread out files and documents around us.

"We're looking for details about the railroad's construction," I said. "Maps would be great. Also accidents, death notices..."

"Cool." She flipped open an old file folder, and a cloud of dust swirled in her flashlight beam.

"Where'd you get that flashlight?" I asked. It looked like a cheaper version of the tactical flashlight I carried as my anti-ghost sidearm.

"I found it on the internet," she said. "It's just two hundred and eighty lumens, but it's aircraft-grade aluminum like yours." Juniper blushed. "I wanted to get the same one but it cost too much."

It was silly how much that touched me—that she'd spent time looking for a flashlight like mine, and that she remembered details from all the questions she'd asked about our methods and gear.

Our search of the paperwork turned up some interesting details, including a hand-drawn map of the rail line built in 1851. It showed the numerous buildings and river docks of the old Silkgrove plantation, almost a small town within itself. The Georgia Canal and Railroad line had crossed the river there, at the same time crossing the state line from Georgia to South Carolina.

The rail line had originated at the Central of Georgia terminal, where lines already extended westward to inland cities like Albany and Macon, but nothing reaching north along the coast.

Isaiah Ridley and pals had decided to gamble on a coastal line, creating a direct connection between the cities of Savannah and

Charleston. There was money to be made in linking the two largest ports in the region.

Unfortunately, the railroad had gone bankrupt instead. The reason why was probably in these papers somewhere.

We found some evidence of a few workers dying from disease and drowning while laying supports in the marshy river islands, and I set those aside for later study. We didn't find any other major ghost-related red flags, no signs that the rails had been laid through, for instance, an old burial ground or graveyard. That didn't mean it hadn't happened, though—Savannah is filled with unmarked graves from earlier generations, not to mention native burial grounds, which are everywhere. The area's been inhabited for more than ten thousand years.

"This is so much fun!" Juniper said, expressing the exact opposite of Stacey's opinion about sifting through crumbling paperwork in search of historical details. Too bad I couldn't hire her as my research assistant.

"I'll have to carry this stuff away," I said. "Any chance you could help me load it into the van?"

"Of course!" She jumped to her feet.

We carted up a few plastic storage bins and packed them with the contents of the old desk. Crane stepped outside to watch us lift them into the van. The boy remained on the porch, half-concealed behind a thin marble column.

"Hi, Crane," I said. "How's it going?"

"It's been really quiet," he said.

"No ghosts?" I smiled, but he didn't smile back.

"Where did Noah and Luke go?" he asked. Those were the two ghost boys, his invisible friends who'd kept trying to lure him to his death.

"Wherever they're supposed to be," I said.

"Do you think they're happy?"

"I'm sure they are."

Crane wore a solemn frown as he returned inside.

"He's getting better," Juniper whispered, with a confident nod. "He's always been kind of a weirdo."

"He's a nice kid. And so are you, Juniper. Thanks for your help."

"Anytime. I can come help you with your new ghost if you want."

"I doubt your parents would be in favor of that."

"Yeah. But you think when I'm older I could come work with you?"

"We'll talk after you're in college."

Juniper rolled her eyes, then gave me another hug. I'm not much of a hugger, but I like that kid. I hope she comes up with better career options for herself, though.

As I drove away, I felt unsettled. I'd been hoping for clues to the identity of the banshee, but no females had died in the construction of the railway. I wanted to trap that ghost before she could attack my client again. So far, though, I had almost nothing to go on. I could feel the minutes slipping away and the night ahead waiting for me. I stepped on the gas.

Chapter Eight

At the office, I pulled Stacey away from her video-editing station, where she'd been reviewing all the raw footage she'd gathered. We heaped the plastic storage bins full of documents next to my desk.

"A little light reading?" Stacey asked.

"There's a lot of homework," I said. "Did you find anything?"

"Sobbing in the basement last night," Stacey said. "That's what drew Ember down there. We caught partials of the banshee. A small, cold little figure."

"Anything from the railroad?"

"Just that weird red light. We'll have to put up thermals and everything out by the tracks."

"Have you seen Calvin?" I glanced around the cluttered workshop.

"He went up to his apartment a little while after I got here," Stacey said. Calvin occupied the loft level of the old industrial warehouse building, which he accessed with a small cage elevator.

"How did he look?"

"Like something was on his mind and he didn't want to tell me about it. You think those people were back, spying on our office?"

"Just keep watch for any black Acuras," I said.

"You sure there's nothing else going on with him?" Stacey whispered.

"I'm sure of *nothing*," I whispered back, a little over-dramatically. "Did you study the satellite images of the rail line?"

"There's not much to see. The woods obscure most of the tracks, or did whenever Google took its pictures. I can see one end of the line at the river, running through the Silkgrove Plantation ruins. It's concealed by woods most of the way. It looks like it ends at the big north-south CSX line."

"It connects to the modern railway?" I asked.

"I'm not sure it really *connects*, but it definitely ends there."

"We'll have to go walk the tracks," I said.

"Today?"

"Tomorrow. Let's head over to the client's. Ember's made an appointment for us to meet with the neighborhood watch guy."

"Ooh, an appointment. We'd better get moving."

While Stacey finished loading extra gear into the van—more cameras and microphones, mostly—I stepped away and called Calvin on my cell.

"We're about to move out," I said. "Are you okay up there?"

"Better than okay. There's a *Rockford Files* marathon."

"Any words of wisdom for us?"

"Watch out for hobo ghosts."

"Thanks so much." It was strange for Calvin to keep himself so distant, as if he didn't want any serious involvement in the case. Even his little jokes felt like deflection and detachment.

"Any signs of the midnight photographers?"

"No, but I suggest you stay alert for them," Calvin said. "Conceal a few cameras watching the streets around your client's home. See if they're spying on you."

"Yeah, that would be nice to know," I said. "See, I knew you had some words of wisdom."

"You caught me. Be safe out there."

We reached our clients' house with a couple of hours to spare before nightfall. A golf cart was parked outside, behind Ember's blue Ford Fusion.

Ember answered the door in the company of a short man with a rigid posture who appeared to be in his sixties. He had a graying comb-over and wore a khaki camping vest over a starched white shirt with short sleeves.

"Hi!" Ember said. "This is Cecil Nobson, president of our neighborhood association. I told him about the prowlers we'd seen." That was the story Ember had given him—that we were investigating suspicious characters Tom and Ember had spotted near their home, possibly related to the break-ins around the community.

"Nice to meet you, Mr. Nobson," I said. He had a firm, quick handshake. "I'm Ellie Jordan from Eckhart Investigations. This is my associate, Stacey Ray Tolbert."

"Call me Stacey!"

"You're three minutes late," Nobson said, looking at us with plain disapproval. "We like to run a tight ship around here."

"I'm sorry," I said. "We appreciate you taking the time to speak with us. Should we sit down, or--?"

"You're professional detectives?" he asked.

I passed him a business card. He spent a long moment studying it, then nodded and placed it in one of his many vest pockets.

"I'll show you the crime scenes," he said. "We'd all appreciate it very much if you could find out who's behind all this trouble. I've put up a few cameras myself, but all I catch is shadows and blurs, no clear faces yet."

"I'd like to see what you have."

He nodded and led us back down the steps to his waiting golf cart.

I sat beside him in the cart with Stacey behind us, facing backwards. Nobson pulled on a pair of wraparound sunglasses and a khaki fishing hat decorated with an American flag pin. Another pin was shaped like a police badge and read NEIGHBORHOOD WATCH.

Only then did he start up the golf cart and pull out into the street.

"Used to be a real promising community," he said, and I correctly guessed that those words would open a long-winded monologue. "There was supposed to be golf, swim, tennis. Old-fashioned values and virtues. There's a word you don't hear too often these days, 'virtue.' The entire concept is just gone from our culture. Everything's so politically correct these days."

"Why wasn't the community ever completed?" I asked.

"Developers ran out of money," he said. "They went over budget, missed deadlines, had those accidents, worker's comp, lawsuits…"

"What accidents?"

"Construction injuries. An excavator fell over on a loose patch of dirt, crushed a man's leg. Things going wrong like that. After the bankruptcy, the quality of people moving in went downhill, if you know what I mean. Tom and Ember are okay, but some houses over on the western streets have turned into *rentals*. And the *renters* don't care about the neighborhood covenants, nor does the property management company that leases them out. All they care about is milking money for the bank. This place never got to be what it was supposed to be." He cleared his throat as he slowed to a crawl near the end of the street, then paused at the stop sign right before the central roundabout. "The Travois family got hit," he said, pointing at a large two-story brick house on the corner.

"What happened?"

"Someone broke in through their back door when they were out of town," Nobson said. "Smashed up the mirrors, the cabinets. Took all the jewelry in the house."

"What did the police say?"

"They haven't caught anybody." Nobson drove onto the roundabout. To the right lay some of the empty or barely developed streets of the community. He turned left, toward the inhabited streets.

Nobson pointed out three more houses. Two of them had suffered similar break-ins—a level of destruction that reminded me of the scene in the concession stand. Stolen items included more jewelry and a collection of antique silver dollars.

"Then you have the Watt family," Nobson said, parking in a cul-de-sac and indicating another house, which was indistinguishable from its neighbors, all of them two stories with dormers on top and a garage on the right side, yards enclosed with the ubiquitous picket fences. "Donna, the wife, she actually saw the prowler in the upstairs hall one night. Ran back to her bedroom, locked the door, phoned the authorities. He was gone by the time the patrolman arrived, though."

"Did she give a description?"

Nobson opened the glove box and brought out a red file folder with the standard neighborhood watch sign logo on the front, a cartoon villain with a black hat and narrow white eyes, a high-collared black coat concealing his face. A red circle with a slash through it were drawn over him. No cartoon villains allowed.

He flipped through the papers inside and produced some handwritten notes.

"Wore a dirty old hat," he read, lifting his sunglasses and squinting at the paper. "A rag over his face, hiding everything but his eyes. Filthy coat. Pants and boots encrusted with mud." Nobson looked up. "That's interesting, because nobody found any dirt or mud in the carpet." He looked down at the paper again. "Oh, yes. Left a smell of whiskey and cigars in the air."

"Sounds like a real charmer," Stacey commented.

I wondered if this was a ghost or not. I noted the location of the house, thinking I might come back and speak to Donna Watt later.

"A couple of these were hit, too," Nobson said as he drove us down a street of mostly uninhabited homes with overgrown, weedy lawns. "Vandalism and property destruction, since there was nothing inside to steal. They marked up the fences, too. The police don't think the fence marks matter because they're all over, not just on the houses that were burglarized--"

"Wait, back up half a step," I said, and Nobson braked.

"You want me to back up?"

"I didn't mean literally. What fence marks?"

"Didn't I mention those?" Nobson switched off the golf cart and stepped out. "I think they're related, personally. Not a coincidence." He started toward one of the empty houses, gesturing for us to follow. "Come on, now. There's nobody to lodge any trespassing complaints. Nobody's ever lived here."

We followed the picket fence around to the back of the house. The yard within the fence was dense with knee-high weeds and brambles. Beyond the back of the fence lay more of the raw red-earth Martian landscape with only a few tufts of weeds. A street with no houses, just sidewalks and fire hydrants, lay beyond that.

"Here they are," Nobson said, leading us to a white picket near one end of the fence. "Have a look."

Three symbols had been scratched into the post, small and crude, as if hastily carved with a penknife. I leaned close to study them.

They were in a column. The top symbol looked like a letter "C" with bars extending from the tips. Beneath that was a squiggly line, as if someone had wanted to represent the rippling surface of a lake or ocean. Below that, the final symbol looked like an oval tilted forty-five degrees to the right.

"Okay," Stacey said, peering over my shoulder. "What do *those* mean?"

"Maybe it's a code," I said.

"Wait, I'm good at these," Stacey said. "Maybe it's *see...something....oh*. Or *zero*? See-ripple-oh?"

"You're right," I said. "You are good at these."

Stacey punched me in the arm.

"I was thinking gangs," Nobson said. "They're always spray-painting those things you can't read."

"Gang tags?" I asked. "These are pretty small for that. Usually the point of a tag is to mark territory, so you want it to be visible. This seems like it's meant to be subtle, so you don't find it unless you're looking for it." I snapped a picture of the symbols with my phone.

"Once you start looking, they're all over," Nobson said. "Teenagers, crooks—whoever it is, they've been marking up the neighborhood for a while."

"I'd like to see some others."

"We could spend all day at it."

"Then just the houses that have been broken into," I said. "And a few that haven't, so we can compare."

"Suit yourself."

We spent another twenty minutes or so driving through the community, stopping so I could take pictures of the little symbols on the fence posts. I jotted down notes about each one—whether the house had been burglarized and what had been taken, if anything.

The last picture I took was a fence post at the back of my

clients' lawn, on the side facing the empty, undeveloped street behind the house. The symbols were small, each no bigger than my thumbnail, etched just under the lower fence railing. It wasn't a shock that I hadn't noticed them last time I'd stood there, since it had been the middle of the night and I hadn't been looking for any such thing. I'd been preoccupied with the ghost I'd just pursued out of the basement.

The marks scratched into Tom and Ember's fence included another oval, tilted the opposite direction with hash lines through it, and a few other marks. Most troubling to me was a stick figure of a woman with an oversized skirt. Another, smaller stick figure was drawn inside the skirt area. Naturally, I thought of Ember and her advanced pregnancy. Why would anyone want to note that on the fence?

"That's a little creepy," Stacey observed, standing beside me as I took a picture. "More than a little, the longer I look at it."

"I don't know what you girls can do that I haven't done." Nobson said from where he waited a few feet away. "If you turn up anything, you'll keep me apprised, won't you?"

"And you'll do the same?" I asked.

Nobson grunted and walked away toward his golf cart, parked in the street.

"Do you really think ghosts might have done this?" Stacey whispered.

"I don't know what to think," I said. "It seems like this place is overrun with ghosts."

"Then where do we begin?"

"I'm spending the night in the basement again. We have to focus on what the clients need. Come on, we have a lot to do before sunset."

We climbed into the van, hurrying to visit the haunted spots we'd already identified and set up our gear before the night's observation.

Chapter Nine

Alone in the basement again, I sat in the dark, on my air mattress, and waited for the banshee. My tablet was propped on my knees so I could check the viewpoints of other cameras around the house, plus the ones we'd set up around the concession stand and the old railroad tracks in the woods.

With the reports of crime in the area, I was worried about non-ghosty types trying to steal our equipment. I'd told Stacey to check the more remote cameras very frequently.

The time passed slowly, as it often does—few ghosts give command performances. They can be elusive when you're looking for them, then suddenly pop out at you when you don't particularly want to find them, like when you're alone in your own house late at night.

It was one-thirty in the morning before I began to sense anything might happen. The air turned cooler, and my Mel Meter slowly registered the temperature drop.

Something scraped along the floor, not far away from me, but I didn't see anything.

"Hello?" I whispered, sitting up a little straighter. My heart was already picking up its rhythm, in case I'd missed the fact that I might be in danger.

I heard it again, closer, as if someone were approaching me.

"Ellie?" Stacey asked over my headset.

"Shhh." I pointed my flashlight toward the sound, but didn't click it on just yet.

The temperature dropped ten degrees, then another five. My Mel Meter flashed as it registered a spike of three to four milligaus. I shivered, feeling a presence in the room.

I pulled on my thermals to see a shape several feet away, drifting closer to me. Pale and blue, almost certainly the same one I'd seen before.

"Rose?" I asked, naming the farmer lady who'd died young and left small children behind. "Rose Whalen? Is that you?"

The small blue form halted where it stood. It was blurry, like a low cloud or patch of fog, making it hard to see any distinguishing features or even to try to get a sense of its exact size.

"You don't have to be afraid," I said. "I can help you escape to a better place."

The shape drifted closer, letting out a deep, mournful sigh, the sound of a girl who has suffered far too much for far too long. I felt sorry for the ghost, trapped in its own grief, unable to escape, probably lost and confused in her death for many more years than she'd actually lived.

"It's going to be okay..." I whispered. I was turning cold and sorrowful inside, feeling bad for her, then for myself. Suddenly I was acutely aware of just how alone I was, how I'd always been that way since my parents died, and would probably always be that way.

In my mind I was at my parents' funeral again. It was dreary, gray, and cold, or at least that was how I remembered it. Completely detached from myself, from everyone and everything, the voices of relatives and other adults hollow and meaningless around me.

Alone.

I remembered walking to the back of our little house, not much more than a shanty by the railroad tracks. My mother lay in the bed there, pale and sweating, with nobody but me to attend her. My father had died at sea a few years before. I knew my mother would be gone soon, and then there would be nobody.

I shivered as a deep winter chill bit into my bones so hard it made every joint in my body ache. I couldn't erase the image from my mind—my mother, feverish, delirious, close to death.

"Ellie?" Stacey's voice was distant. I barely heard her...but I *did* hear her, and it prodded me into just a little self-awareness.

These weren't my memories.

I opened my eyes, though I didn't remember closing them. I was quaking where I sat, my teeth chattering. I felt like I was freezing to death.

"Rose..." I whispered. "Rose, back off. Leave me alone."

"Ellie, there's something else in there with you."

"The banshee..." I managed to whisper. I was struggling to focus, to get my brain moving again under the layer of bitter frost that had buried it.

"Not just her," Stacey said. "There's also--"

A pair of large, rough, invisible hands grabbed me, lifting me off the mattress and high into the air. A male voice grunted in my ear, and I caught the scent of cheap whiskey.

I screamed—I couldn't help it, I was terrified. The invisible specter slammed me against the wall, cutting my scream short by knocking the air out of my lungs.

Pain flared all through my body, a deep gouging pain like somebody was digging into my bones and joints with a rusty scalpel. Every spot that had been freezing cold a moment earlier now shrieked with agony. My teeth clenched together, and I had just enough air to let out a thin moan.

I kicked out feebly with one leg, but I didn't have enough oxygen to put any real force into it—and besides, there was nothing to kick, as far as I could see.

Stacey shouted something over my headset, but I couldn't make out the words through the intense pain drilling into every joint in my body.

This second entity, the one Stacey had tried to warn me about, seemed to be attacking the banshee again...and the banshee had threaded herself all through my body.

Whatever their beef was, I did not appreciate getting trapped in the middle of it.

Another wave of deep, wrenching pain shook my body, my head snapping back and forth. I was shoved up against the ceiling, then finally released and allowed to fall.

It would've been great if I'd landed on my nice, soft, fully inflated air mattress, but this ghost wasn't doing me any favors. I smacked right into the concrete floor and immediately felt bruises forming all over me.

A high-pitched shriek pierced my eardrums, bringing a fresh pain laced with terror crackling through my skull. I knew it didn't come from me, because I was struggling to draw air after my high-speed rendezvous with the solid concrete.

I managed to raise my head, and I saw her with my own eyes.

The banshee was no young mother who'd died too soon, but a girl around seven or eight years old, wearing a frayed and dirty white dress trimmed with torn, crumbling lace. Her hair was a wild dark mane trailing loose ribbons as the other entity hauled her away. She stared at me with wide, desperate eyes, her irises a dusty gray color—her entire form was in whites, grays, and shadows, like an old black and white movie on faded film stock.

She reached out one small hand toward me as he whisked her backward across the room, toward the door to the outside, as if imploring me to help her. Never mind that she'd just been oppressing me and snacking on my energy. I felt completely drained.

The figure who carried her away was less distinct, a broad-shouldered dark shadow with the suggestion of a brimmed hat at its head, maybe a black derby hat. His form seemed larger than life but indistinct, fading to a black fog at the edges.

Her scream grew into a loud, desperate wail, and then the two figures slammed into the basement door hard enough to rattle it in its frame. A crack split one of the door's small window panes from corner to corner.

I attempted to stand, discovered I wasn't quite strong enough yet, and tumbled to my hands and knees.

As I knelt there, catching my breath, the door swung wide open. I reached for my flashlight, feeling far from ready to confront the big, bad ghost, if he was coming back for seconds.

Then Stacey dashed into the room, swinging her flashlight, and I let myself relax.

"Ellie! What happened?" She ran over and helped me to my feet.

"Uh." I leaned on her. I had almost no energy at all. I looked at the open door through which the ghosts had left and she had entered. "Did you see anything out there?"

"Just a cold wind blowing across the lawn. Was that her? The banshee?"

"It was *them*," I said. "The banshee and...the other one. He snatched her away. She didn't want to go with him."

"So he's the bad guy?"

"She was feeding on me at the time."

"So he's the...good guy? The rescuer?"

"Let's not assign any morality-play roles just yet," I said. "Those two are in conflict, and I happened to get in the way. I did get a look at her."

"The banshee?"

"She's just a little girl. Or maybe she just wants to present herself that way, but I don't think she was in control of anything at that moment. I saw some of her memories." Part of me still felt an echo of her deep sadness, and I wanted to sob as the image of her dying mother rose again behind my eyes, but I kept it inside. "We should look back at the Whalen family, identify any girls who died between the ages of, let's say, five to ten."

"Great, can't wait. Are you going to be okay? You look pretty pale."

"I'm..." I tried to take my internal temperature, see how I was really feeling. "Hungry. So hungry."

"I have some raw granola out in the van!"

"I'd even eat that," I said.

"I'll go get some as soon as--"

"*Now!*" I shouted, and Stacey jumped. I felt instantly embarrassed. "Uh...I mean, now. Please. If that's okay. Sorry."

"No problemo. Want to come with me or stay here?"

"Stay. They're gone for now." And I didn't feel like walking for even two or three steps, much less hoofing it out the door and around the house.

Stacey eased me down to a sitting position on my mattress. I slumped, exhausted.

"I'll be right back. Leave her alone, ghosts!" Stacey jogged out the door.

"Nice exorcism," I said, but my voice was too weak for her to hear.

The room gradually warmed to a normal temperature, with the ghosts gone and the fresh warm air from the open door. I clicked my flashlight and pointed it out into the yard. I saw nothing but grass and the support posts for the second-story porch above the basement door.

I reached for my thermals, but they felt too heavy to handle at the moment. I'd have Stacey check the yard and perimeter with them when she returned. I should've had her do that the instant she'd walked in the door, but I wasn't thinking clearly. I was thinking like my head was filled with mud.

After Stacey returned, I slouched on the mattress, reluctantly eating dry, loose granola while she went back outside to scan for any active spirits.

"Nothing out here," Stacey said over my headset, though I could barely hear her over the sound of the hard granola breaking my teeth and shredding my gums. "Wait. Look at that."

"I can't see you," I said. "We're talking over radio."

"Right, sorry. Something snapped the top off a fence picket out here. Looks like they hit it pretty hard."

"Our clients won't be happy to hear that."

"It's okay, I don't think it's a load-bearing picket." Stacey switched off her headset as she rejoined me in the basement and sat next to me while I tried not to pass out. "You took a big risk letting it feed on you like that."

"Yeah, I wouldn't say it was one hundred percent intentional on my part." My head was throbbing, and not just the pain of gnawing the granola pebbles. While the agony and cold in my bones had been ripped away along with the banshee, I was left exhausted, with the sort of headache you might get when you've been awake for six days and haven't eaten in three. Well, I imagine that's what it would feel like.

"You look like you're about to keel over and die," Stacey said.

"Thanks."

"Maybe you should take the rest of the night off."

"I shouldn't..." I rubbed my head. My brain wasn't helping me form words at the moment. "I have to work."

"You've done a lot." Stacey squeezed my hand. "Come on,

Ellie. Just have a quick nap in the van."

"Not a good idea." It sounded like an excellent idea. Even the narrow drop-down cot built into our cargo van, normally about as appealing as an ironing board covered with rusty tacks, sounded as nice as a down mattress just then. "They're paying us to...keep watch..." My voice was slurred, my eyelids dropping.

"I'll keep watch," Stacey said. "You need to recover. How good would you be in a fight right now, anyway?"

She had a pretty decent point there.

"Okay. Just twenty minutes," I said. "Then wake me up."

"You got it, boss."

Stacey helped me to my feet and tried to support me as we walked. I drew my arm away from her, determined to move on my own strength. I might have been badly drained, but I could take care of myself.

After walking several hundred thousand miles on rubbery legs, I made it to the van and let Stacey drop down the horrific back-spasm-inducing bunk for me.

"Just twenty minutes," I said, then I closed my eyes. I couldn't believe how tired I was. The cold little banshee had really gorged herself on me, but at least I'd snagged a clear glimpse of her. We were on our way to identifying and removing her. If only I could keep my eyes open.

I drifted into darkness.

It seemed like only a minute later when the shaking and rattling woke me up. I opened my eyes and they were instantly filled with bright fire.

"What's happening?" I mumbled, covering my eyes. "Stacey?"

"We're just swinging by the park to pick up the cameras," she said. "And the old railroad tracks."

"It's morning?" I sat up on the cot, now vibrating as the van drove. "I just wanted to sleep for a second..."

"You seemed like you needed more," Stacey said. "And nothing really happened. Except, uh..."

"What?" I stood and stumbled toward the front of the van while Stacey drove us along the paved path into the park, stopping when the pavement abruptly gave way to dirt and weeds. "What did you see?"

"Well..." Stacey climbed out, and I followed her. We started across the open space toward the lone concession stand. "The cameras by the railroad tracks sort of...blacked out."

"When?"

"Not long after you started snoring."

"I was snoring? Wait, what happened to the cameras?"

"Lost power, it looks like," she said. "Batteries drained. I checked the footage just before they turned off, and it caught some shadowy figures near the tracks. Not human. At least, not *live* humans. So I didn't exactly want to go running out there in the middle of the night. I hope that's okay."

"You could've woken me up for that."

"Oh, I tried."

"What about here?" I eased open the broken door to the first floor of the concession stand, where a night vision and thermal camera stood on tripods in opposite corners to cover the whole room.

"I didn't notice any action last night, but I'll scan through the footage later."

The cameras seemed intact, which was a relief considering how this place had clearly been visited by a destructive entity in the recent past. We hurried to pack them into the van so we could recover the others ASAP.

I took over the driving, which meant I had to reverse all the way back up the path and out of the park. We went around the park to the stretch of paved road at the very back of the community and followed it until it dead-ended into trees and thorny vines.

Though it was daylight now, the deep woods still felt cool as we walked the overgrown foot path to the railroad tracks. The combination of thick canopy and dense undergrowth made the area feel isolated from the rest of the world, even in the daytime. I had the feeling of things watching us from the shadows.

"My cameras!" Stacey gasped when we reached the green, mossy tunnel that had formed over the old tracks. She ran to the fallen gear. Three tripods had been toppled in the night.

"Anything broken?" I asked, looking up and down the tracks while she inspected the cameras.

"The lenses look okay. I think the weeds cushioned their fall." She sighed in relief. "Looks like all the ghosts did was drain the batteries and tip them over. Thank goodness."

While Stacey broke down and gathered the gear, I did some texting on my phone.

"Busy over there?" she asked me, probably because I was staring at my phone while she did some of the grunt work.

"Just confirming our breakfast plans with the guys," I said.

"I'm so not ready to go out in public." Stacey looked down at her jeans and pink cotton shirt, both of them grungy from the woods. "How long do we have?"

"We're meeting them in ten minutes."

"Seriously?" she gasped, looking panicked.

"Nah, I was kidding about that part. We'll go somewhere super-casual, where nobody cares how we look."

"There's nowhere in the world *that* casual. Where are we going?"

"It's a surprise."

"Why would it be a..." Stacey's expression went from panicked to horrified. "No. Come on, Ellie. *No.*"

"We'd better get moving," I said.

Stacey protested vehemently as we hurried back along the trail, but she quickly fell silent—not because she'd calmed down, exactly, but because the thick shadows of the woods created an atmosphere that made you instinctively want to stay quiet for fear of attracting predators.

The banshee was clearly a kind of predator—it had fed on Ember, then on me. After the previous night, though, I was beginning to doubt that she was the most dangerous spirit in the neighborhood. I needed to know about the one who'd dragged her away.

Chapter Ten

Despite what I'd told Stacey, there was actually time for me to drop her off, head home to shower and change, then pick her up again. We saved time by not swinging by the office to pick up our own cars before breakfast.

Stacey groaned in protest as I pulled into the crowded parking lot of a restaurant located on an interstate exit outside Savannah. The building looked like a giant barn made of weathered gray wood, with a wraparound porch where families waited on rocking chairs and porch swings.

A billboard tall enough to be seen from the interstate showed a smiling, grandfatherly rooster in overalls and glasses, sitting on a rocking chair and holding a corn cob near his beak. The corn cob didn't make immediate sense unless you knew that it had been a smoldering corn-cob pipe in past generations, before massive changes in attitudes about smoking had forced changes in the logo.

The name of the restaurant, as spelled out in the most down-home Hee-Haw font you can imagine, was THE COUNTRY BARN.

"I'm going to kill you," Stacey whispered. She pulled on a pair of very large, extremely black sunglasses.

"What's with the Mary Kate and Ashleys?" I asked. "Are you really afraid someone's going to recognize you?"

"That would be my luck, yes." She sighed. "Let's get it over with."

"That's the spirit! Let's go have some biscuits and gravy."

"Ugh."

We climbed the porch steps and entered the restaurant, where the décor was aggressively folksy—old farm implements on the walls, along with faded signs advertising livestock feed and paintings of barefoot kids in rolled-up jeans on their way to the old fishing hole.

"Welcome to The Country Barn, y'all!" drawled the hostess, a girl of eighteen or nineteen who wore overall shorts over a checkered shirt. The overalls depicted the same rooster who adorned the billboard. "It'll be about forty-five minutes, but go on and make yourselves at home! Most people like to browse the gift shop while they wait."

"Jordan, party of four," I said.

"You made a *reservation?*" Stacey whispered, shaking her head.

"Jordan..." She squinted at something behind her podium. "Oh, yes, ma'am. Your table should be ready in about ten or fifteen minutes." She handed me a black plastic square restaurant pager with an image of Grandpa Rooster on top.

"See?" I said to Stacey. "It pays to plan ahead. Let's check out the gift shop."

She sighed and followed me through the propped-open batwing doors into the cluttered Country Barn Gifts and Notions shop.

"I can't believe you're making me do this," Stacey whispered. "Did you *tell* them?"

"Of course not. That would take about half the fun out of it for me. Look, hillbilly gnomes!" I pointed to a shelf of yard statues, where incarnations of the traditional Germanic sprite reclined in straw hats and patched jeans, playing banjos, jugs, and washboards around their knee-length beards. The gift shop was full of cheesy stuff like that—fake mounted fish and deer heads that could sing songs, flour and sugar jars shaped like wooden barrels and butter churns, piggy banks wearing cowboy boots, faux-folk-art owls and frogs that appeared to be made of spatulas and rolling pins.

"Got any ghost stuff?" I asked Stacey.

She rolled her eyes. "I don't think so."

"Maybe over here. This area looks supernatural..." I approached a corner loaded with figurines of angels and sheep with halos. A rack of postcards offered nature pictures paired with Bible verses. Next to that was a section with audiobooks and kids' travel games.

Country Barn restaurants could be found at interstate exits from Arkansas to Florida, each location basically identical to this one.

The black square in my hand lit up and vibrated, then let out a low *cock-a-doodle-doo!* Just in case I'd missed the lights and vibrations.

"Table's ready," Stacey said, snatching the pager from me and heading back to the hostess station.

"But we haven't looked at the snowglobes yet," I protested as I followed after her. "Hey, that one has Grandpa Rooster in a hammock."

"You're so funny."

"There you are." Jacob stepped forward from the crowded front area, where he'd been standing near one of the benches inside the front door. The benches were packed full of elderly people, maybe from the two small retirement-home buses parked outside.

"Jakey!" Stacey said, in a semi-squealing tone I'm not sure I'd ever heard from her before. She embraced him and kissed him full on the mouth, which drew a few sour glances from the elderly ladies on the bench.

"Hey," he replied, blushing just a little from the sudden public display of affection. "Did you have a good night? Catch any ghosts?"

"Not yet."

"I haven't eaten at one of these in years," Jacob said, looking at the densely packed rural kitsch all over the walls. "Still looks exactly the same."

The hostess led us to a picnic table made of rough-hewn planks of brown plastic. Rooster-and-chicken salt and pepper shakers perched at the center of the table, next to the upright spindle that held the communal paper-towel roll.

"Why'd we pick this place?" Jacob asked as he and Stacey sat across from me. "Is there a haunted house nearby? A haunted gas station?"

"You don't like catfish biscuits?" I asked Jacob, feigning shock.

"Should I?" he asked.

"Ellie picked this place," Stacey said. "To prank me, I guess."

"Oh, because they don't make everything out of quinoa and organic black beans?" Jacob asked.

"Because I'm kind of from The Country Barn family," Stacey said. "My great-grandfather opened the first one in Montgomery in 1931. It really was an old barn. They had to keep it simple and cheap because of the Depression—chicken, biscuits, vegetables. Eventually they opened a second one, then a third, then about sixty more..." She was blushing scarlet. "I don't like telling people."

"Why not?" Jacob asked.

"Because the place is so silly. They used to call me Barn Girl or Rooster Girl at school. And the food's kind of not the healthiest in the world."

"Not healthy?" Michael arrived through the crowd, grinning at me. I couldn't help smiling back like a goofball at my firefighting semi-boyfriend guy. I felt flushed and wished my face would tone down its reactions a little. I stood to hug him, and he joined me on my hard plastic picnic bench. "I saw today's special is deviled eggs and hash browns on Texas toast with sausage gravy. I don't even understand how they came up with that meal. I'll have to order one."

"Are you feeling suicidal or something?" Stacey asked with mock concern.

"Just hungry." Michael was looking at me as he said it, his vibrant green eyes seeming to burn into me. I knew he had questions I couldn't easily answer—like why I'd been avoiding meeting him in person again, though I always did my avoiding regretfully, with some excuse.

The thing was that I really clicked with him, and this feeling of familiarity led me to expose myself in a way that felt dangerous. There was no simple way to explain the war inside my heart and mind, between all the inner voices that wanted to stay safe, shielded, and detached from other people as much as possible—the voices that had been in control for years—and the smaller, more fragile part of me that wanted to get closer to him.

So this was the halfway solution I'd devised, meeting him again as part of a group. Seeing him without getting too close. It made no sense at all and just showed how crossed my wires really are.

All of that flickered across my brain in about half a second, maybe less.

"Are you sure you don't want the breakfast vegetable platter?" I asked.

"Sounds a little healthy for me," Michael said.

"Don't worry, it's all deep fried," Stacey told him. "And served with gravy. You can wash it down with this sugar water," she added as the waiter brought us mason jars full of sweet tea. We hadn't ordered them, they just bring them out automatically at The Country Barn, the way some places automatically bring you water, or some Mexican restaurants give you a free basket of chips.

I thanked the waiter, a burly man with a thick beard wearing a polka-dotted shirt under the rooster-logo overalls.

"My pleasure! Good morning, everyone! I'm Ron and I'm soooo glad you're joining me for breakfast this lovely a.m.! Let me guess..." Ron the burly waiter studied us. "You're all starting out on an exciting road trip today?"

"That's it," Stacey said. "We're going to see Rock City."

"Oh, fantastic! You'll have so much fun, but you'll need a big breakfast. Today's special is the Devil's Scramble Platter--"

"One of those for me," Michael said.

"Feisty!" Ron said, clapping Michael's shoulder and looking at me. "This one looks like fun."

"You should see his mime act," I said.

"Every day in the park," Michael added with a perfectly straight face. "Four o' clock. There's usually a crowd, so get there early."

"Oh, I will," Ron said.

Stacey and I ordered our breakfasts—a Double Cluckin' Biscuit for me (fried chicken and a fried egg), a Fancy Frenchie platter for Stacey (crepes and French toast). As Stacey had mentioned, there was nothing on the menu you could really call healthy. Jacob, looking particularly horrified at the selection, asked whether there was any basic fruit or cereal available.

"You can get the Blueberry Pancake and Waffle Mountain," Ron suggested. "It has a few berries on top, just between the maple syrup and whipped cream. You should try it!"

"Any chance of getting just a piece of toast? Maybe a poached egg?" Jacob asked.

"I suppose." Ron sighed as if disappointed in him, then took our menus and left.

"Okay, here we are," Stacey said, looking at me.

"So why were we all summoned here today?" Jacob asked. "Is there a murder mystery involved? Someone in this restaurant is the killer? I'm guessing it was the chef, in the kitchen, with the sausage gravy. Did the victim die of rapid-onset heart disease?"

"I just thought it would be nice for us all to get together again," I said. Which didn't make a lot of sense, since we'd never gotten together as group before, in a social sense. Maybe a quick change of subject could save the day. "Michael just got back from some advanced firefightery training in North Carolina. What was that like?"

"It was just a lot of hanging off cliffs on ropes," he said. "The scenarios were based on retrieving inexperienced hikers and climbers from dangerous, off-limits areas of the mountain. We also did a night rapid-water rescue scenario at Nantahala Falls, and none of us drowned, so that was nice."

"That's so cool," Stacey said, beaming at him.

"I don't want to make his week sound boring, but I did audit a mid-size chain of shoe retailers," Jacob said. "*Three* cash flow discrepancies. All minor, easily resolved." He leaned back a bit, then suddenly jerked upright again, as if he'd forgotten he was sitting on a bench instead of a chair with a back. "I can't say anything more about it, though. I'm sorry."

"You've been hanging out at shoe stores and you didn't invite me?" Stacey asked.

"I want to know what you've been doing," Michael said, looking directly at me.

"Uh...well, Stace and I had a client with a false alarm a while back," I said. "Possums, it turned out. Not ghosts."

"But possums look like ghosts, don't they?" Stacey said. "Their little pointy white faces and big black eyes. Right up there with owls, somewhere in the top five most ghost-like animals."

"What else is on that list? Cats?" Jacob asked.

"Definitely cats," she said.

"We're investigating a haunted railroad right now," I said.

"Oh, yeah," Stacey said. "We think a ghost train passed by us."

"What kind of train?" Jacob asked.

"Yeah, what did it look like?" Michael asked.

"We didn't actually see the train," Stacey said. "It was just kind of a cold wind. But really eerie. I guess you had to be there."

"Where was it going?" Jacob asked.

"The tracks run from the old Silkgrove Plantation and end at the modern CSX line to Charleston," I said. "Stacey and I will have to walk the tracks soon and see what's there."

"Sounds very *Stand by Me*," Michael said. "You think you'll find a dead body?"

"It would be nice if we found a corpse just lying there by the train tracks," I said. "That would make our job easier." My timing was the opposite of perfect—our waiter had just arrived and now stood at my elbow, giving me a horrified look. "Uh...inside joke," I told him.

"I don't even want to know," the waiter said. "But call me over if you plan to do a rendition of 'Lollipop.'" He refilled the sips of thick, too-sweet tea we'd taken. "Your food should be out in a moment. We're waiting on the poached egg." He glanced at Jacob before walking away.

"Do you think he's mad I ordered off-menu?" Jacob asked.

"I'm sure he'll recover from the horror," Stacey said.

"I want to know more about the ghost train," Michael said. "What does it do? Shuttle souls to the afterlife?"

"The fast train to hell," Jacob said. "I bet the air conditioning sucks."

"I don't know if it takes anyone anywhere," I said. "I'd guess it just runs up and down the track. There must be ghosts onboard trapped in some kind of psychological loop. A train itself wouldn't leave a ghost—it's just a machine—so the ghost train must be some kind of symbolic manifestation."

"Oh, obviously." Michael nodded along.

"We're meeting with Grant from the Historical Society later today," I said. "We're looking for group trauma, maybe a train wreck."

"This whole case has been a train wreck," Stacey said. "It feels like nothing's coming together. There's too much going on."

"So it's not the train to heaven or hell, just a train to some old ruins," Michael said.

"Ellie says there's no heaven or hell, anyway," Stacey said, winking at me.

"I said I *don't know*," I corrected her. "I've never been dead, so I can't say what comes after."

"But you deal with ghosts all the time," Michael said.

"That doesn't mean I know where they go after they leave our world," I said. "Or if they continue to exist at all. Maybe when a ghost moves on, that's the end of its existence. Total peace. Or...maybe not."

"It's strange that you'd work with the dead and have no real opinion about the afterlife," Michael said. "That's kind of...interesting? Confusing?"

"I know!" Stacey grabbed Michael's arm, nodding rapidly. "That's just what I said."

"What do you think, Stacey?" Michael asked her.

"About the afterlife?" She shrugged. "I was raised to believe it was, you know, heaven or hell. I can't say working with ghosts has made me think it's *less* likely there's an afterlife. To me, all these ghosts running around kind of prove there must be something..."

Michael was nodding along, glancing from her to me.

"Jacob?" I asked. "What do you think?"

"I've always thought death was a dead end," he said. "We're just here temporarily, then gone. This did not help me adapt when the dead started speaking to me."

"So what do you think now?" Stacey asked.

"It's definitely more of an open question now. It could be like Ellie says, though—a ghost could be some kind of energy imbalance that needs to be fixed. They definitely indicate that some elements or traces of consciousness must remain after the physical body dies."

"My, you are a morbid table," the waiter said, returning with plates heaped full of sugars and carbohydrates. He distributed them among us. "Double Cluckin' Biscuit...Fancy Frenchie...Devil's Scramble...Your poached egg and plain toast will be out in just a bit," he told Jacob. "Can I get you anything while you wait? More tea?"

"Some water would be great," Jacob replied.

"I'll see what we have." The burly waiter bustled off.

"I really don't think that guy likes me," Jacob whispered.

"Maybe you should've ordered the Gravy Train," Michael said.

"Which one was that?"

"Hash browns with gravy, sausage with gravy, scrambled eggs with gravy," Stacey said.

"Does anybody ever die of a heart attack here?" Jacob asked. "Just eating at a table?"

"Yes," Michael said. "I mean, we did have a heart-attack call right at this location. He wasn't eating, though. He was walking out and keeled over on the parking lot. I think *he* had the Gravy Train."

Stacey hid her face behind her hands, as if supremely embarrassed.

Jacob's food arrived—wheat toast and a poached egg, each item served right in the center of its own large, mostly empty plate, a sarcastic gesture by the kitchen staff.

We began to eat. My Double Cluckin' Biscuit was twice the size of my fist, stuffed with fried egg and fried chicken, implying a kind of philosophical question about which came first. Or which to eat first, anyway. Food like this would leave me drowsy and full of regrets, but I was still feeling drained from the ghost feeding on me. I told myself I needed the calories to rebuild my energy.

"So I'm assuming you want me to walk the tracks with you?" Jacob asked, looking at me. I hoped Stacey hadn't told him anything about the case—she knew she wasn't supposed to, because psychics weren't supposed to get advance information about a haunted site, and Jacob was our main psychic consultant these days. We'd already said too much, really, but all he really knew was that the rail line was haunted, which he would have figured out the moment we arrived.

"Yeah, Jacob should come with us!" Stacey said.

"I want to see this ghost train, too," Michael said. "I'm picturing a locomotive with like a big skull face, a razor-sharp cow catcher for teeth..."

"We'll be lucky to see a shadow of a train, if anything," I said. "But, yeah, it would be great if you both came."

"Yeah, Michael can, uh, put out any fires," Stacey said. "If the ghosts set any."

"He can do more than that," I said, feeling defensive even

though I knew Stacey was kidding. "He has medical training."

"I'm on duty tomorrow," Michael said.

"What about today?" I asked.

"Aren't we meeting with Grant?" Stacey asked. "And I need to rest sometime. I didn't get a long nap like you."

"We're meeting with him this afternoon, but how long could it take?" I asked. "I'd rather look at the train tracks later, anyway, closer to sunset when the ghosts will be more active."

"Does that work for everyone?" Stacey glanced around, and both of the guys shrugged, nodded, and went back to eating. Male communication at its finest.

Then a column of waiters and waitresses emerged from the back, wearing straw hats and plush Grandpa Rooster caps, all of them clapping their hands in time. At the end of the line danced Grandpa Rooster himself, or at least some guy in a big mascot-style Grandpa Rooster costume.

"Cock-a-doodle-doo!" the wait staff sang. "Happy birthday, too! We're so cock-a-doodle happy, let's all crow for you!"

They were coming our way. I gave Stacey a questioning look.

"I slipped the waiter a note," she said. "It's your birthday, right? Didn't want you to miss out."

"You told them it's my--" I began, but the loud, singing wait staff gathered around the table drowned me out. Grandpa Chicken bobbed and ducked around the table, as if scratching for grubs, while a waitress placed a big straw hat adorned with a stuffed rooster on my head.

I glared at Stacey while the wait staff did a chicken dance all around me. Stacey was laughing her head off, having gotten her revenge for me bringing us here in the first place. She snapped an unnecessary number of pictures with her phone, while Grandpa Rooster insisted I stand to be applauded by the entire restaurant, my face beet-red with embarrassment.

Chapter Eleven

Out in the parking lot, Stacey and Jacob stepped aside to talk quietly at one end of the restaurant's big porch. That left me walking alone with Michael, which made me weirdly uncomfortable, especially when I saw the questioning look on his face.

"So, you've been distant and mysterious lately," he said. We reached the cargo van out in the parking lot, and I leaned back against it, crossing my arms as if to ward off any threat of serious conversation.

"Haven't I always been mysterious and distant?" I asked.

"Extremely."

"It's my fault. My nocturnal schedule. This client I have now, she's pregnant. Not just a little bit pregnant, either, but ready to pop out an actual fully-formed infant any day. It would be great to clear the ghosts out of their house before that happens."

"I can see that," he said. "And how long have you been on this case? Three weeks?"

"How long are you going to be on *my* case?" I asked, feeling defensive again.

"Until I've got you solved."

"And then what?"

"And then we'll see," Michael said. "Seriously, breakfast was great. I'll be sweating sausage grease for weeks. How are you spending the rest of the day?"

"Sleeping for a while," I said. "Then Grant wants to meet at the old railroad terminal. You *could* come if you wanted. The train museum might not sound exciting, but it'll still be less depressing than watching your friend's cover band."

"I already apologized for that," he said. "Even I didn't know they were that bad."

"The best part was when the drummer got an earache and they had to cut the show short."

"Yeah, that was pretty great. So we'll do the haunted railroad museum this afternoon, then the haunted tracks tonight?"

"Who said the railroad museum was haunted?" I asked.

"The old terminal, right?" he asked. "Isn't it haunted? I remember going there on Halloween when I was five or six years old. They had a haunted locomotive, one of those huge old black steam trains, with jack-o'-lanterns and spiderwebs."

"You don't think that was just made up for Halloween?"

"I guess, you know, looking back on it, yeah." He shook his head. "Never mind."

"I'm sure it's a little haunted," I said, patting his arm sympathetically, as if he were a disappointed child. "Every other old place in this city is."

"Okay, take me to my bed," Stacey said, leaning against me as she arrived. "Or anywhere close to it. My front steps would be fine."

"You can sleep in if you want," I told her. "Michael's going to the old terminal with me."

"What? I wanted to go there," Stacey said, suddenly more awake. Then she gave me a sly look and patted me on the back. "Oh, sure. You two go have fun. Trains are totally romantic, am I right? The open country, the lost days of yesteryear..."

"Maybe you can swing by the office later and organize the accounts receivable invoices for next week's collection calls."

"On a Saturday? That's a Monday job." She stuck out her tongue, then climbed into the van, looking exhausted.

"I'd better take the kid home," I said to Michael. "We had kind of a wild night."

"I hope I didn't miss all the good parts already," he said.

"Don't worry. We're just getting started. There should be plenty of scary parts still ahead." I stepped closer to him, then went ahead and kissed him, since I'd been the one getting cagey and avoidant lately. He didn't fight back, and pulled me close against him for a few very warm and pleasant seconds.

"It was good to see you again." Michael said.

I watched him stride back across the parking lot, tall and strong, his shaggy brown hair rustling in the breeze, until Stacey laid on the van's horn, startling me into action.

Michael glanced back in time to see me get startled and stumble over my own feet on the way to the van door. That was very cool of me. I'm sure I looked cooler than Scarlett Johansson in a Fonzie jacket as I caught my balance against the van and fumbled with the door handle.

I gave Michael a quick, awkward sort of half-nod and then climbed into the van.

"Took you long enough," Stacey said, yawning and stretching.

"I was just, um..."

"Being a freak?" Stacey asked.

I nodded and started up the van. No point arguing with her when she was obviously right.

We drove away from The Country Barn, the breakfast sitting heavy in my stomach like a pound of deep-fried regret. I couldn't say it put me in the mood for a long walk down deserted, ghost-infested train tracks, but maybe things would be better by the evening.

Chapter Twelve

The railroad museum is a giant brick roundhouse surrounded by a few little spurs of dead-end rail that used to connect our fair city to the rest of the continent, but were now reduced to parking spots for the antique passenger cars, cabooses, and locomotives on display.

Grant Patterson was already there, emerging from the shade of the roundhouse, dressed a little theatrically in a serge suit and boater hat that might have been fashionable back when these cute old steam trains were serious business.

"There we are," Grant said, looking from me to Michael. "Stacey's taller than I remember."

"You'll be surprised to learn this isn't Stacey at all," I said. "This is Michael Holly. Michael, Grant Patterson, from the Savannah Historical Association."

"A new team member?" Grant studied Michael more carefully. "Tell me Stacey hasn't left the firm?"

"No, she's still around," I said. "Michael's a firefighter."

"Oh, a pyrokinetic ghost?" Grant asked, his white, neatly manicured eyebrows rising. "Is this about your--"

"Not him," I hurried to say, before Grant could ask about Anton Clay, the fire-wielding ghost who'd burned down my childhood home and killed my parents. Grant knew about it from helping Calvin research the history of my house, and all the other houses that had burned down on the same site. I wasn't eager to chat about it at the moment.

"Not who?" Michael asked.

"Grant's talking about a different case," I said. "An *old* case."

"Excuse my assumptions," Grant said, with a smile for Michael. "Are you the client? Do you suffer from ghosts in the closet or attic?"

"Basement, actually," I said. "But we took care of the ghosts in his house." *Maybe*, I thought. While we'd definitely removed the boogeyman from the apartment house where Michael lived, I wasn't so sure about the dark well in the basement, which had apparently been infested by ancient evil spirits for many centuries. A demonologist had helped us seal it, but we hadn't encountered much resistance, as if the darkness had simply laid low and let us close the door. I didn't think we'd seen the last chapter on that. "Michael's not a ghost hunter or a client. He's here, uh, socially."

"Socially?" Grant gave me an amused smile. His eyes flicked over Michael again, as if evaluating whether he was a fit mate for me.

"I'm just really into trains. And, uh, old buses." Michael pointed at a long red vehicle parked outside.

"That is a *trolley*, sir," Grant said.

"Right," Michael said. "I just didn't want to get too technical."

"Hm. Well, come along, and let's learn about the fascinating history of Georgia's rail industry."

"Can we do it quickly?" I asked.

"After the time I've spent researching this for you?" Grant asked. "No, dear. Prepare for an earful."

"Is that a real fully restored General Electric diesel?" Michael asked, approaching a boxy black locomotive with fat red stripes across the nose. The old engines and cars sat in individual bays, as if they'd pulled in for repairs. "Looks like a 1947 model. Man, that's a classic."

"You certainly know your trains," Grant said, looking

impressed.

"Don't tell me you're a train buff," I said. "Or any kind of transportation-technology buff."

"Nah, just kidding. I just read the plaques right there. Still, it's impressive, isn't it?" Michael looked up at the engine towering above us. "It must have seemed like a monster back in the day, tearing through the woods and past the old farms."

"In 1827," Grant began, walking out to the little spurs of tracks with cars parked on them, "the South Carolina Canal and Railroad Company was established in Charleston to steal commerce from the Savannah River, and therefore the city of Savannah. Savannah's business community scrambled to compete, chartering the original Central of Georgia line in 1833. It connected the port of Savannah to Georgia's western interior cities like Macon and Atlanta, creating a rapid highway to move cotton from within the state to ships bound for the Northeast and Europe."

"Stacey's already going to be sad she missed this," I said. "She just loves piles of facts, figures, and dates."

"Of course it's fascinating," Grant said. "The railroad marks the beginning of the modern industrial world. After the Central of Georgia was constructed, our Savannah forefathers chartered the Savannah, Albany, and Gulf railroad in 1847, which followed a southerly course and was intended to connect Savannah with the Gulf Coast ports of Florida. There was as yet no northbound line to connect Savannah to Charleston, the next major port along the Atlantic coast.

"This is where your dead friends come in," Grant continued. "The Georgia Canal and Railroad Company was chartered to connect the cities of Savannah and Charleston. It was an ambitious project, including a network of canals through the rivers and salt marshes that would parallel a fancy new rail line. Your Isaiah Ridley was, of course, one of the principal investors. He poured his savings into it, desiring to own as much of the stock as possible, obviously believing it would be extremely profitable."

"Isaiah who?" Michael asked.

"A nasty ghost we had to remove from a client's house," I said. "He spent a hundred years tormenting the ghosts of his own kids.

carried a belt that had evolved into a long, nasty whip lined with buckles and prongs."

"Unfortunately for your whip-wielding friend, the railroad was ill-conceived," Grant said. "The line was to cross the marshy islands of the Savannah River, but the bridge supports proved unreliable at best. The line went bankrupt in 1851. Five years later, other investors would charter the far more successful Savannah and Charleston Railroad, wisely locating the bridge several miles north of the original failed crossing, where the ground was more solid and the river a bit straighter and narrower."

"I wonder why the first guys didn't do that," Michael said.

"Most likely, that was because another major investor in the original line was Andrew Thorburn, owner of Silkgrove Plantation," Grant said. "He wanted the rail crossing on his land so that he could profit as much as possible from it. Instead, that first attempt at a major Savannah-Charleston line ended up as nothing more than a small branch, connecting the plantation and its river docks to the later line that actually succeeded."

"So no trains ever traveled to Charleston on the old railroad we're investigating?" I asked.

"I'm afraid there was never much traffic on that line," Grant said. "Just enough to shuttle cotton from Silkgrove Plantation to the main trunk line. The little spur you're studying fell into disrepair during the Civil War and was never restored to service, as Silkgrove Plantation was out of business, permanently. There was no further use for that bit of railroad."

"That should narrow things down for us," I said. "Were there any train crashes along the line before it was abandoned? Something with fatalities?"

"I found no such events," Grant said, and I felt my shoulders slump a little. "There was, however, a particular incident that may be of some small interest. Follow me."

Grant led us to the far end of the roundhouse. He stood before a massive black steam engine, about two stories tall, the massive smokestack reaching even higher. It was polished to a gleam, the massive wheels bound together by heavy connecting rods, a powerful and dangerous-looking machine with a dark round face. The big cow-catcher at the front jutted out like the teeth of a grinning dinosaur. The locomotive looked like it would snap you up and tear you apart if you stood in its way.

"Hey, that's the haunted train!" Michael said. "From when I was a kid. They used to hang spiderwebs and stuff all over it at Halloween."

"A practice that was soon discontinued," Grant told him. "It's no surprise this was selected for redecorating as a Halloween train. It's an 1890 Baldwin, and once upon a time it ferried passengers and cargo between Savannah and Charleston, along the second, more successful railroad we just discussed. It chugged through the towns and the pine forests in what I imagine to be a quite romantic and charming manner.

"Georgia never saw many train robberies," he continued. "The nineteenth century saw an epidemic of them out West, stealing gold on its way to deposit in the East. The railroads here, of course, tended to be loaded with heavy produce, cotton and timber and such, not the easiest items to stuff into one's saddlebags before riding away. Not in a profitable enough volume, in any case."

"Train robbery?" Michael said. "This is getting good. We should grab some popcorn."

"In 1902, an evening train was halted and robbed after it left Savannah with a sizable shipment of bills and coins en route to the Bank of Charleston," Grant said. "The lead bandit was a man named James McCoyle, a notorious outlaw who'd robbed trains in Nevada and Arizona during his younger years. He was forty-three in 1902, his wilder days behind him. He may have thought trains in the Southeast would be easier marks than those out West.

"McCoyle and his gang blasted the safe with dynamite, took the bank shipment, then robbed the passengers at gunpoint. In a gruesome twist, the gang blasted the most crowded passenger car with some remaining dynamite, killing several aboard. The engineer, conductor, and brakeman were also shot."

"That's terrible!" I said. "Why did he do it?"

"That is a true mystery," Grant said. "Two of the bandits died along with the passengers, so it may be that McCoyle murdered his own cohorts to keep a larger share of the money. It doesn't explain why he killed so many passengers along with them."

"But he was an experienced criminal, right?" Michael said. "Wouldn't he know that killing innocent people would bring a lot of extra attention?"

"I *said* it was a mystery," Grant replied.

"Do you have a list of the people who died?" I asked.

"Of course. I have a folder of information for you. Now if you would simply let me *speak* for just a moment--"

"Sorry," I said.

"McCoyle and his remaining accomplice fled, but as it turned out, there was a railroad detective on board. He was not killed by the dynamite. Instead, he pursued them, killing McCoyle and suffering a bullet in the leg for his trouble. However, McCoyle's accomplice *did* escape with a significant portion of the money."

"Did they catch him?" Michael asked. "The fourth guy?"

"There was no 'fourth guy,'" Grant said. "The fourth member of the gang was a woman. Surviving witnesses described her as pale and freckled, red-haired, wearing a lacy red evening dress that was a bit scandalous for the era."

"Was she ever caught?" I asked.

"Found two weeks later, in a boardinghouse in New Orleans," Grant replied. "Dead of 'unclean living leading to heart failure.'"

"Unclean living?" Michael asked.

"Yeah, like not doing her laundry," I said, remembering how Michael's clothes had been scattered everywhere the first time I'd seen his room.

"Maybe she had a gateway to Hell in her laundry room," Michael said. "That doesn't make it easy."

"I have a copy of the coroner's notes, which were fortunately shared with Savannah authorities at the time. If they hadn't been, I'm sure we'd still be waiting for one of my contacts in New Orleans to dig up the original, if it still exists."

"You have contacts in New Orleans?" I asked.

"The museum and library mafia, my dear," Grant said. "Our tentacles are everywhere. In any case, her name was Maggie Fannon, and this was not her first time at the criminal rodeo. She'd previously been arrested for petty theft and fraud in Savannah and Charleston."

"I wonder if she's our banshee," I said. "This is great stuff, Grant, but you said it didn't happen on the track we're investigating. Right?"

"Your track was already long abandoned by then," he said. "The robbery, however, took place just at the spot where the old line once connected with the new. The gang of robbers may have hidden themselves somewhere down that track while waiting for the train."

"How did they stop the train?" I asked.

"The usual way," Grant said. "A red lantern, warning of emergency. It could mean a medical emergency on someone's part, or it could warn of dangerous conditions on the tracks ahead, so the engineer was more or less obligated to stop because of that risk. It was a frequent ruse of train robbers."

"So they stop the train, blast the safe with dynamite, then end up killing the train crew and several passengers. And two of their own, leaving just...James and Maggie. And only Maggie escapes."

"That's an accurate summary, though without the full flair of my recounting." Grant nodded.

"Sounds like a plausible background for how the tracks became haunted," I said. "We could be dealing with the ghosts of dead passengers and the entire gang of robbers. No wonder the neighborhoods in that community are crawling with the dead. Did you find anything else?"

"Death and birth records for the family who lived on that farm," Grant said.

"Did anybody else ever die on those train tracks? Or near them?"

"If I turn up anything else, you will be the first to know," Grant said. "From your initial request, I thought it best to spend my time digging into the train robbery."

"Definitely," I said. "Thanks so much, Grant."

"It is always my pleasure," Grant said. "We can't have the dangerous and unpleasant sorts of ghosts overrunning the city, can we? There won't be room left for the living."

"And imagine the parking nightmare," Michael said.

"Ghosts don't normally drive cars," I said.

"Do they normally drive trains?" he asked.

"Okay, good point."

"I believe that concludes our tour of the train museum," Grant said. "Unless you want to wait for the museum's next scheduled train ride?"

"Train ride?" Michael looked down the longest track. "What does it do, travel a couple hundred feet and come back?"

"I admit it's not a long ride. There is also the Whistle Stop Cafe, where you can order fried green tomatoes, if your life is lacking in Fannie Flag references."

"I think I had enough fried everything this morning," I said. "We ate breakfast at The Country Barn."

"Then you have enough calories to survive for several weeks," Grant said. "Provided your heart does not explode."

"I should have bought you a hillbilly gnome, Grant. I think one would look great in your garden."

"It is the thought that counts," Grant said. "No need to act on it. I insist you leave the gnomes on the country kitsch shelf where they belong."

"If you insist. Maybe I'll get you a redneck snowglobe instead. It had a little house with a car parked on cinderblocks out front."

"That sounds like a truly inspired work of art." Grant adjusted the brim of his hat. "If there's nothing else, I have a recently acquired trunk of papers to examine at the Association. Legal and property records from the 1840's. We're all very excited."

"How could that not be exciting?" I asked. "Thanks again, Grant."

We walked him to the parking lot. After Grant drove away in his chocolate-colored Mercedes sedan, Michael and I were left alone again.

"So we're going to fight off the ghosts of some old cowboy bank robbers who haunt the abandoned train tracks," Michael said. "Should we bring horses and six-shooters?"

"I'll take my chances with a few high-powered flashlights. Maybe a ghost cannon," I said. "You don't have to come. It might get dangerous."

"If it's dangerous, I'm not letting you go without me."

"It's my job," I said.

"Mine, too. I'm in the 'protect everyone from everything' business."

"Sounds like you've got a Superman complex."

"I had a Superman backpack. No, wait. Spider-Man," he said. "It had this cool spider pull tab."

I checked the time. "We need to get going."

"Cowboy ghost hunting?"

"Some light domestic ghost-proofing," I said. "I don't want to leave my clients undefended while we're hoboing around tonight."

"Did you ever ghost-proof my house?" he asked as we climbed into the van.

"Didn't need to," I said. "I was there the whole time. This new case is more difficult—I have to be in two or three places at once, trying to keep my clients safe while investigating the actual source of the haunting. Usually those things aren't in conflict because the haunting focuses on just one location, but these ghosts are loose and wandering."

"So helping you hunt ghosts counts as a date, right?" Michael said as I drove us toward the highway to the northern suburbs.

I smiled. "There's nothing more romantic than confronting and evicting the unwanted dead. You might get scratched or thrown around, or psychologically tormented."

"Still sounds better than the concert I dragged you to," he said.

"True," I said, pressing the accelerator. We had a busy night ahead, and from what Grant had told us, these spirits might be more dangerous than I'd expected—murderous criminals in life tended not to grow docile and harmless when they became restless ghosts.

Chapter Thirteen

We stopped at the office to gather up supplies. Calvin drew me aside while Michael loaded a couple of boxes into the van.

"I looked over the pictures you took," Calvin said, while tapping at a digital tablet. "The symbols carved into the fence."

"Any ideas?" I asked.

"They look like hobo signs," he said. "Marks they would leave when traveling the rails to share information with each other, usually about opportunities and dangers—charitable people, work available, or police officers who will arrest hobos on sight, notes on the jail conditions, anything that might be of interest."

I looked at the labeled symbols he'd pulled up on his screen. There were symbols for everything from mean dogs (a fence-like scratch mark) to kindhearted ladies (a crudely drawn cat). Some indicated advice like "act religious for free food" (a simple cross). One cluster of curves with an arrow meant "woman living alone," which seemed more than a little creepy to me.

"This is great, Calvin," I said. "I'll have to compare them with my pictures and notes."

"I've already identified several." He pointed to a tilted oval. "That means 'nothing doing.' I found them on the fences of houses you identified as unoccupied. At the houses where jewelry was stolen, there were marks indicating wealth or that the house had already been robbed. The Baker house, the one that lost a collection of silver coins, had these three circles to indicate 'money.' Some of these other symbols don't seem to be common..."

"Do you think ghosts could have carved these?"

"I'm not convinced. There are plenty of instances of spirits snatching and hiding small objects, but this is more like burglary. They're taking jewels and valuables away from the houses entirely. It could be living people studying houses to rob and then carving these marks as a way of taking notes or communicating with each other."

"That seems like a pretty primitive way of sharing information in the twenty-first century," I said. By this point, Michael had wandered over to join us by the long worktable.

"It could be that the people who evaluate the houses don't accompany the robbers," Calvin said. "Those who spy on the houses are at risk of being seen by the neighbors, so they go out and establish an alibi while the rest of the gang carries out the burglary."

"That's getting pretty cloak and dagger for some petty burglary," I said. "They're not stealing the Hope Diamond here. From what Captain Neighborhood Watch told us, the burglars took jewelry and coins, but nothing else. No electronics. What if the ghosts were thieves when they were alive?" I filled him in on the deadly train robbery.

"Then they could be repeating patterns from their lives." Calvin nodded.

"So where are they putting everything they steal?" Michael asked.

"That would be good to find out. Maybe we'll discover something tonight," I said. I pulled up the stick figure of the woman with a smaller stick figure inside her skirt. "This symbol is pretty self-explanatory. It's like somebody wanted to point out that Ember was pregnant."

"This other figure on Ember's fence represents bread." Calvin pointed to the tilted oval with hash lines inside it. "If we're dealing with ghosts, then this might indicate people on whose energy a spirit might feed. Which could be..." He paused, shuffling through the pictures I'd sent him from my phone, until he settled on one. The symbols showed another woman with a big skirt. A smaller stick figure stood beside her, with just the tiniest scratches for arms and legs. Its head was a strange shape, the title oval with hash lines through it.

"Looks a kid with a bad case of breadhead," Michael commented.

"Children are easier marks for ghosts, with more energy to feed on," I said. I made a special note of the house where those symbols were. It was one that had experienced a break-in with a few pieces of jewelry stolen. "They're telling each other where to feed."

"Wow," Michael said. "Disturbing."

"We have to stop them," I said. "Not just our client's banshee problem, but all of them."

"That may not be possible," Calvin said. "Remember to keep your focus on protecting the client, not saving the world."

I nodded. "That's why we need to get going, actually."

"You're helping tonight?" Calvin asked Michael.

"More like getting in the way, probably." Michael offered a smile, but Calvin just nodded with the same grim look he'd been wearing the past few weeks.

"Try not to do that," Calvin said. "Good luck, both of you."

I wanted to ask Calvin whether there were any new developments with the people who'd been spying on our office, but I didn't want to bring it up in front of Michael.

It was late afternoon by the time we reached the Kozlow house, the sun turning fat and orange in the western sky.

Ember looked pale when she answered the door.

"Tom's not home yet," she whispered, shuffling back inside and leaving the door open for us.

"Are you all right?" I asked, after quickly introducing Michael.

"Just tired," Ember said. "I had a nap full of nightmares. Good thing the baby kicked me awake." She turned for us to follow her inside.

She eased herself onto the couch, looking exhausted. I quickly caught her up on the situation.

"We've brought some ghost deterrents," I said. "It's a mixture of technological devices and folk protections that might help and definitely can't hurt. Since your basement is the focus of activity, I'd like to set up a motion-triggered lighting array to blast anything that comes in through the basement door."

"Do whatever you think's best," she said, waving her hand in a kind of dismissive half-shrug. Her eyelids were drooping.

"We'll finish up at the railroad tracks as fast as we can," I said. "But please call us if anything happens, and we'll come right away."

She nodded, her eyes distant.

"Michael, want to start on the front door?" I asked. "Hang both things."

He left, and soon the sound of hammering echoed through the house as he nailed an iron horseshoe above the front door. Wind chimes would go up next.

"Is there anything you want to talk about?" I asked Ember, sitting down beside her. "What were your dreams?"

"The same," she said. "I was alone on the train, surrounded by strangers, scared. When I woke up, I was drained. I've been pretty depressed ever since, actually. But I don't want to bother you with my problems."

"Bother on," I said. "It sounds important to the case, anyway."

"That's the whole story." She shrugged.

"Did you notice anything strange in the house before you went to sleep?" I asked. "Or when you woke up?"

"I felt chills," she said. "That's why I got into the bed. You think it was the ghost? In the middle of the day?"

"Ghosts can come out during the day. They usually don't, but if this one's developed a connection with you, it might make an exception."

"So what do we do?"

"I brought a dreamcatcher," I said. "Part of an array of folk defenses. It's big, almost like a fishing net. I'll hang that over your bed."

"Does that work?"

"It'll just be one deterrent, but since this ghost is digging into your dreams, we should definitely use it." I stood up. "Can I get you anything?"

"A ghost-free house for my little boy," she said.

"I'll get to work on it."

Outside, I found Michael hanging the wooden chimes, their bells tinkling as he anchored them into a potted-plant hook in the porch ceiling.

"So, you'd say this stuff definitely works?" Michael asked. "A horseshoe over the door?"

"Some of the folk protections work some of the time," I said. "We're putting that bottle tree out by the basement door. Any ghosts of people who lived around here would recognize that as a ghost defense. Maybe that will help it work."

"If you say so."

"I'd rather get silly with the ghost protections than leave her undefended."

Back inside, we hung an iridescent blue glass ball in the front window. "A witch ball," I explained. "There are threads of glass inside. Spirits are supposed to get drawn inside by the pretty surface and then get stuck in the threads. It's an eighteenth-century ghost trap."

"I've never heard of them," Michael said.

"You don't use centuries-old magic to put out fires?"

"Only in a pinch."

We grabbed more gear from the van. In the basement, I set up the array of floodlights and the motion detector while Michael hung the horseshoe over the basement door. Then we unwrapped a full-length leaded-glass mirror, freestanding with its own frame.

"How does the mirror work?" Michael asked.

"We line it up facing the door," I said, sliding it into position. "Supposedly ghosts can get confused by their own reflections—it might scare them or send them bouncing back like a light wave." I shrugged. "I don't know about that, but occasionally confronting a ghost with its true nature can shake it up, bring on some greater self-awareness, even help the ghost move on."

"Did you go to ghost college or something?"

I laughed. "No. Armstrong State. Go Pirates."

"I go to Savannah Tech," he said. "Go, um, paperwork? I don't think we have a mascot."

"What do you study?"

"They have EMS and fire certification programs. Right now I'm taking a class in arson investigation, working toward my officer certification."

"Fancy. That's a lot to juggle with your little sister."

"Little sisters are surprisingly easy to juggle. So what did you study? Wait, let me guess..." He stared at me, pretending to concentrate hard. "Nineteenth-Century Depressing German Poetry."

"Close. Psychology. Bring that box." I carried a stainless steel bottle tree frame outside and stabbed it into the ground just beside the basement door. I would've preferred to mount the bottles on an actual tree, but since the basement door was located underneath the second-floor porch, there wasn't one anywhere nearby.

"Sounds useful," he said. He opened a box full of empty bottles padded with brown wrapping paper. "If you ever run across any crazy ghosts."

"The ones I deal with are all pretty crazy," I said. "I mean, they exhibit signs of extreme abnormal psychology. They're in denial that they're dead, or they're obsessed over some event or situation from their lives. The longer they exist as ghosts, the more twisted and distorted their minds become. Especially if they learn to feed on the living. Then they become monsters."

"And you swoop in and help them process their feelings."

"Or haul them out in a trap and bury them in an abandoned cemetery. Either way." My phone buzzed. Stacey.

"The condor has landed," she said.

"What?"

"I'm parking out front. I thought you liked when we talked all secret code-ish."

"Come around to the basement," I told her. "Be ready to wire this lighting array for temperature and EMF."

"I'm *always* ready to wire a lighting array for those things." Stacey found us behind the house, sliding bottles on the slanted, steel-rod branches of the bottle-tree frame. "Oh, nice, I love those. Can I get a picture?"

"Seriously?" I asked, but she was already snapping one of Michael and me with the cluster of inverted bottles between us.

"You forgot to tell us to say 'cheese,'" Michael said, looking almost annoyed about it.

"True photographers never say 'cheese,'" she said. "We'd rather capture a genuine moment."

"Uh-huh, get to work," I said. "Have you talked to Jacob?"

"On his way." Stacey added to the set-up I'd created, so that any detectable sign of ghosts—temperature, a spike in electromagnetic energy, movement—would trigger the floodlights to blast the area around the basement door with a blinding light for ten minutes before they shut themselves off.

"Y'all can go gather the gear for our night hike." I took the big dreamcatcher net from a box and a stepladder from the corner of the basement. "I'm going upstairs for a minute."

"Come on, Mikey, let's load up some backpacks," Stacey said, leading him outside through the basement door.

Upstairs, I glanced into the future baby's room—clouds and rainbows decorated the walls, and a plush white teddy bear sat in a polished new crib with a race-car mobile hanging over it. The sight of that nest waiting to be inhabited strengthened my resolve to get to the bottom of the haunting and eliminate it as soon as possible.

I assumed Ember slept on the side of the bed where hair scrunchies and *Organic Life* magazines were piled on the side table. I climbed the stepladder I'd found in the basement and began nailing the dreamcatcher to the ceiling.

A male voice spoke from behind me, startling me so much I almost fell off the steps.

"What are you doing?" he asked, sounding a little hostile.

I turned to see Tom Kozlow watching me from the doorway, his arms crossed. The tall, thin dentist looked annoyed.

"Ember's been having nightmares about the ghost," I said. "This dreamcatcher could help."

"That's going to stop the ghosts?" He looked incredulous.

"Ghosts exist in a world of symbolism and emotion," I said. "Symbols can become powerful to them, especially if they're backed by a clear intent."

Tom looked doubtful.

"If nothing else, Ember might rest easier if she feels something is here to protect her," I added, and he seemed to consider that for a moment before nodding.

"This is all out of my depth," he said. "I like a sane, rational, normal kind of life."

"Who wouldn't?" I asked. "Sometimes life doesn't give you those options."

"I guess not." He looked at the big dreamcatcher, the spider-web design strung inside the leaf-shaped frame, hung with beads and feathers, and sighed. "I've seen those things a thousand times, but I'm not sure what they do."

"They're supposed to capture bad dreams like bugs in a spider web," I said. "In the morning, the sunlight dissolves them."

"And that works?"

"Nothing's ever certain." I climbed down and folded up the stepladder. "We're going to study the train tracks tonight, but we'll be back as soon as we can." I caught him up on the train robbery and quickly explained the devices we'd set up around the house. "I still strongly recommend that you both stay here in your room if you hear anything unusual tonight. It's not safe for either of you to encounter the ghost on your own."

"Ember's the one who feels sorry for the thing in the basement. Maybe I'll tie her to the bed." He grinned. "Just kidding," he added, almost as an afterthought, rubbing his temples.

I carried the stepladder past him and down the stairs, and he followed close behind. I left it by the door to the basement stairs and found Ember in the living room, typing away at her laptop.

"What are you doing?" Tom snapped. "You're supposed to be resting."

"I'm just finishing up some orders for the store," she said. "It'll take five minutes."

"You shouldn't be working."

"Ever tried making red velvet cake without cream cheese?" she asked, not even looking up at him. "Or hummingbird cake? The staff aren't miracle workers."

"We'd better go," I said, since the tension between them was growing and I didn't feel like hanging around being the monkey in the middle of their argument. "Call if you have any supernatural trouble. And stay out of the basement."

"Maybe you should go on to bed," Tom said to Ember.

"I'm not going to bed this early."

"What have you been doing all day? You didn't exert yourself, did you?"

I hurried on out of there and down the front steps. Michael stood by the van, where Stacey was loading up black backpacks for her and for me, plus an extra camping backpack Stacey had brought for Jacob. Stacey's forest-green Ford Escape and Jacob's accountant-gray Hyundai were parked out on the street.

"Nobody told me to bring a backpack," Michael said as I approached.

"We could swing by your place and pick up your Spider-Man one," I said.

"Unfortunately, Spidey went to Goodwill years ago. I can carry something with my hands."

"What happens if you get into a fistfight with a ghost?" Jacob asked.

"I'll use my ninja death kick of doom." Michael kicked one leg impressively high.

"More like a *Riverdance* kick of doom," I said.

"I thought you weren't going to tell anyone about my secret dance career."

"Too late now. Okay, kids." I turned a little so I was addressing everyone. "We'll be walking more than a mile along the old track. We'll leave Stacey's car at one end of the line and the van at the other. Jacob, do you have any idea what's going on with our case?"

"None at all," he said. "Besides haunted train tracks."

"I didn't tell him anything!" Stacey added, looking annoyed at me.

"Perfect," I said. "Let's hit the road."

We drove east of the planned community, where Stacey parked her car in a strip mall that included a pawn shop, some vacant stores, and a very questionable establishment with black windows and a sign offering to "BUY SELL TRADE VHS/DVD." A run-down gas station occupied one end of the strip mall.

The tracks weren't in sight, but we couldn't get any closer without climbing a high fence and trespassing into a shipping facility full of containers. This was an industrial area next to the river, which meant not many people were around on a Saturday night.

"So," Stacey said, as she and Jacob climbed into the back of the van. "I'm thrilled to leave my car here for an hour or two."

"The gas station's open until midnight," I said. "At least the lights will be on. Did you lock the doors?"

"Obviously."

"Do you have insurance?" Jacob asked. "You might need it."

"Great." Stacey cast a longing look at her car as we pulled away.

She'd parked under an outdoor light in the gas-station parking lot, near an old pay phone stand covered in graffiti. Nothing remained of the phone itself except a limp, frayed cable.

"It's another reason to move as fast as we can," I said. "That and the murderous ghosts."

The parking prospects for the van weren't much better. I drove around the area near the tracks until I decided on the Chet's Discount Grocery parking lot. Chet's was an institution housed inside a grimy cinderblock building with beer and cigarette signs in the windows. It was closed for the night, like the other scattered businesses in the area. I parked behind the store to hide the van. I didn't want to come back to find our array of monitors smashed or stolen.

We climbed out, and three of us strapped on backpacks. I carried thermal and night vision goggles in mine. Stacey and I wore our utility belts, with flashlight holsters and other gear available for the grabbing. I passed Michael an extra tactical flashlight.

Calvin had installed some heavy-duty locks and lined the glass with security film that made break-ins much more difficult. Still, the vehicle would be unsupervised for an uncomfortable amount of time. I double-checked all the doors to make sure they were locked tight.

"Okay," I said. "If anybody wants to rob the van, they're going to have to work for it."

"Maybe they'll give up and move right on to my car," Stacey muttered.

"That's the spirit! Let's get this over with."

We walked down the street from the grocery store to the modern railroad crossing. The striped arms stood upright and the lights and warning bell were dark and silent.

I led the way northward along the tracks, stepping from tie to tie. There were two tracks running parallel, flanked by solid gravel on either side to smother any plant life that thought about invading. Soaring strips of pine forest buffered the railway against a parallel highway on one side and commercial developments and neighborhoods on the other.

We walked single-file, which seemed to be the natural approach to walking on train tracks. I was in the lead, followed by Michael, then Stacey, then Jacob, who'd gone quiet, maybe clearing his mind for psychic impressions.

The night felt full of life—cars whishing by beyond the screen of trees, owls calling in the woods, the buzzing swarms of night insects. A wide path of night sky was visible above us, thanks to the railroad keeping the trees clear for several feet on either side of the tracks. The stars grew more and more visible as we walked.

"Just think," I said. "If we walked this mile-long track a hundred times, we might burn off one percent of the calories we ate at breakfast."

"Hey, you picked the restaurant," Stacey said. "To embarrass *me*, I should add. So now it's your turn."

"My turn for what?"

"Telling us something embarrassing about you, Ellie," Stacey said.

"Yeah, come on," Michael said.

"You do it or I will," Stacey added.

"That's blackmail," I said.

"I like how we're always on the exact same wavelength, Ellie," she said.

"Okay. Embarrassing." I thought it over. "I was really into Britney Spears at one point. For a minute. As a preteen."

"Sorry," Stacey said. "Not good enough."

"Seriously?"

"Dig deeper."

"Uh...you know my cat, Bandit?"

"Fat guy, black eyepatches?" Stacey asked.

"Well, okay." I sighed. "When nobody's around, I've been known to call him 'Mr. Ban-Ban.'"

Crickets sounded in the night. Then all three of them laughed at me, and I felt myself blush. Why had I done that?

"That's great, Ellie," Stacey said. "Say it again."

"No."

"Come on."

"My turn's over," I said.

"Michael?" Stacey asked.

"Where are these other tracks we're looking for?" he asked.

"Up ahead," she said. She clicked on her flashlight and pointed it at him. "Come on. Embarrassing fact about you, Mikey. Spill it."

"Okay. I was in *Peter Pan* when I was twelve," he said. "School play."

"That's only embarrassing if there's video evidence we can all watch," she said.

"The video evidence exists."

"You really played Peter Pan?" I asked, turning around and walking backwards on the tracks, like I'd seen kids do in a movie one time. "How bad was it? Leafy skirt? Green pantyhose?"

"Oh, I didn't play Peter Pan. I was Captain Hook."

"That's like the best part!" I said. "That's not embarrassing."

"The way I did it, it definitely was. The hook was too big. It kept getting caught on everything. My hat. My moustache. My pants. Which is why I ended up mooning the whole audience on opening night."

"I challenge the believability of that story," I said. "I need to see evidence."

"Jacob?" Stacey asked.

"Huh?" He asked, with the voice of a man who'd just arrived on the scene and had no idea what was going on.

"Your embarrassing story? Preferably from your awkward formative years?"

"Oh." His voice was detached, as if his mind were ten thousand miles away. "Um. One time I forgot to close the gate to the back yard. My dog escaped and a car ran him over."

"That...is really sad," Stacey said. "*Not* embarrassing."

"And then I cried at school the next day, and Kelly Brannon and his friends beat me up for it." Jacob blinked. "Wait, what are we talking about?"

"Your miserable childhood, apparently," Stacey said, slowing down to take his hand.

"Sorry. I was listening for the dead. The gate is right up here." Jacob stepped off the tracks and veered across the gravel to the woods.

I pointed ahead of him with my flashlight. He was right. An old wooden gate stood at the edge of the woods, barely visible under its mat of vines and weeds. It looked like a wooden fence might have flanked it at some point, decades ago, but trees, shrubs, and termites had eaten through it. The remaining slats and chunks of fence had all but faded away into the green growth.

Plastic signs had been stapled to the gate. NO TRESPASSING. HAZARDOUS CONDITIONS.

"That could be our stop," I said.

I approached the crumbling old gate and looked over it, into the darkness beyond.

Chapter Fourteen

Past the overgrown gate lay rotting railroad ties and rusty iron track. Railroad workers had clearly disconnected the archaic nineteenth-century line from the modern steel one many years ago, pulling up rails and ties until the old line was truncated back into the woods.

In 1902, the band of robbers had waited here, ready to stop the train as it rolled north along the exact path we'd just walked.

The pines gradually gave way to centuries-old live oaks, their enormous limbs grown together over the tracks during the past hundred and fifty years to knit a solid ceiling overhead, thatched with leaves and Spanish moss. The old railroad tracks appeared to lead away into a dark tunnel, which we knew extended all the way to the woods near our clients' house, and possibly all the way to the plantation ruins by the river.

"Okay," I said. My tone was hushed now, as if in deference to the spirits whose territory we were preparing to invade. "Stacey, all set?"

"Yep." Stacey had extracted the small night vision camera from her bag and held it in her hands. She clicked on the high-sensitivity microphone at her belt.

"Let's get moving." I stepped through the undergrowth, thorns scratching at my jeans. It's always the nasty plants that move into untamed spaces, the sharp brambles and poison ivy. I'd brought some sharp little shears in case we hit badly overgrown patches, but the tunnel effect of the trees seemed to discourage thick undergrowth. Tall, coarse weeds grew between the rails, but it looked walkable as far as my flashlight could reveal.

We entered the tunnel in close pairs, Michael and me first, Stacey and Jacob right behind us. Out on the live tracks, we'd spread out as individuals, joking and laughing, but we pulled together into a tight, quiet group as we entered the confined space, a tiny tribe sneaking into the lair of the monsters.

The air was colder inside, as confirmed by my Mel Meter, which also picked up some electromagnetic activity that increased as we followed the track. The canopy overhead blocked out any hint of stars or the moon, so we could only see the areas illuminated by our flashlights. Everything else lay in darkness.

"Wait," Jacob said. I stopped and turned to see him, eyes closed, one hand extended out above one of the rusty rails, his palm open toward it. "Something here."

I nodded. I'd been wondering if Jacob would pick up on the train robbery at all. We'd been walking away from the place where it had happened.

"Take your time," I said.

He winced, his eyes still closed. "I'm seeing guns and fire. People died here."

"Who?" I asked.

"The people on the train. I don't know how many. I can see an older man..." Jacob backtracked a few paces and pointed in the direction from which we'd come. "He's kneeling on the ground. His hands are tied...he's afraid. His heart's pounding away. He's confused...then he's gone. Blasted right through the back of the head." Jacob paused for what felt like hours but was probably thirty seconds. "I think he worked on the train. Not driving it, but something. Conductor, maybe."

"Who else do you see?"

"There's a lot of them."

"What's a lot?"

"Eight, ten, twelve? They're not all here. Some of them are hiding." Jacob opened his eyes and looked into the woods. "Some of them want to stay in the shadows, they don't want me to see them. But the ones who are talking to me...they're trapped in this tense situation. They want the train to start moving again, to get them away from here. But...these others, these shadows, they're here to take something from them."

Michael glanced from Jacob to me with a quizzical look on his face, as if wondering whether this made any sense to me.

"What does he want to take?" I asked.

"I get the sense of an organized attack, a raid," Jacob said. "Blood was shed. These two groups have been in conflict ever since. The shadowy ones are really slipping away now, hiding from me. They can travel fast down the tracks. They can all do that."

"Do they have any contact with the living?"

Jacob closed his eyes. "Some of them. Some of them, but they're scared of the shadowy ones. They sneak out among the living to feed, but they're always scurrying, whispering. Lately there have been a lot more living within range, so things are keying up around here. Because they can only travel so far from the tracks."

"Do the other ones ever bother the living?" I asked. "The shadowy ones?"

"They probably feed on the living. They must. They have power. The others do it, too, but not as often, I think." He looked down the tracks, deeper into the woods ahead. "They're afraid to leave the tracks."

"Why are they afraid?"

"They're afraid of that shadowy gang. And...they're afraid they'll miss the train." He shook his head. "They're stuck in their memories. The gang of dark ones..." Jacob's eyes widened. "I see them setting these people on fire. Now they're all burned. That's how they died. There are definitely two groups haunting this track. I think one group killed the other. But...everybody died." He shook his head. "It doesn't really make sense."

"Stacey, are you recording?" I asked.

"Never stopped," Stacey replied, gazing at Jacob with the

awestruck fangirl look she got whenever he started channeling information from the spirit world. The portable night vision camera was in her hands, her face glowing an eerie green in the light of its display screen.

"I need you to tell me about individuals, Jacob," I said. "Every individual you see."

He sighed. "You've got the conductor guy. He's tied up with a bullet hole through his head. The dark guys, I can't say much about them yet. The ones who are here and not hiding from us...I'll call them 'the passengers.' Okay. There's a sort of elderly couple, well-to-do, he's got the top hat and coat thing going, she has a hat that looks like somebody used a whole flock of birds to decorate it. Big puffy sleeves. That whole era...she's normally stern, but right now she's afraid. He's always timid, and right now he's *really* afraid."

"Right now?" I asked.

"The moment they're caught in. They flicker. Sometimes they're on fire, screaming. Other times they're just waiting for the train."

"Who else?"

"Young guy, early twenties. Silk tie, tall black hat, smug. Cigarette holder. He's like the yuppie of a hundred years ago. Banker or business guy. Also prone to catching on fire or looking like a horrible charred corpse." Jacob winced, turning away from something I couldn't see. "They can all be pretty scary if they want. They just have to show their death faces.

"Two sisters, traveling together. Not as wealthy as the others. I'd say they're in their thirties. Southern gals, originally from the country. One of them's unmarried, by choice. They're going home...they're trying to go home, but they'll never get there. Burned to death.

"Finally..." He took a quick, sharp breath. "She's *cold*. And stronger than the others. She's been feeding on something, or somebody."

"Who?" I asked.

"Little girl, lost," he said. "Seven or eight years old. She's all alone and...her sadness is so strong it's like a weapon. It can almost freeze the air around you. This one's dangerous."

"More about her," I said.

"She's full of loss, like an emotional black hole. I think her parents are dead. She's alone and doesn't really know where she's going. She has to go live with strangers now."

"What does she want?"

"She wants what they all want," he said. "To escape. But something's not letting them."

"The other guys in the woods?"

"Not exactly. Something to do with the train." He shook his head. "It's like they keep expecting the train to show up anytime."

"Maybe it will," I said.

"They're slipping away now," he said. "They're curious but they don't trust us."

"It's mutual so far. Let's keep walking."

We continued on. The leafy tunnel lay silent around us—no hooting owls or chorus of insects here, as if we'd entered some kind of dead zone.

I heard a crunch of dry leaves and needles, like a footstep, off to one side of the tracks. I swung my flashlight toward it, but found only shadows and brambles.

The heavy, cold air and the complete silence soon grew oppressive. I could hear every step of my boots on the old ties, my breath flowing in and out of my body, my heart thumping. The footsteps of my companions sounded softly as we walked along the weed-choked rails. My meter indicated a steady growth in electromagnetic activity as we went.

My skin had that unpleasant crawling, prickling feeling like I was being watched from the darkness. I continued to hear footsteps and snapping twigs. One time, I caught a shadow in my flashlight, shaped like a human torso, that took a little too long to fade. Shadows ought to vanish the instant you blast them with light.

Then the temperature dropped suddenly, and we were all breathing out plumes of frost. We looked at each other—everybody was aware something had changed.

"Up ahead," Jacob whispered.

A bank of heavy fog obscured the tunnel of limbs and moss, too thick for my light to penetrate.

"Do you sense something?" I whispered back to him.

"I sense a lot," he said. "There's that feeling of anticipation, like just before a storm. The spirits are silent now, waiting. I'm not sure what's happening beyond that."

"Great." I took a breath. "Let's keep going, then."

I moved into the fog. The living walls and ceiling of the tunnel became shadows, barely visible through the thick, frigid air.

The woods broke at a wide creek with a cloudlike fog above its surface, obscuring any view of the other side. A crumbling wooden trestle bridge spanned the water. The rails looked like pure rust, and the ties I could see looked rotten. The bridge faded away into the fog. For all I could tell, some of the ties ahead might be missing, or an unseen portion of the bridge might have collapsed into the creek below.

"A creek like this shouldn't create so much fog," I said. "It must be rolling in from the river."

"Or the Other Side," Stacey said, dragging the last two words out to try and make them extra spooky.

"So," Michael said. "Who wants to go first?"

"Can we go down and cross the stream?" Jacob asked.

"Never cross the streams," Michael intoned.

"Haven't you ever played *Oregon Trail?*" Stacey asked. "Fording a stream is a good way to lose your ox and develop dysentery."

I pointed my flashlight at the rickety old bridge, then at the water below. Walking to one side along the steep, weedy bank, I could see the deteriorated, termite-eaten condition of the remaining wooden supports.

"It's a miracle the bridge has stood this long," I said. "We're not walking on that. We're fording the stream."

"Fine," Stacey said. "But if I die of cholera, you're going to pay."

I walked up and down the bank on either side of the bridge, looking for a good crossing, doing my best to slice the fog with my flashlight. What I wanted: a nice clear path down to the water, maybe with tree roots conveniently spaced like stairs, followed by handy stepping-stone rocks across the creek. What I got: poison ivy, brambles, and glimpses of muddy water through the fog.

"Okay, guys," I said. "This isn't going to be great."

I proceeded cautiously, sitting down before I slid myself along the weed-choked slope. My boots landed in the water with a double splash.

"Ankle deep here," I told them. "I'm going to start across. If I suddenly drop out of sight, then I found a deeper spot."

I started across. The creek sank towards the middle, leaving me calf-deep in water. It was cool but not cold. Here, over the running water, the air was warm again instead of freezing.

"Glad I wore my good sneakers," Michael said, dropping into the creek behind me. I couldn't even see him.

"It's the price we pay for this glamorous work," I replied. The portion of the trestle I could see towered over me like a heap of old bones, casting dark shadows in the scarce starlight. It creaked and groaned in the wind, as if preparing to collapse on top of me. I reminded myself that the bridge had remained standing—more or less—for well over a century of neglect. It probably wouldn't topple over and crush me now. Probably.

Walking blindly through the fog, I made it to the far bank and began to climb almost straight up, through slick mud and thick weeds. My imagination helped me by placing snakes and spiders all through the undergrowth, just waiting to bite my fingers as I ascended.

Behind me, the rest of my team was still sloshing through the water as I reached the top of the bank next to the bridge. Luckily, a big chunk of the muddy earth under my left boot suddenly gave away with slurping sound. I went facefirst into the weeds and began to slide back toward the creek.

My hands made desperate grabs to break my fall. My right found a clump of weeds, which pulled loose at the roots under my weight. My left found a mushy cross-piece of the trestle bridge itself. It creaked a warning, but held.

"Uh, watch your step up here," I called down to the rest of the group.

"You okay?" Michael asked, arriving at the edge of the water and illuminating me with his flashlight.

"You've got serious mudface," Stacey said, joining him. I could feel the gooey mess of wet earth clinging to my skin.

I turned away and pulled myself upward, using the rotten bridge for leverage. I swear I could feel the whole thing shifting, as if the trestle would collapse under the strain of even partially supporting my weight. I really should have had a lighter breakfast.

I kept climbing. At the top, I grabbed onto the iron rail of the track for support as I hauled myself toward the knobby old pines at the top of the bank.

Looking back on it, grabbing that rusty old rail with my bare hand was a huge mistake.

First, the rail was like a solid strip of dry ice, painfully cold as if freezing my skin on contact. Second, it jolted me, like I'd touched a live wire or the third rail of a subway.

I hissed in pain and let go, grabbing onto another clump of weeds I couldn't even see, as if the jolt had momentarily blinded me or the fog had grown so thick there was no light at all.

Kicking and struggling, I regained my balance and my purchase on the steep bank, then pushed myself up to the top, lying on my belly in weeds and brambles, which wasn't all that comfortable.

I stood up, brushing off twigs and mud, and most likely ticks and other little nasties, but I didn't want to think about that. The fog seemed colder and heavier now. I could just discern the branches of a nearby tree. I could hear the creek's slow, sedate gurgle below.

"Okay," I said. "If I can do it, y'all can do it."

Nobody answered.

"Come on." I stepped cautiously toward the bank, but my flashlight only revealed a few weeds through the fog. "Michael? Stacey? Jacob?"

A hand shot up through the weeds and grabbed my ankle.

I screamed and tried to kick and pull away, but its hold was so solid that I ended up toppling backwards, landing on some nice knobby pine roots that jabbed me in the lower back.

Only then did the hand release. A broad-shouldered male figure rose up in the fog, climbing over the bank.

"Michael!" I said. "You scared me half to death. Three-quarters of the way, even." I turned my flashlight on him, right in his face.

It wasn't Michael.

The figure climbing over the bank at my feet was male, dressed in a tattered black suit and a partially burned white shirt. His entire face was charred. His eyes were pinpoints of light staring out at me from deep black sockets.

His jaw dropped open in a loose, lifeless manner. A little hiss escaped, as if he hated my flashlight...and then he grabbed for me again, his strong, cold fingers pressing into my calf. A pale tongue lolled out of his mouth. He looked like a hungry dog.

I managed to scramble backwards. I pushed myself up along a pine trunk, standing to face him while he rose the rest of the way up from the steep bank.

He moved toward me, extending one burned hand toward my chest, a moan boiling from his wide-open mouth.

I wanted to scream for the others to come help me, but my throat was closed tight, my heart beating fast. My friends should have been here by now, anyway. Unless something had grabbed them along the way. I couldn't hear their voices at all.

My own fear held me in place, serving as an accomplice to the approaching ghost. It seemed pretty clear the entity intended to feed on me, or worse.

Move, I told myself. *It doesn't matter where, just start moving.*

My body reluctantly obeyed, turning and lurching over the pine roots into the fog, toward the unseen railroad tracks.

I took another step, and two more pale figures emerged from the fog, blocking my way to the tracks. They were women, their Victorian dresses burned to pieces and clinging to their scorched bodies. They didn't seem entirely solid, as if made of the fog around them, but that didn't mean they couldn't hurt me. Not at all.

Their dark eye sockets fixed themselves on my face. Their hands reached out—one of them had the burned remains of lace gloves between her fingers.

I could smell fire and ashes in the air.

All three ghosts closed in around me, their cold fingers prodding at my arms, my stomach, my chest, my face.

If I didn't do something, I was going to be ghost kibble.

Since my light wasn't driving them off, I reached for the iPod on my belt. I thought I'd hit them with something strong and holy, maybe Aretha Franklin performing "Oh Happy Day."

Then a blast of sound tore through the night, rattling me to the bones. A piercing train whistle called out its lonely cry in the darkness.

The ghosts turned toward it, like parishioners summoned by a church bell. They shuffled away from me, in the direction of the tracks.

I followed, pointing my light toward the ground ahead. If they were done attacking me, I needed to learn more about them.

More shadowy figures passed through the fog around me, all of them slowly approaching the tracks.

I heard the whistle again. A light emerged from the fog-shrouded bridge, burning through the dense fog, high in the air above the tracks.

As it approached, I saw it was mounted on the front of what looked like the skeletal remains of an old locomotive. It could have been the same one Grant had pointed out to us, the steam engine that had been robbed and dynamited in 1902, but there were huge gaps in its frame, through which I could see the fog on the other side. The rusty shaft of the connecting rod had come loose from some of the wheels along the side and repeatedly stabbed forward as the locomotive rolled, as if to spear anyone standing too close to the tracks.

The ghosts approached anyway, standing right at the edge.

I tried to catch a glimpse of the conductor through the soot-coated windows of the locomotive cab, but it was too dark within. I could smell burning coal. The engine, and the broken shells of the cars it towed, did not make a sound as they trundled past me.

The train wasn't moving at top speed, maybe twenty-five or thirty miles an hour. It blasted its shrieking whistle again as the shadowy ghosts closed in from the fog.

Some of the figures reached out their hands beseechingly, as if begging the train for a favor. A couple of others tried to latch onto the side of the train, but were batted back by its motion, unable to hold on.

One figure, wrapped in a pale sheet or dress, rose from the fog and latched onto the side of a ruined boxcar. The boxcar's big sliding door and a portion of its wall were missing, and near the back it was just a bare frame with no roof or walls.

The ghostly figure, a girl or small woman, clung to a ladder on the side.

From the empty space where the door should have been, a tall, solid shadow of a man emerged. It seemed to be dressed in a derby hat and a coat, based on its silhouette.

The man seized the girl and flung her away from the train. She landed in a bank of fog among the gnarled roots of an old oak tree, and I ran to her.

She looked up at me, her face a grim white mask, her hair hanging black and limp. She was seven or eight years old, her dress patched and singed black at the edges.

Her eyes were a colorless pale, and she glared back at me.

I felt cold to my core, as if all the heat had drained from my body. A dark sadness settled in around me, a feeling of hopelessness and loss.

My banshee.

She sat up and reached for me as the other ghosts had, hungrily, as if she meant to feed.

With all my attention on her, I jumped with surprise and renewed fear as hands grabbed me from behind, rough and strong, squeezing and shaking me.

"Ellie?" its voice said.

I turned to see Michael, gripping my arms in his hands. Stacey and Jacob stood on either side of him, shining their flashlights on me.

"Huh?" I said, quite articulately. I looked down at the ground, but the girl had vanished, like all the other spirits. "What?" I added, for clarification.

"You spaced out," Stacey out. "Are you still spaced out?"

"What do you mean?"

"You've been wandering around like a catatonic," Michael said. "Or a sleepwalker."

"What did you see?" Jacob asked me, a reversal of our usual roles.

"The train," I said. "They were all here, waiting for it. It was like they were trying to get on but something wouldn't let them."

Jacob nodded. "I felt it move through here, and the anticipation climbing among the ghosts. Then the let-down after it passed. They're moving back now, into the woods or down the track..."

"Are you okay, Ellie?" Michael had his arm around me, and there wasn't much reason to resist that.

"Yeah, good. I just got a glimpse of their world. Wouldn't want to be stuck there. By the way, everyone should avoid touching the old rails. They're loaded with bad juju."

"I don't have my unabridged ghost hunter's scientific dictionary with me," Michael said.

"They're conductors," I said. "They're rusty, but they're conductive enough for ghostly energy. You said the ghosts were free to move along the rails?"

"But not far from them," Jacob replied, nodding.

"What are you seeing, Jacob?"

"They're drawing back," he said. "I think they're aware of us, and they don't trust us. We're intruders."

"We should intrude further," I said. "Come on."

We continued down the rails, walking alongside them rather than between them. I didn't want to risk touching them again.

The night remained unnaturally cool, but the freezing temperatures had gone away. The fog had thinned but not vanished. The dark woods around us felt alive, full of hidden eyes, watching us make our way through the low, mossy tunnel.

Since I was in the lead, I was the first to see the red light beside the tracks, floating along like a hot ember or a will-o'-the-wisp.

Chapter Fifteen

I stood in place and held up my hand. I guess we'd all seen enough movies, because the others stopped behind me. I motioned at Stacey, then pointed at the red light.

She came up beside me, taking video of it. It moved like a stray flame on the wind, blowing alongside the track, except there was no wind at the moment. It glowed red, but not brightly enough to shed any light on the tunnel around it.

We watched it make its slow, bobbing retreat until we lost sight of it, either around a bend ahead or because of the feebleness of its glow. Or maybe it had vanished altogether.

We followed it silently, and caught sight of it ahead, drifting its slow but steady way along.

It was moving in the same direction we were planning to go, so we continued following behind it, saying nothing. Moving as quietly as I could, I opened my backpack and drew on my thermal goggles.

The same blue shape carried the light, which again looked extra-cold on the thermals, not radiant at all. The shape appeared female, clad in a long dress, her back to us as she walked along the tracks, waving her red light.

I thought of what Grant had said, that someone had stopped the train with a red lantern, signaling an emergency. There had been a female member of the gang of bandits. All things being equal, wouldn't a train conductor be more likely to stop for a woman in distress than a rough-looking man?

Maybe she'd hailed down the train for the robbers. Now she repeated that criminal act, initiating the robbery that had led to murder, night after night, doomed to walk the earth with her cursed light like the original jack-o'-lantern guy.

In time, we passed the hole in the undergrowth Stacey had cut with her shears, revealing the narrow path through the woods toward our clients' house.

"I wonder how Ember's doing?" I whispered to Stacey. My phone showed no calls or messages from them, but it also had only one blinking bar's worth of signal. Reception can be spotty in any haunted place. Being in the woods next to a wildlife preserve didn't help.

"Are we talking now?" Stacey whispered back.

"I don't think we'll disturb Jill O' Lantern if we stay quiet," I said. "She's pretty far ahead."

"I'm picking up some strays," Jacob whispered.

"Cats?" Stacey asked.

"Souls," he said. He knelt and held his hand over the rail.

"Don't touch it," I reminded him.

"Don't have to." He closed his eyes. "There are spirits...apparently...who roam free on the railroads. Not rooted to a spot, but haunting the tracks themselves. Drifters from earlier times who loved the freedom of the rails, back when they were new. A few of them drifted down this way and got trapped somehow."

"Maybe when they severed this line from the main one," I said.

Jacob nodded. "Mostly male, with a wild, restless look..."

"Hobo ghosts?" Stacey asked.

"Basically."

"Then that explains...stuff," Stacey said, probably remembering not to give the psychic too much leading information. It certainly made casual conversation difficult.

We continued on, following the distant red glow along the tracks.

Gradually, the air began to reek of sulfur and sour fumes.

"Does anybody smell cookies baking?" Jacob asked.

"It's the stench of Hell," Michael said. "I knew these tracks would lead us there."

"Paper mill," Stacey said. "South of here, past those pines, is an industrial strip along the river. Everything north of us is wildlife preservation. So are these old tracks, actually, and the plantation ruins ahead. They just haven't gotten around to bulldozing it. Or maybe they're just letting the forest reclaim it all."

"That would be cheaper," I said.

We had to stop when we reached a high chain-link fence built across the tracks, totally blocking our way. Through it, I could still see the distant red ember drifting its way along.

"That's inconvenient," Jacob mentioned, touching the fence. "Tell me we don't have to climb it."

"We don't," I said. "Let's find a gate. I don't want to be trapped inside there and have to climb out in a hurry if something goes wrong."

Working our way around through the dense trees, we finally found a gate. It was wide enough for a car, facing a rutted dirt road that more or less led back the way we'd come. Chains and an old padlock held the gate shut. The signs on the fence welcomed us with greetings like NO TRESPASSING and CONDEMNED.

"Stacey, light." I knelt by the gate and removed my lock picks from my backpack. She held her flashlight above me while I went to work on the padlock.

"Before we get arrested," Jacob said, "I'm a little curious about what we're breaking into here. Just as a conversation-starter with my boss when he fires me."

"Ruins," Stacey told him. "The security shouldn't be too serious. The fence is probably just to keep out kids, vandals, and weirdos."

"Which one are we?" Jacob asked.

I popped open the lock. The gate pulled open with a rusty squeal, moving reluctantly, as if nobody had come to visit in a very long time.

"I'm feeling weird about this place," Jacob added.

"We must be on the right track, then." My light revealed crumbling chunks of old buildings, most of them not much more than weedy heaps of brick and brambles. Silkgrove had been a large plantation, cultivating mulberries for silkworms, then rice, then cotton, but there wasn't much left of it now.

We found the tracks, now reduced to twin iron lines sunken in moss and wild grass. The moist air and earth near the river must have devoured the ties a little faster, because there wasn't much sign of them.

Beyond the rails lay the crooked remains of old chimneys among a few ancient rotten timbers. Slave cabins, maybe. They were located on the other side of the tracks from the mansion ruins up ahead.

The rails led us closer to the river, where two rubble-filled brick walls sat proudly on a hill overlooking the water. The rails ran in the shadow of the hill, to the collapsed and overgrown ruins of long-fallen structures by the water. Mossy, half-sunken pilings remained at the edge of the water where the plantation's docks had presumably been. Its owner had dreamed of a rail and river transportation nexus here, but instead there was nothing but nesting sites for migrating waterfowl.

We followed the rusty rails to the bitter end, where they rose briefly on the collapsed remnant of pilings and support posts and ended at the bank of the wide, dark Savannah River flowing several feet below, the rotten remnants of the last tie still clinging to the sheared-off tips of the rails.

"I vote we stop following the tracks now," Stacey said, as we reached the lip of the steep bank.

"We did it," I said. I turned to shine my light among the ruins. "Anything else, Jacob?"

"Yeah, what happened to Jill-o'-the-wisp?" Stacey asked.

"I thought we were going with Jill-o'-lantern," I said.

"Thumb wrestle you for it!" Stacey offered.

"There's something here," Jacob said, turning back from the water to the ruins. "I don't think she's left."

I looked into the shadowy heaps of the old bricks and crumbling timber around us, trying to glimpse any hint of the red light we'd been following.

"Everybody turn off your lights," I said, clicking mine dark and holstering it.

We stood quietly in the darkness, watching, hearing only the slow lapping sound of the river.

"Maggie?" I called out, the name of the female train robber. "Maggie Fannon?"

"There," Stacey whispered, pointing.

It took me a moment to notice the tiny light, moving among the collapsed buildings like a glowing red firefly. It wasn't alongside the tracks anymore.

I started after it, trudging through the waist-high weeds. The others began to follow me, but I motioned for them to stop. I wanted to check out the ghost without spooking it away.

The tiny light led me to one of the many small, mostly collapsed buildings. This one was made of rocks, maybe some kind of old smokehouse. A live oak had grown up behind it, its heavy limbs wrapped around the sides and top of the little building like the fingers of a giant's clutching hand. The growing tree had applied enough pressure over the years to tilt the building forward, so that the empty front doorway and what remained of the front wall actually leaned toward the ground.

Overall, it looked like the sort of building that would immediately collapse on your head and crush your skull if you poked around inside it.

The red light slipped inside through the tilted cavity of the door. Of course. I sighed as I approached the building.

The front wall was tilted so far over that I had to drop to my hands and knees to look inside. A curtain of vines and moss blocked my view. I used my unlit flashlight to rip and pull them out of the way, worried I would rip some critical vine or root that was quietly holding the old rock building together, and the entire precariously balanced front wall would crash down around me.

"Ellie?" Stacey whispered, approaching me. "Be careful. You're not going in there, are you?"

I shushed her and looked into the darkness inside the building. I couldn't see anything in there—no moonlight was leaking in from above.

I was just about to click my flashlight to life when the red glow returned. It was just a burning pinpoint at first, but this time it quickly flared and spread to form an irregular shape about the size of a burning human head, floating in the darkness just a few feet from me, while I crouched under a ton of unreliable rocks.

My mouth opened, and it was equally likely that I was about to ask a question or scream.

Then it flared a little brighter, and I saw that it wasn't a head or a face—our brains just tend to interpret shapes that way. It's one reason people sometimes think they have ghosts when all they have is an active imagination.

The shape was a rock, and in its faint glow I could see the edges of other rocks around it. It looked like a giant red-hot coal, though it didn't give off any heat.

Then it went dark, and I could see nothing at all.

"Maggie?" I whispered.

Maggie, or whoever the spirit was, didn't respond, not even a tiny dot of red in the darkness.

I clicked on my flashlight, revealing a slag-heap of rocks that had once formed the back wall, before weather and the pressure of the growing tree had conspired to shatter it. I could see the dark bulge of the tree trunk behind the pile, near the top. The limbs and remnants of the roof created a solid canopy overhead, sealing out any light from above.

Slowly, I reached toward the rock that had glowed. It had been a searing red a moment earlier, but my fingers found it just as cold as any of the stones around it. My fingertips left deep trails in the dust on its surface.

"Ellie?" Stacey whispered from outside.

"One sec." I pushed and pulled on the rock. The thing was heavy, but I managed to partially dislodge it, drawing it forward a few inches.

Small rocks and broken pebbles of old cement rolled down from the slag-heap behind it, immediately filling in the small gap I'd just opened. I saw how this was going to go.

"Michael, want to come in and give me a hand?"

"I'd rather you came *out*," he replied, but he dropped to his hands and knees and crawled in with me. Jacob and Stacey hung back, away from the crash zone of the front wall if it decided to flop over. They shone their lights in at us.

"Is there any chance we can move this without creating a rock slide?" I indicated the stone that had glowed.

Michael looked it over, then studied the heap built up behind it.

"It's going to take a minute," he said, lifting smaller rocks from high on the pile. "You should step outside."

"Or stay and help," I said, taking a few stones from the heap and laying them near the wall.

"You should let me do that," Jacob said, but there was no room for an extra person inside the tiny half-collapsed building.

"Maybe in a minute. I've been..." I grunted, moving another rock aside. "I've been meaning to do some...weight training. Just let us know if anything looks like might it come crashing down."

Michael and I continued to work at it, clearing away the rocks higher on the heap so they wouldn't slide down. Finally, Michael rolled aside the head-sized rock. I picked up my flashlight and pointed it at the area beneath it.

More rocks.

"Looks like a bust," Michael said.

"Let's keep digging." I took hold of another hefty rock, and he had to help me move it aside.

"What are we looking for, anyway?" Michael asked.

"In my experience, probably human remains," I said. "We might find a crushed skull or some vertebrae."

"Oh, good, I was worried it might be something scary," he said, lifting more rocks and stacking them near the wall on his side.

"But you called Maggie's name," Stacey said from outside. "Didn't she die in New Orleans? Like a thousand miles away? Why would she be buried here?"

"Maybe Jill-o'-lantern isn't Maggie," I said, panting heavily now. I wiped my sweaty face on my denim jacket sleeve.

Michael moved another sizable rock, revealing something dark and solid underneath.

"Doesn't look like a skull to me," he said. I pointed my flashlight. It was filthy, dusty dark brown material.

Michael had to move a few more rocks to reveal the entire object. It looked like a very old canvas satchel, tied tight.

"Maybe the bones are inside," I said.

"What's going on, you guys?" Stacey asked. "We can't see anything."

"Hold your horses." I held my light steady while Michael carefully unwound the two tight knots holding the satchel closed. Then he lifted the flap and looked inside.

His eyes widened.

"Well?" I asked. "Is it a leprechaun? What's in there?"

"It's...money. Kind of." Michael reached inside and drew out a small stack of green bills bundled together. "I'm not sure if it's real."

He passed me the faded, stiff green certificates. The one on top had the number 20 in each corner, but it was issued by "The Merchants National Bank of Savannah." In 1902. With a picture of a guy I didn't recognize at all, a graying man with enormous sideburns.

"Who the heck is Hugh McCulloch?" I asked.

"Maybe he's the inventor of the muttonchop," Michael guessed.

"Abraham's Lincoln's treasury secretary," Jacob said from outside the building.

"So is it real money or not?" Michael asked.

"I'll have to ask my accountant." I replaced the stiff, brittle money and lifted the satchel away, revealing nothing but more rocks and dust.

We crawled out and away from the slanted building, and I felt the relief of open sky above my head. I stood and handed Jacob a stack of bundled bills. "What do you think?"

"I want to see the funny money, too," Stacey said, leaning close to him.

"Be gentle with it," I said, passing her another stack. "It feels like it'll crumble if you squeeze it too hard."

"Third National Bank of Atlanta," Stacey read from a fifty-dollar bill at the top of her stack.

"Second National Bank of Nashville," Jacob said, studying his stack of hundreds.

"Could we actually cash these in?" Stacey asked.

"I'm not sure," Jacob said. "They're older than the Federal Reserve system, so they might just be worthless paper. Maybe the Treasury would still accept them. I'll have to look it up."

"Still, pretty neat," Stacey said. "Buried treasure."

"I don't think the ghost showed it to us so we could go on a shopping spree at the mall," I said.

"No kidding," Stacey said. "Who goes to the mall anymore?"

Michael, who'd been rummaging inside the satchel, came up with a small leather pouch tied with a string. Its sides bulged out, and it jingled as he moved it.

"Sounds promising," he said. He drew the string and shook out a few coins into his palm.

They were five-dollar coins, with an eagle on one side and a picture of Lady Liberty on the other. Their dates were mostly in the 1890's. They were solid gold.

"Five bucks," Michael said. "We could get a Value Meal at Wendy's."

"How many are in there?" I asked.

He shook the bag. "Twenty or thirty, I think. So, what do we do? Count it up and divide four ways?"

"Keep it all together," I said, taking the bag of coins back from him. I gestured for Jacob and Stacey to replace their cash, too. "It might be worthless paper now, but the ghosts don't know that. This money is part of the case. It's the reason the case exists at all. It's what the robbery was about."

"I don't get it," Stacey said. "How is all the money still here? It's hard to believe."

"The only member of the gang who lived was Maggie Fannon, and I think she's the one who led us here. She must have hidden the money."

"She must have been pretty strong to move all those rocks."

"Or she caused a little avalanche while burying the satchel." I looked back at the old building. "I guess the ruins kept the weather off. And this canvas must be pretty tough."

"And nobody ever poked around back here? Anytime in the last hundred years?" Michael asked.

"It's been part of the national wildlife refuge since the nineteen-twenties," Stacey said.

"We wouldn't have found it without the ghost," I said. "Now we have to figure out what she wants us to do with it. Maggie, are you still there?"

I looked around the ruins, but saw no hint of the little red light. I handed Michael the satchel and drew out my thermal goggles. No sign of the ghost.

"Okay." I replaced my goggles and nodded at Michael. "Now you have something to carry. You are hereby made the treasurer of this expedition."

"Does that mean I have to grow sideburns?"

"Are you besmirching the hallowed memory of Hugh McCulloch?"

"Only the memory of his facial hair." Michael began to pull the old satchel's strap over his head.

"Support it with your arms, too," I said. "It could rupture."

"Either trust me as your treasurer or nominate someone else," Michael said, but he did as I said, supporting the bottom of the bag with his arm rather than trusting the old strap.

We began our return hike, back out the gate—I was even feeling public-spirited enough to replace the padlock—and then along the tracks through the woods. After we'd passed the industrial area, we slipped through the trees and emerged behind the shady strip mall where Stacey had parked her car.

She looked relieved when we found it waiting in the parking lot, perfectly intact. We quickly loaded our stuff and climbed inside.

"So, great hike, everybody," Stacey said as she pulled out onto the road. "Saw some ghosts. Found some cash. We made some real progress on the case. Uh, didn't we?"

"Possibly," I said. "Now I know what our banshee looks like, if we run into her again." I described what I'd seen after touching the rails.

As I spoke, I kept glancing at the road behind us, feeling like someone was watching me. I wondered if we'd brought a presence along with the old money, maybe the ghost of Maggie.

A car was behind us, though the road was otherwise deserted. It felt like they were watching us, but that could have been my paranoid imagination. After we made a turn, I watched behind us again. A pair of headlights rounded the turn after us, just before our road curved us out of sight, keeping their distance but moving in the same direction.

"What are you looking at?" asked Michael, sitting in the back seat behind me.

"Can you tell what kind of car is behind us?"

"I don't see one."

"Just wait."

I caught more glimpses of the headlights, but the car stayed back, mostly keeping itself out of sight behind the last curve or turn.

I had Stacey pull into the first well-lit parking lot we saw—a Waffle House—and wait there a moment. The car eventually showed up, slowed briefly, then picked up speed. A black Acura sedan.

"Follow that car," I said. "It's our turn to spy on them."

"Are you sure they were following us?" Stacey pulled into a parking spot, then reversed, but cut it too widely and had to pull up again.

"You could tail them a little closer," I said.

"Sorry, I missed car-chase day in detective school." Stacey finally managed to turn her hybrid SUV around and nosed back out onto the road, where a red light promptly stopped us.

"Do I run it?" Stacey said.

"If you get a ticket, we can cover it out of that bag of cash."

Stacey hesitated, then stomped the gas and ran through the red light, since no cars were approaching. The Acura was out of sight, though, gone like another ghost into the night.

Chapter Sixteen

When I returned to the Kozlows' basement, the motion detector noticed my presence and the array of lights sprang to life. I turned them off. There were still no messages from Tom or Ember, so either the ghosts had left them alone or our defenses had warded them off.

Jacob and Michael had gone home. Michael had offered to stay, but I knew his younger sister was at home by herself, and I still had reservations about the supernatural darkness that lay beneath his apartment house, sealed for now under lead and steel and a demonologist's rite. For whatever that was worth. I'd encouraged Michael to move away, just to be safe, but he hadn't done it yet.

Stacey sat out in the van, reviewing footage and audio captured by our gear while we were away at the tracks. I sat on my air mattress in the clients' basement, finally getting some time to catch up on the folders of information Grant had collected for us. My top priority was to learn about the victims of the train robbery so I could identify the ghosts.

I read about:

Dr. George Canton, 64, and his wife Ethel, 61, had died from burns and shrapnel. Both were on their way home to Charleston from Savannah. This sounded like the well-dressed older couple Jacob had mentioned.

Ronald Abbot, 26, sales agent for the Albany Pecan Company, made me think of the cocky young man in the suit Jacob had described. A pair of sisters—Margaret Knowles Davenport, 31, and Minnie Knowles, 35, also fit his description. Both were originally from Savannah, but the younger, married sister had lived in Charlotte, North Carolina with her husband and six children, according to the newspaper death notice Grant had copied for me.

Finally, I reached Sophia Preston, age eight, traveling alone. Like the others, she'd died of severe burns and shrapnel from the dynamite explosion in the passenger car. The newspaper reports gave few details, but between my experiences and Jacob's, it seemed she had been recently orphaned and was being sent away, perhaps to live with family in another city. She would have died feeling sad and alone, and had been trapped in those feelings ever sense—even learning to use them as a weapon to feed on the living.

I felt sorry for the little girl who'd grown into a banshee after death. Like me, she'd lost her parents at a young age—even younger than I had—and become a burden to be dropped on distant relatives. I wanted to help her.

I had to remind myself that the living came first, that it was unacceptable for the banshee to still be hanging around to feed on the newborn baby. Time was running out. I needed to devise a trap for Sophia. Surely the little girl's ghost would be happier in the cemetery at Goodwell, full of flowers and trees, than obsessively haunting the site of her traumatic death. Maybe the geographic separation and the new environment could help her move on from this world.

"Ellie, I've got something," Stacey said over my headset. I let out a sigh. We'd only walked a mile across mostly flat land, but my body was tired and full of aches, as if we'd climbed a mountain. The haunted woods and tracks had drained us.

"What is it?" I asked.

"I've been monitoring Captain Neighborhood Watch's hidden cameras around the community," Stacey said.

"You can do that? Hack into his cameras?"

"Apparently he bought one of the cheaper spy camera sets on the market," she said. "Not much trouble to snag the signal. Anyway, I just saw a shadow-man go into a house on another street. It looks unoccupied, maybe not even completely finished."

I weighed how much I wanted to go into an empty house looking for undead hobos and criminals.

"Keep watch on it," I said. "I'd check it out, but I don't want to leave Ember unguarded again." That sounded much better than *I'm just too exhausted, okay?*

"Aye aye," Stacey said. "He just kind of disappeared at the front door, as far as I could see. This camera's pretty shoddy. Everything's gray and fuzzy."

"Grant got us some good information," I said. "I think our banshee's name is Sophia. She was eight when she died."

"Aw."

"Don't forget she's a dangerous ghost now, though. Let me know if you see any more activity."

After jotting down what details I could gather about the dead passengers, I turned my attention to the railroad crew. Benny Wheelwright, conductor, 54—Jacob had seen his ghost tied up near the robbery site. Jacob had said nothing about Lars Olsen, the 28-year-old brakeman from Michigan, or Malcolm Dumont, 46, the engineer. I supposed the brakeman and conductor's ghosts might still be inside the train as it drove back and forth on its isolated track like one of the old locomotives at the museum. I had seen the train moving in both directions now—a wind blowing from the east, an apparition riding the rails from the west.

Each one of them had been tied up with rope and killed with a single shot to the head.

The newspapers, court records, and other accounts offered much less information about those passengers who'd been wounded instead of killed. Angus Kroeller, a railroad cop, had suffered some burns in the explosion, then a bullet in the leg in a shoot-out with the remaining gang members, James McCoyle and Maggie Fannon. McCoyle had died, but Maggie Fannon escaped with the stolen money, probably because of the railroad cop's injury.

As Grant had told us, James McCoyle had been suspected in multiple train robberies out west during his younger years, arrested once but escaped custody. Maggie Fannon was a Savannah native who'd been arrested for crimes like forgery. The other two gang members were also fairly local, Liam and Sean O'Reilly, each with arrest records for assault and robbery, in towns scattered around the Southeast. McCoyle had recruited them locally, not bringing in any of his Old West gang. Maybe he'd ditched them, or they'd died or retired from the increasingly dangerous world of old-fashioned stick-'em-up train robbery.

I tried to piece together what must have happened that night.

Maggie Fannon had waited at the intersection with the old tracks and hailed down the train as it rolled north from Savannah. When the train stopped, the gang had taken the crew at gunpoint and tied them up.

They'd dynamited the safe in the cargo car, helping themselves to a heap of money amounting to about fifty thousand dollars, on its way to the Bank of Charleston in South Carolina.

After that, something went wrong.

The O'Reilly brothers had gone into one of the passenger cars for a little bonus robbery, taking the travelers' cash and jewelry. An additional dynamite charge had gone off while they were in there, killing the brothers and several passengers.

That was where the story ceased to make sense. As Michael had already pointed out, an experienced train robber like McCoyle would know better than to upgrade a simple cash robbery into multiple counts of murder. The heat from the authorities would be intense.

The only scenario I could devise was that the O'Reilly brothers had brought dynamite into the passenger cars to intimidate the passengers, and then accidentally detonated it. Or maybe the kerchiefs covering their faces had slipped, and they'd decided to kill witnesses—they were rough and violent types, after all. And maybe stupid enough to blow themselves up, too.

Another obvious possibility was that McCoyle or Fannon had deliberately dynamited the car with the O'Reilly brothers inside in order to keep more of the loot for themselves. Still, why not double-cross the other gang members later, after the robbery, rather than create a pile of innocent victims? McCoyle's other robberies had been conducted rationally, with no deaths involved.

The dynamite in the passenger car remained a huge question mark.

At some point, the railroad cop Kroeller had exchanged fire with James McCoyle, and ultimately Maggie Fannon had escaped with the money, which would never be seen again.

Until now. I glanced at the worn satchel sitting by my toolbox and backpack a few feet away. Why in the world would Maggie have left all the money behind? Fifty thousand dollars was a huge amount in 1902, easily the equivalent of hundreds of thousands of dollars today. Why suffer all that and then drop the cash?

Maybe she'd been in love with McCoyle or one of the other gang members, overcome with grief at his death. Or maybe she'd been running for her life, afraid, and the bag of money was slowing her down. It certainly wasn't a light piece of luggage. Maybe she'd hidden it at the ruins, intending to return later, but fled to New Orleans and died before she had a chance to return.

I flicked on the overhead lights, opened up the satchel, and began counting the bundled stacks of money, jotting in my notebook the totals given on their rubber bands and also how much money came from each bank, in case that mattered. The money looked so unfamiliar, with the names of individual cities displayed prominently next to faces I didn't recognize at all, that it was as if the currency had come from some alternate reality.

The work absorbed my attention so much that the sound of a creaking door barely registered in the back of my mind. Then a cold breeze blew into the room, and I looked up.

The door to the outside had opened, but there was nobody there who could have opened it.

"Ellie!" Stacey said. "I'm seeing something on thermal in there. Cold."

"Great." I stood up on wobbly legs—they'd fallen asleep while I sat cross-legged on my mattress counting money. Pins and prickles erupted everywhere.

I drew my flashlight from its holster and approached the open door. It was possible I'd failed to close it securely and the wind had blown it open, which would also create a cooling effect on the thermal imaging camera.

"What do you see?" I whispered. I closed the door.

"It went out of range. Northwest corner."

Turning the thermal camera on its tripod, I found the small, pale blue shape drifting along the wall, in the general direction of the stairs.

"Sophia," I said. "Sophia Preston."

The blue form halted, as if pinned in place by my words.

"My name is Ellie Jordan," I said. "I'm here to help you."

It remained frozen in place. Then the overhead lights went out and the basement door blew open with much more force, slamming hard against the wall.

I turned, rotating the thermal camera around with me. The display screen showed a cold haze drifting into the room. I felt it on my skin, too, a cold, clammy presence. The temperature in the room began to drop, as registered by the thermal display. From a balmy September seventy-one degrees to fifty, then forty, then thirty-eight, turning the basement into one big walk-in freezer.

"Ellie?" Stacey whispered.

"Shhh." I needed to assess the situation. Blowing out a frosty breath of air, I rotated the camera, panning slowly around the basement. I was looking for any sign of the tall, dark shape that had dragged the banshee away before.

I found signs of multiple spirits, cold and thin, like spindly pillars of ice floating in a scattered formation around the basement. Around me.

The smallest, darkest one, the one I'd addressed as Sophia, remained where it was, shaped a little more clearly than the others, suggesting the profile of a young girl.

I felt a sinking feeling in my gut. I was surrounded. I glanced at the little cluster of floodlights that I'd pointed at the door while I was away. I'd disconnected its sensors, but I could manually activate the lights and blast them into all the dark corners and nooks where the ghosts lurked. That might send them scurrying. On the other hand, with the kind of focused group intention they were clearly showing here, it might just make them angry.

With my thumb on the button of my flashlight, I took a deep breath of the frozen air and addressed them.

"Okay," I said. "You've got my attention. What do you want?"

The deep cold spots remained where they were. If anybody answered, I didn't hear it. Stacey would have to review the audio later in case there was a reply out of the range of human hearing.

The money for which they'd died sat out in stacks around my

mattress. I had to wonder how they felt about that. It certainly made the situation awkward for me.

Since the ghosts weren't responding or moving, I took the opportunity to sweep the camera around and count the large cold spots. Six. Among the deceased were six passengers. Sophia, our banshee, was one of the six.

"Sophia Preston," I said again, then I read the other names from my notebook. "George Canton. Ethel Canton. Ronald Abbot. Margaret Knowles Davenport. Minnie Knowles. I understand you had a difficult death and, so far, a pretty troubled afterlife. You're trapped here and you want to move on. All we want is to help you do that."

The six cold shapes remained where they were, making no sound. I could feel them watching me from every side. My back was always to one or two of them, and I didn't like that at all. My heart was thudding, my instincts screaming at me to fight or flee. Preferably flee. The basement door still stood wide open, but I resisted the urge.

"Any ideas how I can help?" I asked. I was feeling a little desperate for a response here. If they had a message, they needed to tell me already. If they were going to attack, let them go ahead and do it.

Cold silence was their only answer.

"Stacey," I whispered. "Get into position."

"Okay! Uh, what position is that?"

"Come around back," I said, through gritted teeth. "Stay outside by the door until I call for you. Watch for nasties along the way."

The six figures still hadn't moved. I wrapped my arms around myself, the intense cold eating through my denim jacket. I really needed to replace my leather one. It had been a much better insulator against the cold, plus those pesky psychokinetic ghost attacks.

When trapped in a basement surrounded by several ghosts who are acting way too interested in you, the smart thing is to get out of that basement, and preferably out of that house altogether. Get thee to a Motel 6 if necessary. Unfortunately, my job is to protect my clients from ghosts, and my activities that night might just have drawn them all to my clients' house instead. I'd turned one or two ghosts into six. Huge failure on my part, the exact opposite of the job I was supposed to do.

So I had to stay there and face them, even if it meant getting slammed all over the concrete floor by irate ghosts.

"What's the plan, Jan?" Stacey arrived in the back yard at top speed, with both her flashlights drawn.

"The ghosts are stonewalling me," I said. "I want to test something out. Stay in the doorway and make sure it doesn't close."

I walked several steps deeper into the cold, lightless basement, feeling eyes all over me, observing me from the darkest parts of the room. I moved as quickly as I could, returning all the cash to the satchel, then bringing it to the open doorway.

"Take this," I told Stacey. "Carry it away."

"So they'll come after me?" She frowned, understandably.

"I hope they do," I said, which only deepened her frown. "Then we'll know why they're here."

"Okay." Stacey sighed, then carried the satchel to the far side of the lawn and set it down by the fence. She stood next to it, a flashlight ready to fire in each hand.

I didn't feel any change in the basement. The thermal camera showed the ghosts staying put, not reacting at all to the money.

After a few minutes, it seemed apparent that they weren't planning to react at all. That was bad news. Either Sophia had bragged about feasting on Ember's rich pregnant-young-woman energy, and brought her friends along for a taste...or the ghosts were here to watch me. I wasn't fond of those options.

"What do you want?" I asked the unseen spirits. "Why are you here?"

I had the cold sweats now, standing in the freezing air and waiting for a response. I've faced some dangerous and violent entities before, but I almost would have preferred a clear attack to this complete uncertainty, this indifferent and endless staring at me like a gang of obsessed stalkers.

I fought the urge to scream at them. My clients, after all, were sleeping upstairs, and I didn't want to have to explain why they had more ghosts than ever in their house tonight. I wasn't even sure of the reason myself.

"Okay, Stacey," I finally whispered. "Come on back."

Stacey dashed across the yard and into the basement. She eased the satchel to the floor and drew her second unlit flashlight, then stood with her back to mine, helping me watch for any attack.

"What are we doing?" she whispered after a minute.

"Waiting," I said. The ghosts hadn't moved so far, and I was desperate to learn anything I could from them, as long as my education didn't take the form of scratching and biting. I hate the scratchers and biters.

The ghosts remained implacable, and I tried to pretend the cold and fear weren't wearing me down.

Finally, after twenty or thirty more minutes of their silent staring, they began to withdraw. I felt it in the temperature first, as the warm outdoor air tumbled in through the open basement door. On the thermal camera, the cold spots were fading away.

"Okay." I let myself breathe for a change. "I guess they're gone. You should get back to the monitoring station."

"You mean the van? I'm not leaving you here tonight. They could come back."

"We have to watch everything, Stacey."

"The server's recording everything." Stacey dropped onto my air mattress, stretching her legs across the floor. "I'm staying."

"Suit yourself." I sat down with her, feeling a lot more grateful than I was acting. I didn't especially want to spend the rest of the night sitting alone, waiting for the dead to emerge from the shadows. Sure, that may be a typical Tuesday for me, but I'd had more than enough for one night.

"You know, I think we only found about half the money," I said, to change the conversation away from dead spirits who watch you in the night. "I was almost done before the ghosts came, but the total was only up to about twenty-four thousand dollars."

"So where's the rest of it?"

"That's the question." I sighed and leaned back against the wall. "We need to trap Sophia the Banshee Girl. I don't think she's the worst ghost in the area, but she's the only one anybody's paying us to stop."

"Really? And we just leave all these other ghosts running wild?" Stacey asked. "What about Maggie?"

"What about her?"

"I mean...she hired us, didn't she?"

"You think the ghost was trying to hire us?" I laughed a little.

"That would be a first."

"Seriously, though. She led us to all that money. She's stuck haunting the tracks. Maybe she didn't intend to do it, but she hired us."

"You're crazy, Stacey."

"Sure, but that's irrelevant right now. I know you, Ellie. You aren't going to be content to just capture one ghost and leave all these others running wild. Are you?"

"We need to talk to the other witnesses around the neighborhood," I said. "Captain Neighborhood Watch said some of them had seen intruders. I think they might have seen ghosts."

"So we won't give up even after we get Sophia tomorrow night?" Stacey asked.

"We'll be lucky if we *can* catch her," I said. "But you're right. We can't leave all these ghosts here, terrorizing the neighborhood, feeding on these people. We have to find a way to stop them all."

Chapter Seventeen

The next morning, I stopped off at the office on the way home. After the way the ghosts had swarmed around me the previous night, I didn't want to leave the satchel of possibly-cursed money in our clients' home. I didn't particularly want to leave it in the van, either, in case ghosts tried to bother Stacey the next night, and of course there was the threat of regular, everyday thieves who still had a pulse.

The only place to leave it was in the giant steel safe in the basement below our office. The safe was designed to hold large firearms, but Calvin and I had stocked it with more dangerous items than that over the years, supernatural bric-a-brac—a voodoo doll, a few old murder weapons, a possibly-possessed skull of an ancient tribal shaman—that might still carry a spectral charge and wasn't safe to leave out in the wild.

I parked inside the workshop and walked down the stairs to the basement. By the time I'd opened the safe, the cage elevator was rattling its way down.

"Sorry, I didn't want to wake you," I told Calvin as he rolled out of the elevator. Hunter jogged over to me, jowls bouncing and tail wagging. "There's no silencer on the garage door, though."

"It's seven o' clock," Calvin said. "I've been up for two hours. What's happening here?" He glanced at the satchel I was placing inside the safe.

"Want to see?" I put it on a built-in counter and untied the straps.

Calvin whistled at the sight of all the money inside.

"Jacob's researching whether the cash is worth anything. I'm pretty sure these have some value." I opened the pouch of five-dollar gold coins. "There's twenty-four of them."

"Oh, yes. Where did you find this?"

I gave him a quick rundown. "It's amazing it survived all this time. I guess it's been in a wildlife preserve for about a hundred years, and it's been fenced in for part of that time."

"Oiled cotton," Calvin said, touching the lining of the canvas. "Linseed oil. Nineteenth-century waterproofing. The pressure of the rocks heaped on top would have kept most of the air out, slowing the process of decay."

"Okey-dokey. What do you think about what Stacey said? Was the ghost hiring us?"

"More likely, the hidden money was one of the strands binding Maggie's ghost to this world. A part of her guilt."

"So we freed her?" I asked.

"It's possible, but the only way to be sure is if you see her again, haunting the tracks," Calvin said. "Then you'll know you didn't."

"A few other things don't make sense to me. Why did they murder the railroad crew? Why dynamite the passengers? And why did Maggie hide half the money instead of taking it all with her?"

"It could have been a form of insurance," Calvin said. "If she were caught, she could go back and collect the rest of the money at some later time."

"Seems like a desperate move," I said.

"The circumstances might have been desperate. She was on the run, weighed down by two satchels stuffed with money. Another possibility is that she may have been leaving the money for someone else. An accomplice."

"But the whole gang died," I said. "And she knew it. The court records said that she and McCoyle both shot at the railroad cop. She would have seen McCoyle die, right? And she couldn't have missed the passenger car exploding."

"The rest of her gang died." Calvin nodded as he thought it over. "At least, the ones we know about died. Maybe there was a fifth that we don't know about."

"Ugh. How would I even begin to figure that out?"

"You've been focusing on those who died. Maybe you need to spend more time thinking about those who lived."

"That's easy to say, but the information on the passengers who weren't killed is pretty sketchy. I might have to contact Grant for more help." I considered the idea. "But wait. We know the other person, if there is one, never collected the money. So that person might have died in the robbery. But why would she have left half the money for someone who was already dead? Maybe she didn't know he was dead?"

"If there was an accomplice, Maggie must have believed that person was alive in order to leave the money behind."

"The plan must have gone wrong somehow." I rubbed my head. "If only I had any idea what the original plan was in the first place. Would Maggie have known about the double-cross, killing the O'Reilly brothers in the middle of the robbery? If that *was* a double-cross and not a stupid accident. There are too many possibilities..."

"Focus on just one at a time," Calvin said.

"Okay. Starting over. If there was no other accomplice, then she buried the money because it was too much to carry, or as security in case she got caught. But then why the mysterious death two weeks later in New Orleans? And where did her half of the money go? Well, that part's easy. Any number of people would've been happy to steal that money from her, before or after her death. Maybe she was killed by somebody unrelated to the train robbery, somebody who'd discovered she had money to steal.

"Second possibility: she's leaving the money for an accomplice, but not one of the gang members we know about, because she knows they're dead. And we're back to having no leads on the accomplice."

"Don't you think it's interesting," Calvin said, "that the entire railroad crew was tied up and shot except for the railroad detective?"

"He was burned. And shot in the leg. That's a serious injury, especially in 1902 and several miles out of town. If it struck the femoral artery, he would have bled out and died fast."

"But he did not die," Calvin said. "And Maggie escaped the scene unharmed, with the money. In fact, if she was found in New Orleans, how did the investigators connect her to the crime?"

"She had a canvas satchel...probably just like that one." I pointed to the one on the table. "They found it near her body, with three hundred dollars in Third National Bank of Atlanta notes, a few gold coins, and one crumpled piece of paperwork with the date and intended destination of the cash transfer. The Bank of Charleston."

"Convenient," Calvin said.

"Extremely. Why would she keep that with her? It's almost exactly like somebody planted that there to make it an open-and-shut case."

"Did any witnesses to the robbery corroborate that Maggie was among the gang?"

"The robbers all wore bandannas on their faces," I said. "Like any old-timey bad guys. I guess the engineer must have seen her face when she hailed him down, since she probably wouldn't have worn a mask for that, but he didn't survive. None of the surviving witnesses saw her face, unless I missed something in the file. But they did say one gang member was female, in a red dress and leather boots. She had a derby hat like the men in the gang—like millions of men wore at that time. Red hair, like Maggie."

"The contents of her satchel are convenient for us, too," Calvin said. "If some other person unrelated to the train robbery killed Maggie in New Orleans in order to take her money, why would they leave any cash behind? You said the satchel was found near her body—not hidden anywhere?" split

I nodded, getting his point. "Whoever killed her wanted to make it clear she was connected to the robbery. That the last member of the gang was dead and the authorities could stop searching for her."

"Was that all the money ever recovered from the robbery?" Calvin asked. "Three hundred dollars and change in her satchel?"

"Until now." I pointed to the cash on the table.

"What scenario does that suggest?"

I thought it over. "If we're suspecting the railroad cop, then he must have tracked her to New Orleans. Taken her money and killed her. He must have used poison, right?"

"Possibly. He might have smothered or strangled her. Forensics was not much of an issue at the time."

"So the railroad cop and Maggie would have been cahooting together," I said. I began pacing, seeing the scenario come together in my head. "James McCoyle wasn't in on it, or he wouldn't have shot the railroad cop, right? So Maggie and the cop—what's his name? Kroeller. Maggie was double-crossing the rest of the gang, maybe she and Kroeller were going to kill the others and then split the money.

"The O'Reilly brothers go to rob the passengers, and either Maggie or Kroeller blows up the car. Probably Kroeller, he would have had more time to set it up, since he was already on the train before the robbery. So, boom, there goes half the gang. Then Kroeller just has to kill James McCoyle, the leader."

"Which he did," Calvin said.

"But not before McCoyle shoots Kroeller in the leg," I said. "Maybe Kroeller kills the train's crew because they see or hear something that tells them he's in on the robbery. So Maggie runs away with the money and Kroeller hangs around acting innocent. He's been burned a little by the dynamite explosion—maybe he stood too close—and he's been shot, so he's not an immediate suspect.

"Maggie doesn't know whether he's going to live or die, so she hides his half of the money in the plantation ruins." I shook my head. "That still doesn't make sense. If he dies, she can keep the money. If he lives, she can give him his half."

"Their original plan, whatever it was, must have been shaken by Kroeller taking that bullet," Calvin said. "Hiding the money must have been a last-minute attempt to make the hand-off. Perhaps she intended to write him and tell him where to find it. While he convalesces in the hospital, she flees the state with her half of the money, without stealing his."

"But before she gets that information to Kroeller, he tracks her down, despite his wounded leg, and kills her," I said. "That eliminates the last witness, and he keeps her money. Well, it's speculative, but it fits what we have. Wouldn't the railroad company or the state investigators be suspicious of Kroeller, too? When the whole train crew dies except for the one who's actually supposed to be providing security..."

"Maybe they were suspicious," Calvin said. "What happened to Kroeller subsequently?"

"I have no idea."

"Then you'll need to get one."

"Okay. I'll look for follow-up information on Angus Kroeller, and on the little girl, Sophia Preston. I'm pretty sure she's our banshee. We're going to trap her tonight if we can, but I don't really have any good bait. The cash from the robbery seems like good bait for the bandit ghosts, but they aren't the immediate concern." I thought of the large, dark figure that had dragged Sophia's ghost out of the basement the other night. "From what Jacob said, it seems like the bandits are trying to rule the area. The passengers' ghosts have to sneak around and avoid them."

"You mentioned another ghost on the train, keeping the passengers off," Calvin said.

"The passengers seem to want to get on the train, but the train won't stop," I said. "Maybe the engineer's ghost is afraid to stop. Or Kroeller's ghost won't let him."

"If Kroeller killed them all, that can give him a lot of power over the other ghosts," Calvin said. "He would be the alpha ghost in this haunting."

"And he's on the train, stopping the others from leaving. Why?"

"He could be obsessed with keeping his crime a secret," Calvin said. "Which means staying in control of all witnesses. For all time."

"Assuming Kroeller was actually working with Maggie Fannon to rob the train, and wasn't just an innocent man who got shot in the line of duty."

"We haven't established anything for certain."

"Any chance you want to tackle some of that research today?" I asked. "Maybe give Grant a call? Anything we could learn about those two people, Kroeller and Sophia, would be pretty great right now."

"What will you be doing?"

"Pounding the pavement, talking to witnesses about these intruders around the neighborhood," I said. "Unless you'd rather do that while I focus on the historical research."

"I'll stay inside with the computers and the air conditioning."

I caught him up on the case, which took a much longer time than I'd expected. He leaned in a little when I told him about the Acura tailing us, seeming more concerned about that than a trainload of ghosts.

"That's multiple incidents," he said. "I'm going to see if someone at the department can do me a favor, maybe just pull those guys over and check their licenses."

"Hopefully we won't see them again," I said, my head too full of our problems with the ghost world to begin worrying about the living.

"Hoping for the best is rarely the soundest strategy," Calvin replied.

"You should put that on a poster," I said. "Maybe with a kitten dangling from a limb. Okay, I'm hitting the road. Let me know if you turn up anything on Sophia before tonight. And I'll call you if I get kidnapped and murdered by some guys in a black Acura."

"Please do."

I drove away from the office, wondering whether we'd actually made some progress on the case, or were just spinning our wheels in the dark.

Chapter Eighteen

That afternoon, following a quick sleep and shower at home, I parked my Camaro in front of the Kozlows' house and checked my make-up in the mirror. I was trying to look professional and sane. I'd even dressed in my rarely-seen black pantsuit, which clashed with my sneakers, but I was not going door to door in heels.

I picked up my pen and notebook, slung my purse over my shoulder, and paused for a deep breath. Introducing myself to strangers and asking them questions is far from my favorite way to spend a Sunday afternoon. I'm not exactly a people person—not a misanthrope, just not the peoplest person around. I'd rather be quietly reading by myself.

Stacey would have been useful in this situation, but she was even more useful reviewing our past footage and setting up the van to record the feeds we were swiping from Cecil Nobson's mail-order spy cameras around the neighborhood. She was doing all of that back at the office.

Armed with my notebook, I set off down the sidewalk, doing

my best confident-and-together act. My first stop was the home of Donna Watt, who had recently seen an intruder who'd vanished before the police arrived, leaving no trace of himself.

It was a five-minute walk over to her cul-de-sac, just enough time to get my social anxiety nice and keyed up before I approached a total stranger out of the blue to ask about her ghost problems.

The two-story Watt home sat at one side of the street, enclosed by a picket fence. From our previous tour with Captain Neighborhood Watch, I knew that the symbols carved into the back of the Watts' fence included a woman and one bread-head stick-figure child. I was interested to see whether that matched the occupants of the house—if there were no children or multiple children, we might have misinterpreted what that small child figure was meant to indicate.

The trees in the yard were spindly and thin, probably no older than the house itself and clearly not thriving. I passed an old white Chevy Malibu and a red Big Wheel with Iron Man decals in the driveway and climbed the half-story of brick steps to the front door. A concrete angel, about as tall as my shin, crouched on the corner of the brick stoop, clutching a concrete bucket full of crushed cigarette butts.

I straightened up my spine, put on a smile—hopefully a gentle one, not a too-big creepy one—and rang the doorbell.

The solid front door swung inward, leaving the screen door as a barrier. The pudgy woman who looked out through the screen had long, tangled brown hair, glasses, and wore a pajama-bottom-and-stained-t-shirt ensemble that made it clear she was not expecting company. A television blared somewhere behind her. It sounded like a loud kid's show.

A boy of three or four dashed up behind her, peering around the woman to look at me.

"Hello?" The woman gave me a suspicious look, probably expecting me to try and sell her magazine subscriptions or a new religion.

"I'm sorry to bother you, ma'am," I said. "My name is Ellie Jordan, and I'm a private detective with Eckhart Investigations in Savannah." I held out a business card.

The woman creaked open the screen door and accepted the card. She looked skeptical at first, then relaxed a bit as she read it over. Our cards resemble any detective agency's, no little cartoony ghosts or anything to indicate that we walk on the weird side all the time. The mere sight of a professional-looking card seems to help people relax and open up, even though anybody can get a thousand of them for a few bucks at Staples.

"I'm looking for Donna Watt," I said. "Is that you?"

"What's this about?"

"I'm sure you know there's been a pattern of break-ins and intruders around the neighborhood," I said. "We've been retained by some of your neighbors to look into them." That made it sound like more than one household had hired us, but it wasn't strictly a lie—Tom and Ember were two people, after all, so it wasn't totally inaccurate to say *some of your neighbors*. Just a little misleading.

She looked hesitant.

"Some of your neighbors have had...abnormal experiences," I said, as if I'd been chatting with her neighbors all day. "Sometimes there's no sign of a break-in, and it's not clear how the person entered or left the house--"

"That's what happened to me. Cody, go watch *Paw Patrol*," she said to her son.

"Paw Patrol! Paw Patrol!" the boy sang, running out of sight toward the sound of the television.

She watched him go, then stepped out and closed the door firmly behind her. She glanced furtively at her next-door neighbor's house, where nobody was outside, then pulled a red pack of Marlboros from her pajama-pants pocket.

"Can you tell me what you saw?" I asked. "And when it happened?"

"About a week ago." She lit the cigarette, coughed, spat something ugly over the porch railing and into the bushes. "Sorry. Cody's been saying he sees somebody at night. An 'evil cowboy.' Of course, I thought it was all made up until I heard him screaming last Friday night. I got out of bed to check on him. When I opened the door from my room into the hall, I saw it walk past. It looked at me." She shuddered.

"What looked at you?"

"A man. I guess. He had an old hat and a coat, and he had a bandanna over his face like he was about to rob a bank in some old

John Wayne movie. He looked like an old movie, too, I mean everything was gray, there was no color. His eyes were solid black. I'm sure that was all some kind of lighting trick, the moonlight from the window, maybe." She was shivering, though, like she hadn't completely convinced herself that her eyes were playing tricks on her.

"What did he do?" I asked.

"He just moved on down the hall, like he didn't care whether I saw him or not. He smelled bad. Like rotten meat soaked in bad whiskey. And cigars. All that rolled up together. I thought I was going to be sick. I was so surprised, and scared, too, that all I could do was stand there and watch him walk away.

"Cody screamed again, so I looked over at his room. When I looked back, the man was gone. He must have gone down the front stairs, but he would've had to be lightning-flash quick to do that. He must have, though."

"Did you hear any sounds?" I asked. "Footsteps on the stairs?"

"Nothing. And to be honest...well, anyway. I screamed for Evan, my husband. Ex-husband, soon to be. I guess I was so tired or scared I forgot he left us four months ago. High and dry. He's the manager down at Chet's Discount Grocery, and he moved into that girl's apartment. The cashier."

"I'm sorry," I said.

She shook her head. "Anyway, I checked on Cody and he wasn't hurt, just scared. I called the police, but they couldn't find where he might have broken in. They searched the house, but they didn't find any sign of him."

"Does anybody else have a key?" I asked. "Your ex-husband, maybe?"

"I had all the locks changed," she said quickly, as if eager to share that information. "Only my friend Jenna has the new key, and she didn't give it to anyone."

"Was anything missing?"

"Not a thing."

"Did anything else happen? Bear in mind I've heard a lot of strange things today, things that are hard to believe. So if you saw anything else strange, it'll actually fit right in."

"What else are people seeing? Who did you talk to?"

"Of course, I want to keep people's information confidential," I said. "I won't repeat anything you tell me to your neighbors, either."

"Fine." She cupped her hand to hide her cigarette as a hulking gold Mazda SUV pulled into her next-door neighbor's driveway. With her other hand, she waved at the blond woman in yoga pants who climbed out, who didn't seem to notice. She was several years younger than Donna and looked like she split all her free time between aerobics class and the tanning salon. Donna waved again and shouted "Tammy Lee!"

Tammy Lee glanced over with a slight wave and distasteful smile, then turned her attention to lifting her baby out of a carrier in the back seat. She strode away at double-time toward her house, never looking back.

"Has your neighbor seen anything strange?" I asked.

"We haven't talked about it." Donna took a long pull on her cigarette as soon as her neighbor was inside the house. "She can be cagey."

"You were about to tell me something else about your experience," I said, hoping that was true.

"Oh. That's an interesting word for it." She paused, then sighed. "I didn't even tell the police all of it. I didn't think they'd believe me."

"What did you leave out?"

"It's not important. Probably just me being tired and confused. But I could swear...as I watched the masked man walk off down the hall, I could just about see *through* him. I could see the big hallway window on the other side of him."

"That's very interesting."

"You probably think I'm crazy now."

"I don't. Something about this community is crazy, but it's not you."

She laughed and crushed out her cigarette in the angel's bucket, coughing again as she straightened up. "That's all I can tell you, really. That's all there is."

"How long has your son been seeing this person?"

"Off and on...months, I'd say. More of it since Evan left us. And now I'm scared of it. I want to leave this house, but we can't move. We can barely afford to stay, only because my parents are helping..."

"Has he seen the figure again since you called the police?"

"Just three or four nights ago."

"What does he tell you about it?"

"That he's a bad man. That he could hurt us. I don't see how my son's nightmares are going to help you, though. Or me telling you I saw a ghost."

"It helps a lot," I said. "There are ghosts in the area. I'm here to get rid of them."

Her eyes widened. "Are you yanking my toes?"

"No. It's one of my firm's specialties, actually. This area has a lot of haunted houses."

"Uh-huh." Despite everything she'd just told me, I could see the suspicion creeping into her eyes. Denial. If she accepted I was a ghost-hunting professional charging her neighbors money to de-haunt their houses, it also meant she had to accept the reality of the ghost she'd seen. It was safer to dismiss me as a crazy person or scam artist. Her voice became coldly professional, a distant and formal tone clearly developed at one job or another. "Ma'am, I'm going to have to get back inside now. You have a nice day."

She retreated into her house and closed the door. Good thing I hadn't introducing myself as a ghost exterminator right up front.

I tried her next-door neighbor's house, wondering if Tammy Lee or her baby had attracted hungry ghosts, but Tammy Lee had no interest in talking to me and shooed me away from her door before I could finish explaining why I was there.

A number of doors closed in my face pretty quickly that afternoon. Not even my pantsuit could make me seem like a normal human being, I guess. Some people did speak to me, though. From Mr. Nobson of neighborhood watch and homeowners' association fame, I had a small list of people who'd been robbed or encountered intruders in their homes.

Checking the symbols carved into fences gave me more leads. People who'd been robbed—always of jewelry or coins—had marks indicating *wealthy person* (a small top hat by a big triangle) and *already robbed* (hash lines that resembled a tilted split-rail fence). Those were standard hobo signs we'd learned about from the internet.

Houses with bread-head figures always had kids, and one of their moms told me she'd seen a dirty, diseased-looking man in their garage, which they used for storage rather than parking, but he'd just disappeared when she turned on the lights. Her daughter, eight years old, had reported seeing a strange man of the same description a few times late at night, in her bedroom and in the kitchen.

Those were the kinds of stories I heard throughout the afternoon, from those occasional neighbors who were willing to talk.

Late in the day, I approached the uninhabited house where Stacey had seen the dark figure enter through the front door the previous night. The house sat at the end of a street where two houses were occupied, several stood vacant, and some were only wood frames, their unfinished rooms and interior staircases open to the weather.

The yard was red earth, with occasional clumps of weeds and scrub brush laced with briars. The house looked mostly finished aside from a couple of empty window holes. Two full stories, including a second floor above the garage that connected to the second floor of the main house by a glass-walled sunroom.

As I'd been doing all day, I walked around to the back of the fence. It had an unusually large number of carvings for an empty house. The symbols included *danger* (a rectangle with a dot inside), *man with gun* (a triangle holding up sticks arms, as if to say "Don't shoot!"), and *keep out* (which looks like an inverted "Y"). Among these were others we hadn't found in the keys on the internet, like a crude skull and crossbones, though that one seemed fairly self-explanatory. Somebody was serious about telling the other spirits to stay out of the house.

I called Stacey. "Are you on your way yet?" I asked.

"Uh, working on it," she said. "I was planning to get there by sunset. Do you need me there? Is something up?"

"Just checking. Come as soon as you're ready."

"Roger that," she replied in her super-serious movie-action-hero voice.

After I hung up, I looked up at the house for a minute. Vines had snaked their way up the walls over the years of neglect, and some of them encircled the windows. I could see nothing inside, with the windows reflecting the red glare of sunset.

I slid the rusty bolt, and the back gate opened with a creak that sounded very loud on the quiet street, announcing my presence to anyone who might be inside the house.

The brambles and weeds in the yard slowed me down as I approached the back door. It was locked, so I stepped up onto the rear deck and looked into the windows, cupping my hands around my eyes. The glass panes felt as cold as the freezer doors at the grocery store, though the house's air conditioning unit was a weed-choked box on the side of the house that had probably never been used.

The inside of the house was far from finished. Floors were bare plywood, walls looked like particle board. It might have appeared nice on the outside, but it looked like the house was actually built on the cheap.

Bare wall studs and wiring were visible in one room. In another, clearly the kitchen, the cabinets had all been smashed and lay in ruins on the counter, reminding me of the wrecked concession stand at the nonexistent baseball field.

More of the assorted *danger* and *keep out* signs were carved all over the walls, much bigger than the thumbnail-sized marking on the fences. I took snapshots with my phone, feeling a little spooked. The place was definitely some kind of center of activity among the spirits.

I wanted to pick the lock and explore inside the house, but the sun was getting low in the sky. Calvin's voice in my head steadied my eagerness, reminding me that walking alone into a nest of ghosts, with no back-up at all, was always a fairly stupid move.

Reluctantly, I walked away from the house and back through the gate, even locking it behind me as if to hide the fact that I'd been there. I was pretty sure they knew. As I departed down the sidewalk, I could feel something watching me from the house, but I only saw empty windows when I looked back.

I passed one empty house after another, attractive and modern two-story homes with badly overgrown lawns, most of them flawed in some way—a gaping hole where a window or door should have been, an unfinished roof, an exposed attic. The houses had an oddly soulless feeling to them, hollow shells that had never been home to anyone, except for the wandering spirits of the dead.

Stacey texted me. She was on her way. Tonight, we'd do our best to remove the banshee from our clients' home.

Chapter Nineteen

When Stacey arrived, we carried a trap into the basement, along with the pieces of a pneumatic stamper that could seal the trap at high speed.

We assembled the stamper, and I set it to close automatically if it sensed a temperature drop combined with an electromagnetic spike, indicating the ghost might have entered the trap to investigate the bait.

"Are we setting up cameras by the tracks again tonight?" Stacey asked. "It's getting dark."

"No, I'm more interested in watching another place," I said. I told her about the house. "We'll go over there after dark so there's less chance of somebody spotting us." I didn't want to draw curious neighbors, for one thing, but I was mostly worried about somebody breaking or stealing the expensive thermal camera. "Let's finish the trap first. Banshee Girl doesn't usually show up until after midnight, but we'll leave it burning for her in case she makes an early appearance."

I'd written Sophia Preston's full name on an index card in heavy black marker, and I dropped that to the bottom of the cylindrical trap. I weighed it down with some small items I'd picked up earlier in the day—marbles, bright ribbons, a couple of finger-sized Melissa and Doug wooden dolls with a simplistic design and materials that I thought might seem familiar to Sophia's ghost. Modern plastic toys would be alien to her.

"I don't know," Stacey said. "The kid lost her parents and died a miserable death feeling all alone in the world. You really think she'll care about toys and ribbons now?"

"Maybe there's enough of a kid left inside her," I said. "I'm open to suggestions if you have any."

"Nope, just nitpicks and criticism."

"Calvin couldn't find out much about her. It's not easy on Sundays when all the libraries and institutions are closed. We've picked up that her mother died of an illness. Back in those days, it could have been influenza, tuberculosis, a rusty nail, goat bite, anything."

We lit the candles arrayed in a spiral up to the open top of the trap. Ghosts hate light if there's too much of it, but seem to feed freely on fire and ambient heat. The candles would, hopefully, draw Sophia's attention and lure her inside, along with the weak bait we'd scraped together. Then the lid would slam down, triggered either by my remote control or by the temperature and EMF sensors within the trap.

Then the banshee would be sealed inside the cylinder, walled in by leaded glass and electrically charged mesh, and we could take her away to a better life. Or a better post-life, anyway.

With the trap set, we left the basement and drove over to Town Park Way, where the house I'd investigated earlier was located. Only the first two houses on the street, facing the roundabout and the community park, appeared inhabited. Beyond them, the streetlights were off, probably disconnected to save power. The empty houses ahead lay in darkness, barely touched by the weak moonlight.

We parked at the end of the street—not a cul-de-sac, just an abrupt dead end that gave way to pines and undergrowth. Jacob called Stacey as I was getting out, in time to save her from helping me unload the cameras and tripods.

As I started toward the empty house, she hopped out of the driver's seat and grabbed my arm with such force that I nearly lost my balance.

"Careful!" I warned her, adjusting the cumbersome gear in my arms.

"Sorry. Listen, Jacob says that...uh, well, you tell her, Jacob." Stacey held her phone to my ear.

"What?" I asked, mildly annoyed at the delay.

"Hey, Ellie. So I looked up some things. First, those gold coins are worth more than five dollars each."

Not exactly the shocking news of the century. "How much?"

"More like four to five hundred bucks apiece," he said.

"We have twenty-four of them."

"Easily ten thousand dollars," he said. "And then I looked up the situation with the banknotes. National banknotes were completely replaced by modern money, Federal Reserve notes, in the 1930's."

"So they're worthless?"

"No, technically the Treasury will accept them at face value."

"And you say 'technically' because..."

"Those old bank notes are extremely rare now. Among currency collectors, they could be worth ten to twenty times their face value."

"So that's..." I felt my mouth drop open. "Jacob. You're telling me that we don't have twenty-five thousand dollars in the safe, we have...a quarter million dollars or more?"

"That's what I'm telling you. Well, expect some discounting because coin dealers have to make a profit, but yeah. A few hundred thousand."

"I...don't know what to say," I replied, because that was the truth. After scraping by from month to month for years, an amount like that doesn't even sound real, especially in reference to a bag of cash you just basically found on the ground.

"Ellie?" Jacob asked. I'd about forgotten he was still on the phone.

"Yeah," I said. "Great. Thanks, Jacob."

After we hung up, I returned the phone to Stacey.

"Isn't that amazing?" Stacey asked, with an exciting squeal creeping in at the edge of her voice. "Holy cow!"

I admit the thought *What do you care, you're rich anyway?* might have flickered across my mind, for one-tenth of second. She was excited for a different reason than me, I guess, just the discovery that it was so much more valuable than we thought. Like buying something cheap at a garage sale and learning it was a precious antique.

"Okay," I said, trying not to look too stunned in front of Stacey. "Stay here and keep watch on our clients' house. I'll go set up the cameras."

"But you're not going inside the house, right?"

"If I scream your name, come and help."

The house looked larger at night, a looming dark mass casting the area around it into deep shadow. It seemed to absorb the moonlight that fell on it.

My heart was already thumping as I unbolted the gate. I nudged it open with my hip so I could carry the cameras into the yard. The yard seemed stonier than I remember, tripping me up as I walked.

I set up the night vision camera in the front yard, facing the front door, lowering the tripod until it was concealed behind the picket fence as much as possible. The black windows of the house seemed to watch me, waiting.

Around back, I pointed the thermal camera at the rear door. It registered a slight coolness radiating from the doors and windows, as if the air conditioning were running hard inside, though the actual outdoor unit remained as silent and overgrown as ever.

With the camera set into position, I again climbed the three wooden steps to the back porch and peered into the dark windows.

"Uh, Ellie? What are you doing?" Stacey asked over my headset. She must have been watching me on the thermal.

"Just looking." Since I could see absolutely nothing, I turned on my flashlight and pointed it through the windows. The house looked somehow worse now, the plywood warped and stained, doorways sagging as if water-damaged, the destruction in the kitchen more thorough. Maybe the high beam of my tactical flashlight revealed things more clearly than the low-burning afternoon sunlight had. If not, then the ghosts had a heavy presence that distorted the house by night.

My flashlight again found the large warning marks carved into the kitchen walls, with every hobo-script symbol for danger and death. Something important was happening here.

I drew the lock picks from my jacket pocket and went to work on the back door, pushing it open a minute later. Its hinges let out a harsh squeak, loud as an alarm bell, and I winced. Cool air drifted out over me.

"Ellie?" Stacey said. "Did I just hear a door open? Because it looks like you're messing with the door..."

"I'm just taking a quick look," I whispered. "If I scream your name, come help me. That'll be our secret code."

"I should just go in there with you. The banshee probably won't hit Ember's place for a while, right?"

"Keep watch anyway." I stepped inside the house, sweeping my beam around. Nothing pounced on me or bit my face right away. I left the door open behind me in case I needed a fast getaway.

The first room I entered was probably intended to be a living room, with a brick fireplace flanked by windows looking out onto the back yard. The ceiling soared above, a full two stories, and a staircase ran along the back wall to an upstairs loft area with a half-wall, which would almost certainly be called a "bonus room" on the sales brochure.

Everything was bare wood, with more of the cheap particle-board stuff mounted on the walls. A faint lumber smell still lingered in the air.

The plywood floor bowed and creaked under my boots as I walked from one barely-built room to another, checking for monsters in closets and the kitchen pantry. I'd decided not to bring my bulky thermal goggles with me, because something told me I might want to escape this house at a run. If I had, I likely would have found a cold ghost-residue all over the shattered cabinets, like the concession stand. They seemed to have been smashed with the same sense of unfocused anger and frustration.

The ceiling creaked, as if someone in a heavy shoe or boot had taken a step in the room just above me. I froze, listening.

A second creak sounded, then a third. Definitely like a person walking up there. I traced my flashlight beam across the ceiling, following the creaking steps.

They stopped as suddenly as they'd begun, leaving the house silent again.

Cold sweat broke out all over my skin. I already felt jittery. I wasn't alone in the house, and whatever was upstairs probably wasn't here to sell Girl Scout cookies.

I remained still and listened.

A moment later, a loud bang sounded from the living room, and I, being a tough and experienced ghost hunter, jumped and screamed. I just hadn't expected any sounds from that direction, since I hadn't heard anything descend the stairs.

"Ellie?" Stacey asked.

"It's okay," I whispered, while making my way back to the living room. "I didn't scream *your* name. Remember your instructions."

"Okay, but why the shouting?"

The back door was now closed. The banging sound had been somebody slamming it into place.

I heard another long, wooden creak from the back stairs leading up to the loft, but didn't see anything when I turned my flashlight toward it. The banister posts cast tall, bouncing shadows on the walls as my beam moved among them.

"They must like me," I whispered. "Because they don't want me to leave."

"Get out of there!"

"One sec." I started up the steps. The sixth stair let out the exact same creak when I put my foot on it.

Trembling, I continued upward. *Just a quick look around*, I assured myself. *Then I'm out of here.*

My instincts told me that I needed to get out *now*. For all I knew, I was locked inside, trapped in some malevolent spirit's hunting ground.

I reached the top of the stairs and quickly moved away from the railing and the half-wall, into the lofty bonus room. It was at least a ten-foot drop to the living room floor below, and it doesn't take a powerful or sophisticated spirit to nudge you over and let gravity do the rest of the work. Thousands of people die in simple household falls every year, and rarely do investigators bring in a paranormal forensics team to determine whether a ghost might be at fault.

The shadowy loft area had one small window that let in very little light. I found nothing creeping around the bare, empty room, but I definitely felt like I was being watched, probably from the dark doorway to the next room. Naturally, I walked over there and through the empty doorway, which had never been hung with an actual door.

The next room was probably meant as a den or spare bedroom. It was the terminus of the upstairs hallway, which I would have to traverse to reach the source of the footsteps I'd heard below.

I stepped into the hall. A row of empty door-holes lined the left side of the hallway, while the right side overlooked the foyer below. Presumably there was supposed to be some kind of railing along that side, but that had never been added, either. Instead, a long stretch of the hallway's right side opened onto a straight drop of ten or twelve feet to the foyer floor. The front stairs were the same way, circling down along one wall with no banister on the outer edge, an open invitation to trip and fall to your death.

I clung to the left side of the hall, near the unfinished doorways, as if the hallway floor were a thin, crumbling ledge on a high mountainside.

The first door led into an empty room, about twelve feet by twelve feet with a double-paned window, probably meant to be a bedroom. I checked the rectangular cavity of the closet, found no wraiths in heavy boots, and moved on to the next bedroom and the hallway bath, identifiable by the pipes in its incomplete walls.

I crept along the final stretch of the hall toward the last doorway, keeping close to the wall on my left and away from the dangerous drop to my right.

The air grew thicker and colder, harder to breathe. I forced myself to step through into the final doorway, though it seemed like the air itself was resisting me.

A much larger room lay beyond, obviously the intended master bedroom, with two sets of windows and more door-shaped holes along one wall, leading into a bathroom and a walk-in closet. The whole upper floor, with the doorless entrances to every room, made me think of some kind of cave system or pueblos carved into cliffs.

The air in the master bedroom was even thicker and colder, and I began to smell what my witness had described earlier: whiskey, then a strong tang of rotten meat that made me queasy.

I heard a grumbling, like a rough male voice muttering under its breath. Panning my light around the dark room revealed nothing.

My flashlight beam seemed weak, unable to penetrate very far into the gloom, which is never a good sign.

"Ellie, are you still alive in there?" Stacey whispered. I tapped the microphone with my finger, a signal that I was still breathing but that she needed to be quiet.

A floorboard creaked within one of the dark doorways. I stepped toward it, and my flashlight revealed the long throat of a walk-in closet. It was empty, like the other rooms, but something glinted at the very back, on the floor.

I approached cautiously. A floorboard had been pried loose, and in the small cavity below it lay a little rat's nest of items—or more of a raccoon's nest, maybe, since raccoons are attracted to shiny objects. It was a heap of glittering jewelry and polished silver antique coins.

I crouched down to examine it. This would make excellent bait for the bandit ghosts, alongside the money recovered from the robbery. Clearly, the ghosts had been attracted to these jewels and coins already.

It was interesting to find this little stash. I'm familiar with a number of cases where ghosts pilfer small objects from the living. Usually it's a mischievous ghost hiding items like keys or glasses, or maybe a kid ghost who swipes small toys. The stash is usually found, if at all, in the ghost's lair—the attic, the basement, or wherever it feels most comfortable. Still, I hadn't heard of ghosts focusing on items of monetary value, or carrying them from one house to another, before this case.

As I reached out to scoop up some of the treasure—the second stash of buried treasure we'd found in this case so far, a new record—I heard another long, slow creak on the floorboard behind me.

I froze, feeling dread. It was right behind me.

I turned my head. The shadowy man stood less than a foot away, looking down at me. His eyes were twin black holes under the brim of his hat. A pale cloth concealed most of his face, but the portion I could see around his eyes looked decayed, bits of skin clinging to bone.

He was a partial apparition—I could see the buttons of his coat but not his hands or legs, or at least those were totally hidden in shadow. I began to swing my light around to get a better look at him, plus blast him with a few thousand lumens as a "back off" warning.

Then something slammed into the back of my head, an unseen fist sucker-punching me right in the skull. I toppled over to my hands and knees. My forehead banged against the wall, but I was so numb from the shock of the initial attack that it took almost two full seconds to register the cracking pain in my temple.

I swayed, trying not to fall over altogether. The ghosts decided to help me with that, I suppose, because the next thing I felt was a hard boot kicking up into my guts. It lifted my whole body off the ground in the most painful way, with its sharp toe caught under the lower lip of my rib cage. I howled in agony.

The inhumanly strong kick sent me flying up and back against the closet wall. The flimsy particle-board sheet splintered on impact. My head bounced against the ceiling. It must have done some damage because white plaster dust spilled down all around my face.

I fell toward the floor, unable to see anything below me. My flashlight had fallen from my hand and gone dark, as if they'd sucked all the energy out of it.

Rough, unseen hands grabbed me all over my body. There must have been two or three unseen assailants. They punched my face and stomach, then grabbed my hair and slung the side of my head against the wall. Somewhere through the ringing pain between my ears, I was vaguely aware of Stacey's panicked voice over my headset.

The ghosts flung me out of their closet, away from their stash. I banged into the ground and rolled until I hit the far wall.

Nothing happened for a moment, except Stacey shouting that she was on her way. I didn't have the strength or the air to reply.

Then the house groaned. Sure, houses groan from time to time, but this was like a deep, aching voice rising from every joist in the house, shuddering the air all around me. It was like being trapped inside a speaker cabinet while a group of angry, disturbed ghosts try to moan out some karaoke. I could feel my bones trembling in their sockets.

Hands grabbed me again in the pitch darkness—the cowboys weren't done with me yet. I kicked and punched uselessly as the entities closed in around me. The air grew much thicker and colder now, like someone was shoving frozen cloth into my nostrils and down my throat. I couldn't manage to choke down even a sip of air.

They were going to kill me. I felt my body go limp, out of oxygen. Fists and boots continued to pound as a black fog rolled across my brain. I began to lose consciousness.

"Ellie!" Stacey shouted. Her boots thumped toward me down the hallway. One nice thing about the ghosts slamming me all over the place, I supposed, was that Stacey had no trouble determining where I was inside the house. I comforted myself with that thought while choking to death.

I wanted to call out, to warn her there were multiple strong entities in here, but I could do nothing except fight to draw air against the immense pressure crushing in around me.

The room turned blinding white, every grain of plywood and particle board seeming to transform into a glowing filament of light. I was sure I was finally dying. *Go into the light, Carol Anne.*

Then I gasped and pulled in a huge breath of cold, whiskey-scented air. Maybe I wasn't so dead, after all.

"Ellie!" Stacey set down the bulky ghost cannon, the heaviest light-thrower we have. She'd brought the searing brightness, but she'd brought the fire hazard, too, because the room was nothing but dry, exposed wood.

She ran over, helping me sit up while I enjoyed the glorious feeling of drawing more fresh oxygen into my lungs.

Breathing again brought another wave of agony from my bruised body. The ghosts had fled from the intense light, but there was a chance they'd recover and return. The ghost cannon is also very unreliable, and the batteries don't last long.

"What happened? You look awful," Stacey said.

"Go," I croaked. "Go now."

"No way. I'm not leaving you here, Ellie. Never." She put an arm around my shoulders and hugged me.

Yeah, that hadn't been my intention. I'd meant we *both* needed to go now. The lack of a clear subject in my sentence had made Stacey think I was being noble or self-sacrificial for her sake. Actually I was just having trouble speaking.

She helped me up to my feet. As I was finding my balance, the ghost cannon cut right out, plunging the room back into darkness.

The house shuddered with another deep groan.

"Go," I said. Then, to clarify: "*Let's* go."

"That's right, Ellie! We're both leaving together." Stacey tried to help me, but the return to darkness had fueled a nice, useful panic that got my legs running.

She grabbed the ghost cannon as we left the room, muttering angrily as she tried to activate it again. The hallway was gloomy, lit only by touches of moonlight seeping in from the big windows over the front door. I kept close to the wall again, avoiding the open drop to the foyer floor below.

Then Stacey screamed and pitched over onto her side, the wrong way, toward the drop-off. I tried to catch her, but wasn't close enough or fast enough on my feet at that moment.

I'd lost one flashlight, but I carried two on my utility belt, so I drew the second one and fired it up, aiming it at Stacey and expanding its iris so that light saturated the area around her.

The light revealed the same apparition I'd seen in the closet, dust gray, a pale cloth hiding its face. Its hollow skull-eyes looked down at Stacey, and then it began to reach its bony hand toward her. One solid push and Stacey would be over the edge, in danger of breaking a limb or her neck if she landed the wrong way. The bulky weight of the ghost cannon wasn't going to do her any favors, either, whether she landed on it or it landed on her.

Stacey screamed again when she saw the thing assaulting her.

"Leave her alone!" I shouted again. Remembering the train robbers' names would have been an extremely useful thing right then, so naturally my brain completely blanked on them.

He leaned closer to her, reaching toward the golden stud in her earlobe as if he meant to steal it.

Stacey desperately thumbed the ghost cannon switch, trying to torch his head with a million lumens, but the device wasn't cooperating.

"Leave her alone!" I shouted. The apparition's head snapped toward me, and though its eyes were black and empty, I could feel its cold, hellish stare.

Somewhere in my brain, a pin dropped, a connection was made, a little cellular gear turned in its socket.

"McCoyle," I said. "James McCoyle. Is that you? Or are you one of the O'Reilly brothers? Liam? Sean?"

The apparition drew itself up tall, gaining a foot or more in height as it did so—ghost's appearances can be flexible like that—so that it towered above me. It studied me, as if trying to decide what to do.

Two dark, faceless shadows, the size of broad-shouldered, broad-waisted men, rose in the doorway behind him. Maybe the O'Reilly brothers, responding to their names.

By then, Stacey had enough time to regain her feet. We backed away slowly, together, and the three ghosts advanced on us.

Stacey tried to make a break for it down the front stairs, but I pulled her back. The lack of any railing made it too risky, too easy for the ghosts to try and kill us both.

"This way!" I shouted, right in her face, probably a little too loud in my general panicky desire to survive and escape. I yanked her arm, and we took off down the hall, past the bedrooms, across the loft and down the back stairs.

The ghosts had helpfully locked the back door, which slowed us down. I heard creaking footsteps on the stairs behind me, but I didn't turn around.

I pushed open the door, and Stacey and I burst out onto the back porch at a full run. We didn't stop running until we were across the lawn, through the gate, and leaping into the van.

Stacey heaved the ghost cannon in back, cranked up the van, and spun out as she accelerated into a tight curve, turning a fairly impressive one-eighty in the middle of the street. I could smell our tires burning.

We rocketed away from the house, then Stacey slammed on the brakes, flinging me against the dashboard. I'd forgotten my seatbelt. Should have listened to Safety Bear.

"What is your problem?" I asked her, disentangling my hair from the air-conditioning vent.

Stacey didn't say anything, but she was white as a sheet. One of those sheets cartoon ghosts wear.

Wordlessly, her hand shaking, she pointed ahead through the windshield.

In the middle of the road stood Captain Neighborhood Watch himself, Cecil Nobson, clad in his official fishing hat and khaki vest. He'd parked his golf cart sideways in the middle of the road, and placed one bright-orange traffic cone on either side of it, creating a roadblock across the uninhabited street. We had to be the targets of it, considering we were the only people here.

He clung to the slender roof-support column of his golf cart as if his life depended on it. I could see the expression on his blanched face clearly, because he was only inches from the grill of our van.

Stacey, speeding as fast as she could down the street, had nearly crushed the man to death against his own golf cart.

Chapter Twenty

"Good Lord have mercy!" Stacey said, flinging open the driver's-side door and leaping out. Reluctantly, I climbed out the shotgun door. Why had I let Stacey drive? Oh, because the ghosts of three dead men had just beaten me to a soft and gooey pulp.

I stumbled toward Nobson, who still cringed and trembled against his golf cart. Stacey ran toward him, rubbing his arm.

"You...you could have..." He swallowed, then straightened up, shaking Stacey away. "You could have killed me! Do you know the speed limit on this road is twenty-five miles an hour?"

"Uh," Stacey said. "I think I was going about that."

The cloud of smoldering tire residue in the air seemed to contradict her.

"What are you doing out here, anyway?" I asked, ready to put him on the defensive. "Blocking up a road like this isn't legal."

"I'm on official neighborhood watch business."

"Doing what?"

"Don't try to deny you two were up to something. I got it all on video. The two of you breaking into that house. Just what were y'all doing in there?"

Stacey looked at me, probably curious to see how I was going to answer that. I know I was.

"Uh," I said, trying to weigh my options as rapidly as I could. "We've...been...studying the fence carvings around the neighborhood. You know, the symbols you showed us? It turns out that some of them are hobo marks. This house has an unusual number of signs warning us away."

"Oh, yeah!" Stacey said, nodding her head like a little Garfield in a car window. "You can go look at those on the fence."

"Or maybe we should call the police and let them sort it out." He reached for his cell phone, mounted at his belt next to a can of pepper spray.

"You'll just annoy them," I said. "There's been no forced entry into that house. The locks are still intact, I can promise you. All they'll see is a man with too much time on his hands setting up weird, totally illegal little roadblocks in his own neighborhood."

"You clearly aren't familiar with subsection C of the community charter," Nobson said. "I am the law here."

Stacey snickered—I could tell from her guilty look that she knew better, but couldn't help herself—and he flushed dark red.

"So you're saying that if I bring the police out here and have them search that house, you'll have no problem with that at all?" He spoke through gritted teeth, giving me a taste of the dark side of Cecil Nobson, neighborhood compliance officer.

He did have me there, though. I didn't want anybody going into that house tonight, not even annoying little Captain Neighborhood Watch himself, considering how violent the ghosts inside were. I strongly doubted he would believe me if I explained it was dangerously haunted, the robber's roost of a gang of dead bandits. The police wouldn't, either.

On top of that, if the ghosts didn't attack the police, they would discover a stash of stolen jewelry taken from all around the neighborhood. Considering Stacey and I had just left the house—and our friend here had caught that on camera—things could only get awkward from there. If we tried to keep Nobson and the police out, especially with some flimsy story about a ghost, we'd only look even more guilty when the coppers found the loot (see, I was already thinking like a criminal).

If I told him up front that we'd located his neighbors' stolen property, though, he'd surely insist on recovering it right away.

I only had one option—bluff and bluff some more.

"Call the police all you want," I said. "There's nothing in that house right now. You'll just look foolish if you did it tonight. But if you waited until..." I shook my head and turned back toward the van. "Come on, Stacey."

"Wait!" He held up one hand, palm out, with the authority of an experienced crossing guard. "What's going to happen?"

"Don't tell him," I said to Stacey, as if she were about to speak. "He'll blow the operation."

"What operation?" Nobson looked from me to her, bewildered. Then he folded his arms and drew himself up a little. "You'll have to coordinate your activities with the neighborhood watch going forward."

I glared back at him, just to hint at how mean I could get if he really wanted to push me. Then I sighed and slumped my shoulders, as though the weight of his authority had defeated me.

"Fine," I said, "We'll coordinate with you. But anything we say needs to be kept in strict confidence. Top secret."

"Of course." He nodded as if we were now on the same wavelength.

"We broke their code," I said. "The walls in there are covered with markings—you can see them through the window. We think they use it as a rendezvous point before and after their burglaries, and a drop-off and pick-up point for stolen goods. Not just from your community, but all over town."

Nobson's eyes widened and he nodded, gaping a little as he took in the wider conspiracy I had invented.

"The markings are one way they communicate," I said. "Pretty smart, if you think about it. There's no cell phones, no way to listen in at a distance. We've determined the date of their next robbery and their next drop-off and pick-up."

"When?" Nobson was just about salivating for the information.

"That's classified," I said.

Nobson frowned at me and huffed impatiently. Behind him, Stacey was fighting to keep a serious look on her face.

"I thought we were coordinating," he said. "This is a joint operation now. We need to share intel."

"We operate on strict compartmentalization," I said. "I can tell you that it will be within the next month, and we will bring you in for the planning phase three days in advance. That should be more than enough time."

"Okay." Nobson seemed to accept this, probably realizing that meant nothing was going to happen anytime soon. "Three days should be plenty. We'll need to coordinate with local authorities. The police are familiar with me from neighborhood watch business."

I bet you call them twice a week. "That can be your department, as soon as we give the go-ahead," I said.

"If I had a better idea of when it was all going to happen..." he said.

I shook my head. "I'd need clearance from my boss to give out that information."

"Understood." Nobson nodded sagely, really buying into this cloak-and-dagger stuff. I hoped it would keep him at bay long enough to wrap up the case.

"It's good to have another security professional in this field with us." I held out my hand, and he looked surprised for a moment before shaking it. He turned and shook Stacey's hand, too.

"Glad to be of service," he said.

"We're actually done for the night. So...you know." I nodded at the golf cart.

"I'll disassemble the roadblock," he said. "I appreciate you briefing me on the situation."

We returned to the van—I was ready to drive now—and Stacey gaped at me from the passenger seat while we waited for him to load up his cones and move out. Each orange traffic cone had a yellow stripe down the front, with NEIGHBORHOOD WATCH USE ONLY printed sideways in bold type.

"What was all that?" Stacey laughed. "You really pulled some rabbits out of your hat there."

"I just hope it keeps him at bay long enough for us to close the case," I said.

"But to be clear, he's not going to actually be involved with anything, right?"

"Of course not," I said. "Unless he sticks his nose in again."

"Doesn't sound like something he'd do at all." Stacey shook her head.

After taking another long look around, Nobson finally puttered away in his golf cart. I grimaced as I followed behind him, until we reached the roundabout encircling the park and I could pull around him.

"How's the trap at our clients' house looking?" I asked.

"I'll check." Stacey unhooked her seatbelt and climbed into the back with the monitors.

Chapter Twenty-One

Nothing had disturbed the trap yet, unfortunately. It would have been handy to come back and find the banshee all bottled up and ready to go, but my luck rarely turns that way.

I settled down in the basement to wait for her, watching the candles flicker in the ghost trap.

Sophia never arrived, though, and neither did any other ghost. They tend to do that. Just when you're actually prepared for them to show up, ready to trap the ghost and finalize the case, they decide to go on vacation. I'm not sure where the dead take their vacations. Cape Fear, maybe. Or the Dead Sea. I'll be here all evening, folks, tip your waitresses.

After sunrise, Stacey and I stopped for breakfast at Henry's on Drayton Street. Even though it was not really on the way between the client and the office, the place has an amazing breakfast selection. It's a buffet but it's not gross. I filled on up fresh fruit. Okay, and bacon. I was almost positive bacon would somehow help me heal from my injuries, which included an attractive purple bloom on my face, a scratch over my eyes, and a swollen lip. I was getting a lot of glances from other patrons.

"How bad do I look right now?" I whispered to Stacey. I should have taken more time to clean up before going out in public.

"Uh...on a scale from month-old zombie to mummified Egyptian corpse?" she asked.

"That's what I thought."

I finished breakfast as quickly as I could. We shut the van away inside the garage door at the office, then split up and went home.

I slept a little, but I was restless, turning all the loose pieces of the case around in my head. I kept seeing flashes of the ghosts behind my eyes. The ice-cold eyes of Sophia, the banshee who'd fed on me. McCoyle, the ruins of his face hidden behind cloth. Sleep would just bring nightmares.

Eventually, I gave up and drove back to the office, thinking I'd look again through the information we had and review more of the video footage. I was tired but keyed up at the same time. Maybe some work would knock me down to just tired. There was an old couch in the workshop for naps. Anytime you get a job where there's a nap couch at the office, hold onto it for dear life, that's what I say.

A black Acura sat by the front door, parked slantwise the way police do, taking up multiple spots but enabling a fast getaway.

My pulse quickened. The sight of the car, knowing Calvin was alone in there, filled me with as much dread as the dark, empty eyes of the ghost I'd seen the night before.

Panic filled in the details for me. Maybe they'd been casing us for a robbery, but we didn't have too much to steal beyond obscure and specialized ghost-hunting equipment. A few video cameras didn't seem worth the effort. The only other thing we had was a giant safe full of potentially cursed items from past cases, plus a few hundred thousand dollars' worth of cash...

They knew about the money. Maybe they'd known about it the whole time, or maybe they'd been spying on us for other reasons and seen us with the cash.

Now Calvin was the only thing between them and a small fortune.

If they'd taken over the place, they'd probably be watching the front door, so I pressed the accelerator and shot around back to the loading docks. I reminded myself to slow down and come to a quiet halt outside.

I snatched the stun gun from my purse and stalked toward the back door, next to the garage door where we kept the van. I couldn't help remembering the night I'd found Calvin in that attic, lying in his own blood after a highly focused attack by a powerful fearfeeder ghost. I was terrified of finding him that way again, injured or worse.

If they'd hurt Calvin, I would zap them, then I would beat them. Fear and fury competed for dominance inside me. I decided, at the moment, it was probably safest to side with fury.

I found the back door unlocked, so I threw it open and charged recklessly inside. A tiny voice told me I should have called for help before barging into the situation, but I wasn't going to leave Calvin alone in there.

My dramatic entrance into the workshop, stun gun held high and ready to blast the first goon I saw, went entirely unappreciated. Nobody was in the room.

The safe and the money were down in the basement.

I didn't hear Hunter barking, and that worried me, too. The bloodhound would probably not get aggressive in a home-invasion situation—he was more likely to hide his droopy head under the nearest sofa—but they might have shot him anyway.

I listened carefully as I crept down through the very no-frills concrete stairwell that connects the three floors of the buildings, but I didn't hear anything. Putting my ear to the door didn't reveal anything, either.

I sighed, then raised my stun and burst through in another dramatic entrance, ready for a fight, expecting to dodge bullets.

Again, nobody and nothing. The big safe was closed, but there was no sign of Calvin. On the bright side, there was no blood or signs of a struggle. Maybe, hopefully, things hadn't reached that point. I certainly didn't care about the missing money as long as they'd left Calvin unharmed.

I checked the store rooms and closets, but didn't find anything. Back on the first floor, I looked out into the lobby, but nobody was there.

The door to Calvin's office was closed.

I crept up to it, trying to move in the way that cats and ninjas do, making no sound. I'm not sure I was successful. I put my ear to the door and listened.

Voices. Low, murmuring.

Time for dramatic entrance number three. I flung the door open and leaped into the room, raising my stun gun, ready to zap anyone who stood in my way. For maximum effect, I screamed at the top of my lungs, hopefully startling the intruders and slowing their response time. It was a nice little stress-breaker for me, too.

I landed in the middle of the cluttered office, just inches from Calvin's desk. His walls were lined with bookshelves bowed under by the weight of everything: bundles of old paranormal journals and tabloids, arcane texts on the occult, obtuse texts on parapsychology and ESP. More of them were heaped around the floor. I was lucky I didn't crash into any of it.

Calvin sat behind his desk, eyebrows raised at how I'd chosen to enter his office. Hunter, on the carpet beside him, lifted his head just a little in acknowledgment of my presence, then resumed his one-eyed nap.

Two other people sat across from Calvin. One was a severe, pinched-looking older woman, gray hair, maybe in her sixties. She wore a peach suit that was no match for the sour set of her mouth and the glittering cat-green of her eyes. It was as if the Wicked Witch of the West had tried to pass herself off as a human resources person at some mid-size American corporation.

Beside her sat a younger man, maybe a couple years older than me, dressed in an actual three-piece suit—I'm not that attuned to fashion, but I know lavishly expensive clothes when I see them. His dark amber eyes looked me over, taking me in.

Everybody in the room was perfectly calm and relaxed. Except me, of course. I'd just come running through the door screaming, a stun gun crackling in my hand.

"Don't shoot," the young man said, and his smooth English accent caught me off-guard. "We surrender."

"What's going on here?" I asked, looking among the three of them.

"I should ask you the same," Calvin said, turning and rolling toward me, concern in his eyes. "You like you lost a fight with a grizzly bear."

"Don't change the subject," I said. I glanced at the severe old woman and the quietly smiling man. "Who are they? Why have they been watching us?" My gaze shifted to the table, where I saw a lot of very unfamiliar paperwork plus a few glossy brochures. A company name stood out, its logo at the top of every page.

PARANORMAL SYSTEMS, INC. The logo was a triangle encircled by a tilted ring that made me think of Saturn. The symbol was familiar to me. I'd definitely seen it somewhere before.

"They're from a company called Paranormal Systems," Calvin said.

"My sharply honed detective skills are picking up on that," I said, gesturing at the brochures.

The English-sounding guy stood up and extended his hand. His closely trimmed hair was midnight black, his eyes a sky blue. He wasn't tall and broad-shouldered like Michael, but he exuded some kind of strength and power. I might have even found him attractive, if I hadn't also disliked and distrusted him on sight.

"Nicholas Blake," he said. "Or Nick. Most people skip the second and third syllables. You must be Eleanor Jordan, lead investigator."

"You would know, since you've been spying on me," I said, shaking his hand. Weird electric tingling. I felt like his eyes were looking through mine. His expression reminded me of Jacob, when he was focused on the spirit world, scooping up impressions. I pulled away quickly.

"Sorry about that, Miss Jordan. It's standard procedure during the assessment period," he said.

"During the...?" I asked.

"With me is Octavia Lancashire, our general director." He presented me to the older woman, who nodded very slightly as she looked me over, but she let Nick do all the talking. He seemed to slip into some kind of sales-presentation mode. "Like your agency, we identify and remove spectral entities for our clients. We have offices in Baltimore, Philadelphia, Providence, and several other cities."

"None in the UK, though?"

"We are one-hundred percent all-American," he said in his polished Oxford accent. "Wave the flag, have a hot dog with crisps.

Aside from our branches in England and Wales, of course."

"Right," I said. I noticed Calvin was being completely silent. "And you're here because..."

"Just a general assessment of the region," he said. "We're curious as to what sort of activity you have down here and what your approach has been."

"They want to buy the agency from me," Calvin said.

"What?" I did my best not to scream the word at him, or to look as horrified as I felt. "No. That can't...you're not going to do that, are you, Calvin?"

"We are just in the early stages of a friendly dialogue," Nick said, smiling a little more. The lie detector in my brain was pinging off the charts. "Nothing serious. We've not even made a formal offer. This is our first conversation with Mr. Eckhart."

"Does this mean you're done following me around?" I asked.

"I am sorry, once again. As I said, just an assessment of the degree of activity, really, and your methods."

"Uh-huh." I nodded, trying to look calm and collected, like my world wasn't crumbling around me.

"Naturally, an acquisition would bring a substantial investment on our end," he said. "This agency could be providing entity-removal services to the entire region. Atlanta, Augusta, Charleston--"

"We already do," I said. "That's my job."

"And we would obviously want an experienced investigator like yourself on our team," he said. Just the way he said *team* made me ill. "Ghost removal, however, is just one of our multi-tiered suite of services."

"How many tiers does our suite of services have?" I asked Calvin, who only replied with a brief, humorless smile.

"I'm sensing just a little tension in the room," Nick said, and I raised my eyebrows at him. *Ya think?* "I propose we break for now and pick up our conversation later. Unless Mr. Eckhart has any additional questions for us?"

"Good idea," Calvin said. "Let's have a break."

"I hope we've given you something to think about." Nick offered his arm to the older lady and helped her stand, though she didn't seem at all fragile to me. Her face remained stern as she looked at me. I wouldn't say she radiated grandmotherly warmth. If she ever baked cookies, they'd probably be laced with broken glass and arsenic.

"You certainly have." Calvin accepted a handshake from Nick, then from the very bubbly and chatty Octavia Lancashire.

"It was a pleasure to make your acquaintance, Mr. Eckhart." she told him, her raspy voice low and measured. I've heard murderous ghosts with sweeter voices.

"You, too, ma'am," he replied. "Let me walk y'all out."

Nick turned to me with another smile and handshake, which I reluctantly accepted.

"I hope we can speak again soon," he said. "It's so rare to meet anyone who can chat about the work."

"You're a ghost hunter?" I asked him.

"A ghostjacker, they call us at home." He smiled, and I noticed he hadn't let go of my hand. His dark eyes again seemed to look through me, reminding me of Jacob.

"Are you a psychic?" I asked him.

"We're all a little psychic," he said, releasing me and really trying to turn on the charm with his smile. "People, animals...probably plants, too, if we found a way to test them for it."

"It sort of feels like you're dodging the question," I said.

"I would say it feels as though you knew the answer before you asked," he said. "Until next time, Miss Jordan."

I wanted to tell him that only telemarketers called me that, but I didn't want him to mistake it as an invitation to get more friendly and familiar with me. So I just raised my hand and waved for him to leave, as if he were standing much too far away for me to reply.

While Calvin escorted his guests to the front door, I remained in the office alone, looking over the papers from Paranormal Systems, Inc. I recognized them a little more now—I'd skimmed past their internet ads several times, probably because of my own ultra-weird search history.

I sat down to read. The paperwork was full of alluring headings like DUE DILIGENCE PROCEDURES and OPERATIONAL ASSESSMENT. The slick brochure featured four people, two men and two women, in black coveralls, the first coveralls I've ever seen with built-in turtlenecks. Their uniforms featured the letters PSI in bold red, along with the triangle-plus-Saturn-ring logo, and they each wielded a piece of gear: a parabolic microphone, an ionometer, a tactical flashlight, a sleek silver video camera whose shape suggested a gun. They were young, beautiful, smiling, happy, and probably models and not actual paranormal investigators. Their suntans alone gave that away.

"So that was crazy," I said when Calvin returned to the office. "When were you going to tell us about it?"

"They only just made contact," he said. "I was curious what they had to say."

"You wouldn't do that, though, would you?" I asked. "Sell the company to those strangers?"

He didn't say anything, just quietly looked at the papers on his desk, like they were the keys to some prison where he was trapped. Which made me his jailer, I guess. Trying to keep him here.

"What is going on with you?" I asked. As withdrawn as he'd been, talking about officially retiring from work, I knew something major was on his mind. I could think of a hundred terrible things that could be happening, several of them involving major terminal illnesses, all kinds of nightmare scenarios. I would have preferred to deal with just one, the real one.

"I know about their company," he said. "There's training I can't provide you, Ellie. They have corporate retreats with classes and workshops. Hey, it's a free trip to Saratoga Springs."

"Did you really just say 'corporate retreats' and expect me to take it as a positive?" I asked. I held up the brochure. "Would I have to wear coveralls? Really? Because I'm saving up for a new leather jacket, and if you're going to make me wear coveralls, I'd rather spend it on a new microwave."

"You'd probably make more money, too," he said. "Heaven knows you deserve it. And, unlike me, they know how to turn a profit."

"Yeah, no kidding." I opened the brochure and showed it to him. "*Identification and removal of spirits, poltergeists, presences, and other dark entities.*"

"The same thing we do," Calvin said.

"*Spirit communication*," I continued. "*Séances – individual or small group. Guided ghost-hunting expeditions. Courses in metaphysics and paranormal investigation. Psychic testing and training. Meditation, yoga, and tantra to enhance psychic sensitivity.* Calvin. Calvin! I am *not* teaching yoga classes."

"I'm sure you wouldn't have to do that," he said. "They don't offer it at every location."

"Why are you doing this to me?"

"I haven't done anything. They haven't made an offer. They may not, especially now that we've established my lead investigator is hostile to them. So there goes my retirement money, if there was any."

"I'm...really sorry. You shouldn't retire, though. I want to work for you, not Cruella De Vil and Jude Law over there. Holding séances and encouraging people to contact the dead? It's like they're trying to stir up dangerous ghosts. Or they're complete frauds."

"They aren't fraudulent," he said. "Just distasteful."

"Then why sell to them?"

He sighed. "All I've done was listen to them. We can discuss it later after I've actually had time to think."

"If it's about the money--" I pointed toward the basement and the safe full of cash.

"It's not about the money. Leave it alone."

"Then why--"

"I said *leave it*." Calvin's jaw clenched slightly, which is the equivalent of a major show of fury from him.

"You've got it pretty good right now," I said. "Stacey and I do most of the fieldwork, you can sit here and watch *Matlock* with Hunter, just make an occasional phone call or do some research...by the way, did you get a chance—"

"James McCoyle robbed a train in California in 1883," Calvin said. "Gold. Six months later, he was apprehended by an investigator from the Pinkerton Detective Agency, but gave him the slip while on a train to Chicago. That Pinkerton detective was fired over the incident. His name was Angus Kroeller."

"So, wait." I was caught off-guard by the sudden change of subject. Maybe he thought he could distract me with juicy details about the current case. For the moment, he was right. "How big of a coincidence would it be for Kroeller and McCoyle to run into each other in 1902, about twenty years later, during another train robbery thousands of miles away?"

"Very big," Calvin said. "At that time, McCoyle hadn't

committed a robbery in ten years. He was retired. Something brought him out of retirement."

"You think McCoyle wanted revenge against Kroeller?" I asked.

"Why would he want revenge against the detective who was incompetent enough to let him escape? Seems like he'd want to buy the man a drink, if anything."

"Then Kroeller, the railroad cop, wanted revenge against James McCoyle," I said. "But how did he lure McCoyle into doing it?"

"A beautiful young redhead might be an effective lure for a middle-aged man," Calvin said. "That and the promise of a big, easy score. Maggie Fannon must have been a double agent, secretly working for Kroeller. She would have approached McCoyle, gained his trust, and proposed the robbery to him."

"It seems pretty elaborate for a revenge killing," I said.

"This way, Kroeller gets to kill McCoyle in the line of duty, which is more easily explained than, say, shooting him in the back outside a tavern some night," Calvin said. "And he gains a share of the stolen money, or all of it if he intended to double-cross Maggie."

"So he tracked her down, killed her, took her half of the money...and then what did he do with it? Did the railroad ever investigate him as a possible robbery suspect? His job was to protect the crew, the passengers, and the money, and he failed at all three."

"I wouldn't be surprised if they suspended or fired him," Calvin said. "I haven't tracked down that information, if it's out there to be found. The Lower Atlantic Railway has been absorbed by multiple acquisitions since then. I wouldn't be surprised if their records were entirely lost by now. They didn't have much time to investigate him, anyway. I did eventually track down a death notice for him. He died three weeks after the robbery, one week after Maggie's death in New Orleans."

"No. So there's a *sixth* person involved in the robbery? What happened to that half of the money?"

"I don't know about the money—it would again be useful to locate some of the old rail company records. You forgot to ask how he died."

"How did he die?"

"Infections and complications arising from a gunshot wound to the leg," he said. "At the home of a doctor in Kansas City."

"But he went to a hospital in Savannah right after the

shooting."

"Let's imagine the situation. He has just robbed his employer. He might already be suspended, fired, or under investigation himself. His accomplice has disappeared with all the money."

"So he doesn't convalesce until he heals," I said. "He leaves the hospital as soon as he can manage—maybe sneaks out at night, if he's under suspicion—and sets out to track down Maggie. It takes him two weeks to catch up with her in New Orleans. He might have put a lot of strain on the wound. But ultimately he died from..." I stood up so fast that the office chair rolled away behind me. Light bulbs were popping on all over my brain. "That's what we need to do."

"Die of lead poisoning and gangrene?" Calvin asked.

"Not part of my plan, but we need to get to work. I'm going to call Stacey and make some coffee."

"I might be of more help if you shared any details of this sudden fantastic idea of yours," Calvin said.

"We can start by seeing how many working floodlights we have in the storeroom," I said. My phone was already dialing Stacey.

"What?" she answered drowsily, and her voice immediately made me picture her with droopy eyes, her short blond hair sticking up around her.

"Get up," I said. "We have a train to catch."

"Huh? When?"

"In about ten hours."

"So I can sleep for seven or eight more--"

"We have to get to work now," I said. "Come over to the office."

"You're an awful boss," Stacey said with a yawn, then she hung up.

Chapter Twenty-Two

I called Michael while I waited for Stacey to arrive. He was at work, but he seemed relaxed and free to talk, so I guess he had no urgent fires to put out, real or metaphorical.

"Let me guess," he said. "You finally have a night off and you want to head to Tybee Island for plantains and salsa and a walk on the beach. That works for me, too."

"Long walks on the beach, huh?"

"And snuggling quietly by the fire. Have you not even read my online dating profile?"

"No fires," I said, a little too quickly. Pyrophobia is not a form of insanity if you ask me. It's totally rational. "I want to ask you a favor, but it's not a big deal if you're busy."

"You want to eat at Gerald's Pig and Shrimp instead of North Beach? Okay, but there's no deck on the ocean there."

"As tempting as that sounds, I have to round up a posse of ghosts tonight."

"Your date ideas are always more exciting than mine. Next time I'll invite you to a monster truck show, with one of those big robot dinosaurs that crush cars."

"If it works, I really will have a few nights off. But we're doing the long walk on the beach and not the monster truck thing."

"Maybe we'll do both."

"What I need you to do sounds pretty simple, but it's also the most dangerous job." That wasn't strictly true, but if he knew my whole plan, he might not be so willing to wait half a mile away and might try to stop me altogether. "It's as easy as jump-starting a car, but then you have to get out of the way, and I mean far out of the way, really fast."

"What happens if I don't?"

"Um...splat," I said. "But you'll be fine."

"Unless I'm splat."

"Exactly. Want to back out? I can probably find someone else."

"Will I get to see the ghost train you were talking about?" he asked.

"That's what you'll be dodging."

"I'm there."

After loading the van, Stacey and I stopped by a theatrical supply outlet before driving over to the Town Village community. We pulled a little bit of a *Smokey and the Bandit* routine, with me driving ahead in my Camaro and scoping the streets for Cecil Nobson and his patrolling golf car. We didn't want any questions or interference from the man with the local police department on speed dial. We planned our routes to avoid his hidden spy cameras, since Stacey had determined where each one was located.

We parked at the dead end at the back of the neighborhood, where the high scrub pines along the undeveloped road conveniently helped conceal us from view as we unloaded the van and hiked back to the old rail tracks.

Stacey looked at me like I was crazy when I described what I wanted her to do, but she went to work with the lights and wires. We'd brought two generators, one for each side of the track, so that no wires would lie directly in the path of the ghost train. This set-up was one reason we'd had to get to work early. Well, early afternoon, which is early for us.

We made our preparations throughout the afternoon, testing as we went.

By nightfall, I was ready to get things rolling. We had to return to the McCoyle gang's hideout house, but we had to park on another street and make our way over by foot to avoid the spycams of Captain Neighborhood Watch.

Reaching the fence, we stopped and looked up at the house, as forbidding as a block of black ice, radiating coolness into the warm night. The Weather Channel predicted rain later, but I hoped to be done with our work before then.

"So this is definitely our plan?" Stacey asked, frowning up at the house with worry obvious on her face. "I didn't, like, misunderstand it or anything?"

"This is it," I said.

I took a deep breath and led the way through the wooden gate, which let out its usual rusty squeal.

My sense of foreboding grew as we approached the back door, and I hoped I wasn't about to get us killed.

I had to pick the lock all over again. Then we pushed into the cold, heavy air of the dark living room.

I clicked on my flashlight since it was the only way to see, but kept it pointed at the floor to avoid threatening the ghosts with it. Stacey had her light drawn and ready in case she needed it.

Footsteps creaked ahead, maybe the ghosts responding to our entrance. I saw nothing there.

From my jacket pocket, I drew out a thick stack of faded green cash. I shook it gently as we walked, dropping a bill here, a bill there, like Hansel and Gretel, if Gretel had used twenty-dollar notes from the National Exchange Bank of Augusta instead of breadcrumbs.

Stacey and I ascended the stairs, both of us trying to look tough and stoic when the house around us inspired nothing but fear. I would have felt safer if Michael or Jacob were with us, but I didn't want to put them in danger. Besides, a smaller team can make a faster exit if things get hairy.

We passed through the loft and down the hall, avoiding the huge drop on the side. You didn't have to be psychic to feel the heavy, dark presence in the house, and the epicenter of it lay dead ahead, in the master bedroom.

I kept dropping money as we went.

The master suite was pitch black, despite its pair of giant windows. They'd gone completely opaque—even shining my light directly at the glass panes revealed nothing of the world outside.

It was freezing and growing difficult to breathe, just as it had the previous night. I heard a low male voice murmuring in one corner, near the walk-in closet where I'd received my bashing. Turning my light toward it revealed nothing but wood and dust.

The feeling in the room was tense, and I knew they would attack if we didn't move fast. Even then, they still might attack, and we would have to do our best to avoid getting killed.

I had some hope that things might go the other way, though.

Standing in the middle of the room, I loosened my grip on the banknotes and shook them faster, spreading them around in a way that reminded me of the times I'd helped my dad shake fresh pine straw over the tree islands in the yard, back when I had a yard and a dad.

The bills drifted slowly to the floor, landing all over the place, with a soft patting sound like falling snow.

Then I dropped several gold coins, and they let out a heavy ringing tone as they struck the floorboards. I couldn't help wincing as some of them rolled out of sight. Four or five hundred bucks each, Jacob had said. And I'd just scattered ten or twenty thousand dollars' worth of antique currency all over the floor.

If this failed to get their attention, I'd be very annoyed.

Beside me, Stacey poured a pint of cheapo whiskey into a wooden bowl. The bandit ghosts often smelled of whiskey, so I thought a nice libation of it couldn't hurt. Maybe it would help establish a somewhat friendlier tone than our previous encounter, or at least keep them curious enough to wait and see what we did next.

"James McCoyle," I said. "Sean O'Reilly, Liam O'Reilly. I have something to tell you." I felt weirdly like Maggie Fannon must have more than a century ago, trying to recruit these rough men into a plot. "The railroad detective Angus Kroeller drew all of you into a trap. He killed all three of you. He planned it that way."

At the mention of Kroeller's name, the room grew even colder. A dark mass formed in front of me, the outline of a man in a hat, possibly the same one I'd seen the night before.

"McCoyle," I said, and the apparition became a little clearer. Ghost-cloth still covered his face, and his skin still looked old and decayed, but at least his colorless eyes were present so I wasn't in the unnerving position of staring into his skull-sockets again. "You may not know it, but you killed Kroeller, too. When you plugged him in the leg, he ended up dying from it. That gives you power over him.

"There's only one train out of here," I said, speaking louder, a little more confident now that they didn't seem intent on my immediate death. Throwing money at people can go a long way toward improving their opinion of you. "Kroeller controls the train, doesn't he? And as long as he does, everybody's trapped. You and the passengers. But we can take it back from him. We can do it together. And there's more of this cash when you're done. What do you say? Money? Revenge? Do these things move you?"

McCoyle's apparition grew sharper, though still dark, most of his body hidden in shadows my flashlight couldn't penetrate.

He spoke a word. His voice was a rough, inhuman whisper that made me think of a match head rubbing coarsely against a rough striking strip.

The word was *"Maggie."*

"Maggie, sure," I said, and didn't really know where to go from there. Did he know Maggie had been conspiring against him? I didn't want to complicate things with too much information. Ghosts are intensely backward-looking, so it can be difficult or impossible for them to learn new things. I figured, if nothing else, McCoyle knew Kroeller had killed him and might be interested in revenge.

The intense glow of hate in his pale eyes indicated I might be right. Either that, or all that hate was just for me, intruding on his territory and getting all up in his business.

"Maggie walks by the tracks," I said. "Are you looking for her?"

He continued staring at me.

"Will you help me get the drop on Kroeller?" I asked.

After a long pause, three more words came, at the very low end of my range of hearing.

"Kroeller will die."

"Great! Just what I was saying. Do we have a deal?"

The apparition looked at me for another long, drawn-out moment, slowly turning my guts to icy slush, and then faded.

A cold wind arose in the room, though the windows were sealed tight. The old banknotes blew along like tumbleweeds, rustling against each other. Coins lifted up on their sides and began to roll.

The money swept away into the closet, clinking as it dropped away into the stash at the back.

"Meet us at the train tracks," I said to the bandits, though I couldn't see them anymore. "Before the train comes. Don't be late."

I nodded at Stacey, and we left without another word—not running, but definitely not taking our time as we left that house of the dead.

"Do you really think they'll help us?" she whispered as we made our way across lawns and between houses back to my car.

"Worth a try," I said. "They took our money and didn't attack us. Those might be good signs."

"I'm sure they'd take the money either way," Stacey said. "Good luck trying to spend it down at the saloon and the general store, guys."

Before we returned to the dead-end street, I stopped at our clients' house. A light was still on upstairs, but I didn't alert them to our presence.

I walked around to the back of their fence. With a boxcutter, I scratched through all the symbols carved by the ghosts. Then I drew new ones, indicating "nothing happening" as well as "keep away." We needed the stamper out by the tracks tonight, so we couldn't leave a trap set for the banshee. Hopefully this would discourage her, or any other spirits, from visiting while we were away.

If things went as I hoped, the banshee would be gone after tonight. We were killing a dozen birds with one stone.

I called Michael to let him know we were ready. I waited for him at the dead-end street, leaning against the van and watching the woods around me. The night was extremely quiet.

Michael finally arrived, in his ancient and badly scratched Wrangler, and I explained his job to him.

"Are you serious?" was his response.

"Don't hook it up until you hear from us," I said, while Stacey passed him a brick-sized military-surplus walkie-talkie from the van.

"Cell phones aren't cool enough, huh?" he asked.

"Not reliable enough," I said. "We have to get the timing right, but we won't know when the train's coming until it's here."

"And what are you going to be doing?"

"Trainspotting," I said. "Maybe trying to help a couple of

ghosts hitch a ride."

"Be careful," he said.

I hugged him, and he took the opportunity to kiss me, which was nice.

"You be careful, too," I said. "Move fast and get out of the way."

Stacey hugged him before he left, seeming to linger against him a few seconds longer than I would have strictly preferred, but maybe that was my imagination. I had bigger fish to fry tonight. Sharks, even.

After he drove away, Stacey and I hiked again down the narrow path through the dark woods. At the railroad track, we triple-checked our gear, then we waited. Stacey had wisely brought a pair of camping chairs for us. She's spent a lot more time than I have sitting around in the woods doing nothing.

"I feel like we should have a campfire," Stacey said.

"Probably not a great idea." I glanced upward at the dense, leafy canopy that formed the tunnel shape over the tracks.

"Should we sing?"

"I know you're kidding," I replied, and she shrugged.

"I'm in position, over," Michael said over the walkie-talkie.

"Ten-four, what's your twenty?" Stacey asked, while I reached out to take it from her. "Ten-twenty-three, Ellie's taking the horn." Ten-twenty-three means *stand by*, in the sort of radio code that Stacey usually made fun of.

"How's it look over there? Do you think you can set it up?" I asked him.

"Yeah...I guess I can run them under the fence. It's going to take a few minutes."

"Thanks, Michael. Be careful. Don't forget to watch for the real trains, too."

We waited, and the hour grew later. The temperature in the tunnel dropped slowly but steadily over time, and the air seemed to grow tense, as if packed with static electricity. I heard occasional murmuring in the woods, and the crunching of a leaf or breaking of a stick, like people creeping through behind me.

"Shouldn't we have done something about the real locomotive?" Stacey asked, speaking just above a whisper in the cold silence. "Over at the museum? I guess the museum probably wouldn't let us."

"I'm not sure the ghost train has much connection to the physical locomotive that inspired it," I said. "The train is the focus because that's what all the ghosts have in common, since most of the people would have been strangers to each other. It's compiled from all their memories. For the passengers, it represents the way out, maybe the way to move on altogether. Kroeller doesn't want them to leave—doesn't want his own dark secrets to get out, maybe—and so he's keeping them off the train. He's controlling the train and not letting it stop, not letting it pick up the passengers."

"So the ghost train's like...symbolic?" Stacey asked.

"Of the passengers' desire to leave and his desire to keep them here."

"Then what about—"

"Shh." I gestured at what I'd seen down the track—a red ember of light, drifting slowly in our direction. Maggie Fannon was out walking, and last time we'd seen her, the ghost train hadn't been far behind. She'd come from the direction of the river and the plantation ruins.

I put on my thermals and watched the pale blue shape of Maggie approach, carrying her icy-cold light.

"Maggie Fannon," I said, moving closer to the tracks. It's *so* much easier to get their attention once you know their names. "Is the train coming?"

She stopped walking and seemed to look at me, though I could only see suggestions of her form on the thermal.

"Angus Kroeller controls the train, doesn't he?" I asked. "And he betrayed you. Left you dead in a cheap hotel room. Did you love him?"

Maggie's cold form stood unmoving for a moment, then advanced on me in an eyeblink. I reached for my flashlight to defend myself, but she was much too fast. I could feel the anger radiating from her.

A sudden pressure squeezed inside my chest, as if an ice-cold hand had seized my heart, stopping it from beating. You've seen *Temple of Doom*. I gasped and swayed on my feet.

Then it stopped, and I stood in the middle of the tracks, alone. A red glass lantern hung from my hand, burning brightly, casting an infernal glow around me. I wore an alluring red dress with puffy silk around the sleeves and a heavily brocaded bust. The body inside it was not my own.

Maggie. I'd thought she was killing me—and maybe she was—but she was also shoving her memories into my head. For a ghost, that seems to be easier than creating a series of auditory apparitions to simulate a speaking voice.

As Maggie, I walked along the same stretch of tracks, but they were not nearly so rusted out and overgrown. A wide streak of night sky was visible overhead, ragged at the edges from oak and pine limbs just starting to claim the empty space above the disused track.

In front of me waited the junction with the main north-south line. The old spur line on which I walked hadn't yet been truncated, sealed with a fence, and forgotten. All of that still lay in the future.

I stood a few feet away from the junction and lifted my lantern high as the bright glow of a train's headlight approaches. The ground rumbled as it grew closer. I swung the lantern, drawing my long red hair in front of me to hide my face, hoping the engineer would be too distracted by my dress to remember anything else.

A high metallic screech filled the night, and clouds of sparks flew from the train's wheels. The engineer, seeing my emergency lantern, had thrown the brakes, stopping for me.

Across the main line, the O'Reilly brothers and James McCoyle hid in the woods. When the train stops, and while the engineer looks my way, the three of them will climb up behind him with their guns drawn.

I became aware of guilt and conflict swelling inside me. I never meant to have feelings for McCoyle, never meant to see him as anything but a mark for Kroeller's scheme, a pawn to help carry out the heist Kroeller and I had planned.

Maggie's thoughts were bleeding deep into mine, our identities blending. I tried to get some psychological distance from her within our shared head.

McCoyle was fifteen years older than Maggie, but he had a confidence that put her at ease, and an adventurous attitude that made her feel alive. He was filled with colorful stories about life on the Western frontier, and he wanted Maggie to escape to the Caribbean with him after the robbery, where they would supposedly buy a sailboat and a house by the beach. Sounded pretty idyllic.

She was supposed to be working with Kroeller, but she detested him. The man was a piggish worm, and he kept trying to take her to bed, an idea that revolted her. She wanted no more contact with him.

She'd been wrestling with how to tell McCoyle the truth and still keep him. So far, she couldn't see a way, but she had to act before Kroeller came to track them down at the safehouse in Florida. Maggie had stupidly given that information to Kroeller before deciding she was going to turn against him and stay with McCoyle.

The train ground to a halt, the locomotive passing me by several feet before it fully stopped.

"Bonsoir, mademoiselle." The engineer looked down on me as though from a balcony, tipping his hat. Malcolm Dumont, I remembered from the file, French Canadian. His enormous mustache puffed and waved in the wind. "What troubles the beautiful lady this evening? Malcolm is here now, you need cry no more."

He shouted, and I heard a struggle as McCoyle and the O'Reilly brothers arrived from behind him.

I took a man's hat and a black bandanna from the canvas satchel by my feet, tying the cloth over my face before I draw out my revolver.

The memories flickered forward.

In short order, the engineer, brakeman, and conductor were tied up and kneeling on the tracks in front of the huge grill of the cowcatcher. Then the gang hunched in the woods as McCoyle dynamited the safe in the cargo car.

The mood among the robbers was jubilant as McCoyle and I unloaded the cash and coins. The O'Reilly brothers entered the passenger car with their revolvers raised to shake out some extra money.

There was no railroad cop on duty. Kroeller has assured me of that. The lack of security around the big bank transfer made the heist appealing to everyone involved. I told McCoyle and the others that I had the information from a friend who worked for the railroad and just wanted a cut, which was true enough, as far as it went.

Inexplicably, the passenger car erupted and ripped open along one side, flames exploding through the shattered windows. A chorus of screams rose from the fire.

Gunshots thundered near the front of the train. Clutching my canvas bag full of cash, I backed away toward the woods until I could see the front of the locomotive.

The lanky blond brakeman and the doughy, middle-aged conductor laid across the cowcatcher, shot dead. The flirtatious engineer knelt, his arms still bound, his eyes wide with horror. He looked me right in the eyes, and then his forehead erupted as the bullet took him from behind. He drops across one of the rails, dead eyes still gazing at me, at the woman who'd flagged him down and brought him to his death.

The shooter stepped over the dead engineer, toward McCoyle and me. It's Kroeller. Why was he here? That wasn't part of the plan.

With rising horror, I understood. He'd killed a slew of people tonight. His intention must have been to kill McCoyle and me, too, and keep the money for himself. I'd taken him for a corrupt but generally bland and mediocre man, but there was a monster inside him.

I seized McCoyle's arm and screamed for him to run.

We escaped into the woods, each carrying a satchel of stolen money, but Kroeller chased us.

The memories became fast and confused. We traded gunshots with Kroeller in the dark woods. I desperately wanted to kill Kroeller, because then I would never have to tell McCoyle the truth.

McCoyle shot Kroeller in the leg, and the railroad cop collapsed to the ground, crying out in pain. McCoyle's was hit, too. He had two dying words for me: "Run. Live."

Then I ran alone, lugging two canvas satchels. I followed the old disused spur line toward the river, racing along the ties, simply because it was the fastest path away from the burning train. I was spattered with my dead lover's blood, and I had nowhere to go and nobody left on my side.

Chapter Twenty-Three

"Ellie!" Stacey shouted, gripping my elbows and giving me a hard shake. "Earth to Ellie. Come in, Ellie."

"Huh?" I blinked, trying to disentangle my thoughts and my general sense of self from Maggie's memories. "How long was I out?"

"Like ten, twenty seconds? Your face went all pale. I took off your thermals."

"Did I miss the train?"

"No train yet." Stacey eased me toward one of the camping chairs.

"Maggie answered my question. She was definitely *not* in love with Kroeller." I stopped walking and looked around. "Where is she?"

Stacey checked through the thermals. "Not seeing her right now."

"I was hoping she'd help me flag down the train," I said.

"Well, it's not like she's very good at it, right?" Stacey asked.

"Still..." I shrugged. Stacey had a point. "The last time the engineer stopped for her, he ended up dead on the tracks."

"Maybe it's better if she hides, then," Stacey said.

"Is it just me, or is it freezing?" I checked the Mel Meter. Not only was the temperature sinking fast, into the thirties already, but the electromagnetic readings were off the charts.

Up and down the tracks, I heard whispers and soft footsteps. I didn't want to point my flashlight at them, but I felt the rising anticipation, and I could imagine the shades gathering alongside the tracks for yet another try at catching the next train out of here, as they must have been doing for years and years.

A low, cold wind blew along the tracks, rustling through the high weeds like an invisible creature.

"Here it comes," I whispered.

"Ellie, are you sure about this?" Stacey asked.

"When am I sure about anything?" I stepped into the middle of the tracks, facing into the wind. It blew westward, from the direction of the river, carrying more frigid air with it.

"Ready?" Stacey asked. She stood with remote controls in her hands. The stamper was beside her, with a trap loaded and ready to go, and then we'd set up three more, which Stacey or I would have to seal by hand if their sensors detected a ghost. All four traps had a heap of old banknotes at the bottom. Stacey hadn't lit the traps yet, because we didn't want to distract the bandit ghosts too early.

"Hold steady..." The wind picked up, roaring faster. A rattling sound rumbled along the tracks. "Now, Stacey!"

"Finally!" Stacey said, clicking buttons.

The array of floodlights switched on, arranged in rows on either side of the tracks, all of them pointed at the approaching sound. Intense red light flooded the tunnel, like the glow of a volcano, painting everything a hellish hue. We'd picked up red stage light gels and placed them on every floodlight we had.

The skeletal old train became visible, still many yards away from me but approaching fast, rattling and belching black smoke. The train apparition was a good sign that we'd gotten the driver's attention, I thought.

"Dumont! Malcolm Dumont!" I called out, holding my ground as the rattletrap train chugged toward me, wheezing out black smoke, plates of metal hanging loose from the locomotive like the scales of a dying lizard. I figured the engineer's name might help, or at least couldn't hurt.

The train rolled on, directly toward me, with no obvious sign of stopping.

I raised the ghost cannon, which had also been fitted with a gel, and fired it up, casting a massive beam of blinding red light directly into the locomotive cab. There was no way the engineer could ignore it, I hoped. I waved it side to side, the old train lantern signal for "stop."

Through the cracked windshield, I saw the engineer. Dumont did not resemble the eyebrow-waggling French-Canadian I'd seen in Maggie Fannon's aggressively overshared memory. His face was a sooty, grimy skull under his engineer's hat.

I shouted the engineer's name again, three times, as if I were summoning him in a mirror at a slumber party.

I can't say whether it was the ghost cannon or his name that did it, but a long, awful peal screeched through the night. If you've ever heard the sickening crunch of a bad car crash, imagine that, but stretching on and on and never seeming to end.

Jets of growing sparks sprayed out from the wheels on either side. My pulse quickened as the front of the locomotive filled my view. Greasy trails of flame erupted all over the locomotive, letting off thick, acrid black smoke, as it screamed and rattled its way to a halt in front of me. Blistering heat rippled off the enormous black grill, which was taller than I was.

I coughed at the eruption of greasy smoke. My eyes watered. I switched off the ghost cannon and tried to shake the red gel filter away from the lens, but the gel had melted in the intense light and welded itself to the glass. It was going to take some time to clean it up, and I had none at the moment.

He emerged from the smoke, a bulldog of a man, the kind who might have thick muscles under all the fat. His face was piggish, as far as I could see through its layer of soot and ash. He wore a derby hat, tie, overcoat, and a cigar smoldered in his fingers.

I recognized Angus Kroeller from Maggie's memory.

"You should really quit those things," I said, nodding at the cigar, which smelled like burning engine grease instead of tobacco. "They can kill you."

"Get off my line," he said. His voice was powerfully clear for an auditory apparition. Usually they're incoherent, or low and scratchy like McCoyle's three words had been. His voice was almost human.

"You can let it go, Kroeller," I said. "Everybody knows the truth. You killed everyone. You were the mastermind of the robbery. You wanted revenge against McCoyle, because he escaped your custody on the way to Chicago, humiliated you and got you fired. Why not make some cash along the way? You could pin the crime on the man who wrecked your career, then kill him and his whole gang to cover it up."

Kroeller's small, angry eyes glared at me from their sooty pockets of flab.

"Kroeller, there' s one thing I don't understand. Why kill so many innocent people? Just a little added fun?"

His lips peeled back, revealing crooked yellow teeth.

Then he punched me in the nose.

It was a classic straight punch, his body squaring up in a practiced boxing stance. The crack of the impact echoed in my skull, and my head rocked back on my neck.

I dropped my head forward to face him again, and blood ran from left nostril into my lips. I stared at him in a confused haze of pain. The apparition was blurry—no way to tell whether he was losing focus or I was.

"Really?" I managed to say. "You just punch a girl like that? No preamble, no—"

He hit me again, and I felt blood gush from my other nostril as I staggered backward. My boot heel caught on a railroad tie, sending me off-balance. I stumbled and tried not to fall, while Kroeller advanced on me through the smoke.

"Quit." That low, striking-match voice was beyond creepy, but right now I welcomed McCoyle's ghost like a guardian angel. Okay, I still would have preferred an actual guardian angel, but I don't have the phone numbers of any.

Shadows emerged from the smoke, surrounding Kroeller—three men with their dark hat brims pulled low, pale rags hiding their faces. I could almost hear a steel guitar lick in the background as the bandits arrived.

Thick, acrid smoke made me close my eyes, but I heard the muttering, and then the shouting.

It occurred to me that right next to this fight was not the ideal place to stand, so I hurried off the tracks and went to join Stacey by the stamper. The smoke grew thinner as I walked away from the train, but I was coughing pretty badly. It felt like I was breathing in the rancid dark fumes of a tire fire.

"What happened?" Stacey touched my face, looking at the twin streams of blood from my nose.

"I sneezed too hard," I said.

"Look." She pointed at the train cars, which I hadn't been able to see behind the smoking, burning locomotive.

Among the shreds and hulls of the damaged cars, illuminated by our array of red lights, I could see pale shapes. I thought I recognized Maggie, and Sophia, too, in a blurry white dress and hat. Maggie had switched off her lantern. She didn't need it now that the train had, at last, stopped and allowed them to board. I could no longer see Kroeller or the three robbers anywhere.

"It would be pretty convenient if the train pulled away now," I said.

"Let's do it." Stacey threw the switches on her remote controls, and all the red floodlights died. We could still see by the light of the greasy fires that burned here and there on the locomotive, and also by the red glow from its partially ruptured coal-car, where some of the stored coal was smoldering.

I pointed a tactical flashlight at the locomotive cab. A small gel on the lens turned the white light into a cool, glowing green beam. I moved it up and down in a vertical line, the signal for "go."

The train did not go.

"Come on, Dumont," I muttered, waving the light more frantically at the cab. "Come *on*."

The train led out a metallic shudder and lurched as the brakes released.

"Yes," I whispered, urging him on. "Yes, yes...."

The train shrieked out a loud, piercing whistle as it began to roll forward, a little faster than honey dripping from a cold jar. I winced. I would've preferred if the engineer hadn't gone out of his way to alert Kroeller that the train was moving again.

I radioed Michael and told him to proceed.

Stacey and I watched the train inch forward, very gradually gaining speed, smoke drifting out all around it. All the pale apparitions who'd boarded seemed to stir in response to the movement.

The stamper let out its unmistakable pneumatic hiss, followed by the thunk of the trap lid slamming into place. Something had tripped the automatic sensors.

"What the hay? We didn't even light that yet," Stacey said, stepping over to inspect it.

"Check the others," I said. I looked into one of the three open cylindrical traps standing in a row near the stamper. The sensors on the inside indicated that the temperature was ten degrees lower than the ambient outdoor temperature, and the EMF meter was spiking between four and five milligaus.

Even without the candles lit to lure the ghosts, something had found its way into the trap and was currently wallowing in the loose leaves of old money piled at the bottom. If this trap had been loaded into a stamper, it would have closed automatically, too.

I slammed the lid in place by hand and smacked it with my fist a few times, making sure it was sealed tight. Stacey was doing the same thing next to me.

We both looked into the single remaining trap. Forty-eight degrees, the same as the temperature outside it, at least since the arrival of the train had burned away some of the deep freeze caused by the presence of so many ghosts. No electromagnetic activity.

"Three out of four ain't bad," Stacey said.

"It depends on which three we caught,"

"Maybe the brothers are sharing a trap?"

"I don't think so." I glanced up at the tracks and immediately grabbed Stacey's arm, probably digging a little too hard with my fingers. "Look," I whispered.

The rusty, smoking skeleton of the train chugged away down the tunnel, its loose wheels rattling as it gained more speed. The fire-stained caboose, its ceiling steeply dented and partially collapsed, was almost out of sight.

That wasn't the problem.

In the middle of the tracks, where I'd just been standing, the soot-stained figure of Angus Kroeller glared after the train as it rolled away.

He turned toward us, his small eye sockets black and smoking, literally smoldering with anger. Then he turned back toward the train and vanished.

"What?" Stacey whispered. "Where is he?"

At the retreating tail of the train, oil lanterns cast a dull red glow, the equivalent of tail lights for the benefit of other trains, I supposed.

Kroeller stood on the platform at the back of the caboose, his hands in his pockets, looking back at us as the train pulled out of sight. I couldn't see his face, but I could imagine his sooty, piggish smirk.

I took off after the train, following the fading red lights westward through the leafy tunnel.

"Ellie!" Stacey shouted. "What are you doing?"

"I have to catch that train!" I shouted without looking back. I ran along the center of the tracks, stepping high and trying not to stumble in the thick weeds.

"I thought we *wanted* the train to take the ghosts...Ellie!"

I didn't slow down a bit, because the train was still picking up speed. I had it in sight again, but I couldn't spare another second. Kroeller was already gone from the caboose platform, away inside the train.

I put on speed, sprinting as fast as my non-jogger legs could carry me, my lips curling into a determined snarl. I drew close to the rusty, rattling grab rail at the back of the caboose. It looked like it was missing a critical support bolt or three, but I didn't see any other options.

The train whistled and put on another blast of speed just as I leaped for the railing. I grabbed on, but the railing let out a terrible, rusty squawk and wobbled under my weight, on the verge of breaking loose and dropping me onto the wooden rail ties rushing by below.

I managed to climb up onto the platform without dying, though. Stacey jogged along behind the train, but it was really building up steam now, and the gap between us widened until she was lost in the smoke and darkness. My tiny head start had made all the difference.

The caboose's rear door was missing. My flashlight revealed the ruins of the caboose, but the partially collapsed roof blocked most of my view ahead. The remains of the second-story cupola, from which the brakeman keeps watch over the train, had fallen inside along with the roof.

I ducked around and under it, and I smelled fire, never a comforting scent to me. I emerged from around the twisted metal in a hunched, wobbling position that made me feel vulnerable.

In the front corner of the car, a tall figure knelt at a wood-burning stove bolted into the wall. I could see him in profile, his hair long, blond, and wispy, his colorless eyes entranced by the flames as he fed more wood into stove. I recognized him as the brakeman from Maggie's memory.

He didn't immediately react to me, so I crept around him, hoping to reach the forward platform of the caboose without any incident.

As I reached the empty doorway at the front of the caboose, the tall blond man flickered into place in front of me, blocking my path. I could see the gaping bullet wound in the center of his forehead, the rivulets of blood dried into veins of black crust all over his face.

"Lars Olsen," I said, recalling the brakeman's name. "Don't engage the rear brakes, no matter what they tell you."

"I do as the engineer says," he replied, his voice a flat monotone, as if reciting memorized text.

"Just *don't*. Hey, your stove's spilling hot coals everywhere." I pointed, and when he turned, I darted out through the door. I hopped the gap to the next car, where the rear door was loose, swinging from one hinge. I pushed my way in, bracing for a fight.

I was also trying to do the math in my head. If a train leaves point A heading west at thirty or forty miles an hour and climbing, and the tracks end in half a mile, how long until Ellie gets splattered? What if the train is a ghostly apparition that could disappear at any moment, leaving its sole living passenger hurtling through the air until she lands on a rusty iron rail? Show your work.

I figured I had no more than one or two minutes to stop Kroeller before he reached the engineer in the locomotive. Then he would order the train stopped, evict all the unwanted passengers who'd boarded, and we'd be right back where we began, the ghosts trapped along this old length of track and feeding on our clients and their neighbors. We'd never get rid of the banshee before Ember's baby was born.

The door opened onto a strange scene lit by an oil lantern on a corner hook. The car was made of weathered old boards, though it hadn't looked that way from the outside. The furniture—a round table, two wooden chairs, and a single bed—was not bolted down, so it was scattered in disarray around the car.

I hurried toward the far door of the railroad car, which was closed and blocked by the bed, as if someone had meant to leave the furniture in my way.

Someone lay on the bed. I slowed as I saw Maggie in her red dress, her skin bleach-white, her glassy eyes staring up at the ceiling. She lay cold and stiff with rigor mortis, her fingers clenched around the unlit red-glassed lantern hanging over the edge of the bed beside her, swaying with the motion of the train.

Maggie's ghost was reenacting her death. Maybe Kroeller's ghost had encountered her and "killed" her again, restaging the murder.

The bed was heavy, and I had to lean against the headboard and shove with all the strength in my legs and back to move it away from the door. Time was running out fast. I didn't even have time to try and do the algebra.

I heaved the bed across the warped wooden floorboards, which seemed like they belonged in an old building, maybe the boarding house where Maggie had died a hundred years ago. As soon as it was clear of the door, I pushed my way out, flashlight drawn.

The next car was the ruins of a boxcar—only one side of it still remained, full of holes and rust, with remnants of metal roof still clinging to it along the top.

Sophia sat in the shadows here, her knees against her chest, her white dress filthy with soot. Her face and arm were badly charred. She rocked slowly, weeping to herself. I wished I had time to stay and try to comfort her, but I kept moving.

Next was a passenger car, very probably a replica of the one where the dynamite went off, judging by the rows of blackened seats and the floor-to-ceiling rupture in one side of the car. All the windows were shattered. An acrid smell hung in the air, as if I'd just missed the explosion.

My flashlight found the bodies of a man in a top hat and a woman in a puffy-sleeved dress sitting in one row, both of them cut by shrapnel and burned. Like Maggie, they looked like they'd been dead for at least a day or two, their corpses stiff and their blood dried. I passed more bodies, one man sitting alone, two women badly burned and unrecognizable, who I assumed were the two sisters that had been traveling together.

A hand seized my arm as I passed them. The closer of the two sisters, the one in the aisle seat, had grabbed me. Her charred head turned toward me, creaking on dried and shriveled muscles and tendons, and her empty sockets seemed to stare me in the eyes. A few long strands of brown hair clung to the sides of her head, brushing against the singed shreds of her traveling dress, through which I could see bone and scorched flesh.

She opened her jaws, leaning closer, and I shined my flashlight into her face. It didn't seem to deter her.

"How long until we reach Charleston?" she asked, her voice low and smoky. "We've been waiting a long time."

"Uh, soon," I said, pulling away from her with a strong shake of my arm.

I ran out the next door. An empty flatbed car lay ahead. At the far end of it, Kroeller jumped onto the ladder to the coal car ahead, which sat just behind the locomotive. He was almost to the engineer, who would no doubt stop the train at his command.

If I survived all of this, I thought, I was going to take McCoyle's ghost out of his trap and do my best to give him a good thrashing. If the bandits had done their job, Kroeller's ghost would be defeated, not running wild and ruining my night. Never trust a gang of thieves, dead or alive.

I bolted across the platform as Kroeller went over the top. He walked right onto the heap of smoldering coal in the ruptured coal car.

The ladder was unpleasantly warm to the touch and grew hotter as I ascended. By the time I reached the top, it was blistering hot. Kroeller crossed the bed of smoking coals as if the heat and smoke didn't bother him at all.

From this vantage, I could see where the tracks ended just a few feet ahead.

Michael had clamped a copper wire at the end of each rail, then run them under the old wooden gate and out to the modern steel line. I'd needed somebody to sit out there and wait until the last possible minute to connect the wires. Jacob had said that certain spirits roamed freely around the railways, so I was worried that plugging our isolated little track into the continental rail system might bring in all kinds of unknown entities and energies to interfere with our work.

Those wires were meant to serve as paths for the ghosts' energy to follow, allowing them to escape the haunted stretch of track and move out into the world, and hopefully even to move on to the next one.

If the wires didn't work, then I supposed we were all about to come to a crashing halt.

"Kroeller!" I shouted, since that seemed like the best way to distract him, but the dead railroad cop didn't look back. He just kept strolling across the smoldering heap of coal. I jabbed my flashlight at him, but the beam wasn't much of a weapon with all the smoke and soot in the air. It can't stop a powerful and determined ghost from doing what he wants, anyway, if his intention is strong enough.

I did the only thing I could think of, and it was stupid: I shot off to a running start over the smoking coal, my boots hissing in the heat, and then I jumped on him.

This is rarely a good idea, because while ghosts may look solid, they usually aren't. They're made of energy, and they can hit, bite, and scratch all they want, while all you can do is punch and kick at empty air.

Still, I'd encountered a couple of ghosts who became dense enough to fight, and certainly the apparition of the train itself was so strong I could walk on it. I thought there was a small chance that this time, in this situation, the ghost I was attacking might have a solid form, too.

I was wrong. I passed right through and sprawled across smoldering black coal, howling in pain at the heat. It was awful, but I'm not sure this ghost coal was quite as hot as actual burning coal, or I might have been incinerated fairly quickly.

I pushed up onto my hands and knees just before Kroeller's beefy arm locked around my throat, choking me with the crook of his elbow. His coat sleeve was scratchy, stiff wool against my skin.

He had a sulfurous smell, like rotten eggs, and it was so strong I probably would have gagged if I were able to breathe at all.

His other arm locked around my waist, and his heavy gut rested on the small of my back, his lifeless weight pinning me in place. His flesh was corpse-cold, and he wasn't breathing at all.

"You're mine," he whispered. His thick, clammy lips brushed my ear.

The locomotive reached the end of the line, and chunks of wood rained down as we bashed through the old gate and fence. The entire train slung from side to side, writhing like a snake, but it managed to keep rolling forward on the copper conducting wires. We broke free of the woods and hurtled toward the bright steel tracks gleaming under the moonlight.

I struggled enough to make Kroeller tighten his grip on me. I wanted to make sure he forgot about reaching the locomotive and stopping the train, at least for a few more seconds.

The locomotive reached the steel rails and made a ninety-degree turn that would have been impossible for a real train to execute. The coal car whipped around after it, and the sudden lateral shearing motion sent me flying out through the ruptured side of the car, high into the space above the two sets of steel tracks, the northbound line and the southbound line.

The impossibly sharp turn probably wouldn't have affected Kroeller's ghost at all if he hadn't been clinging so tightly to me. He dropped off the train with me, his cold, soft weight pressed against my back. I hoped separating Kroeller from the train would give all the ghosts onboard their chance to escape his control forever.

As we fell, I had time to see the ghost train transform upon reaching the steel tracks, shifting into something like a mirage of fire, a locomotive and cars sculpted entirely of thin, transparent sheets of pure flame.

Then it rocketed away along the track, streaking north like a comet, melting into a shapeless cloud of flame that instantly vanished into the distance.

I had about half a second to appreciate my good fortune in escaping the train before that had happened. Then I belly-flopped into the gravel railbed with Kroeller's immense clammy weight on my back, and everything went dark.

Chapter Twenty-Four

My eyes opened. I found myself sitting in a softly upholstered seat, gently rocking from side to side, sunlight warm on my skin.

I occupied a seat near the middle of an oak-paneled passenger car, which looked almost luxurious, the wooden seat frames intricately carved with little floral designs. All the wood was polished and gleaming, the deeply piled red carpet below my feet completely spotless. I didn't see a grain of dirt or dust anywhere, not even motes dancing in the generous shafts of sunlight pouring in through the windows.

Nobody else was there. As I got moving, standing and stepping out into the parquet-floored aisle, I noticed the accumulated aches, pains, bruises, and burns from all that I'd suffered in the past few days had vanished. I felt healed, revitalized, light as a feather and full of happy energy. I should have been covered in coal dust, but it was as if I'd had a long soak in the tub. My hair was clean and brushed, there wasn't a speck of dirt on my skin or even under my fingernails, and even my clothes looked as if they'd been washed, dried, and ironed, though I'm not somebody who typically irons her jeans or her denim jacket.

"Hello?" I asked the empty car, as if I expected somebody to pop up between the vacant rows and explain where I was, how I'd arrived there, and what I should do next.

I walked down the aisle toward the door at the back. My polished boots clicked on polished wood. The situation seemed beyond surreal, but I didn't feel like I was dreaming. I pushed open the door and stepped through into the next car.

It looked like the one I'd just left, but several scattered passengers occupied the seats. I saw the man in the top hat with his wife, both of them having tea and cookies and gazing out the window. The wife glanced at me and smiled. All their injuries were gone, and they appeared to be brimming with good health and cheer.

Then I saw the two sisters, no longer burned or injured, clad in lovely dresses and traveling hats piled with feathers. The young man who worked for the pecan concern in Albany gave me a languid smile as I passed him. He was also fully restored.

I found Sophia a few rows ahead, sitting alone. She no longer looked like a suffering burn victim nor a pale and weeping banshee. She was a healthy, vibrant little girl in a white dress and a matching hat adorned with a bouquet of colorful cloth flowers, held in place by a lace chinstrap. Her black hair had been gathered up in little coils. She smiled at me, radiant in the sunlight from the window.

"Don't you look pretty?" I sat down beside her.

"Thank you," she replied. "You look pretty, too."

I laughed. I'd felt on the verge of laughing since my eyes had opened, as if the happy feelings bubbling up from inside me just had to be given expression.

"I don't know about that," I said. "Do you know where this train's going?"

"It's taking us home," she said. "I can't wait to see my mother and father again. I miss them so much."

"I miss mine, too."

"They'll be waiting for you at the station." She stated this with supreme confidence and another big smile. "They'll be pleased to see you."

I wanted to cry with happiness. At the same time, I was starting to feel uneasy. Something was not right.

"I think I'm on the wrong train," I said. Outside the window, the landscape was unfamiliar but beautiful, with gently rolling grass hills dotted with wildflowers. Shimmering streams ran between the hills, collecting in sparkling blue ponds in the little valleys.

Iridescent lights swirled in the sky, like a glowing daytime aurora from horizon to horizon. I couldn't see the sun, but every inch of the sky was radiant.

The uneasy feeling nagged at me again. As marvelous as everything around me seemed, I didn't want to be here.

"I have to go back," I told Sophia.

She squeezed my hand as if to comfort me, in a very mature gesture for a little girl. I ran to the back of the car, which led me into the apple-red caboose. The middle-aged conductor sat at his desk, poring over a ledger. He tipped his hat at me.

I glanced up the ladder to the small second level of the caboose, the cupola, where the tall blond brakeman sat in his chair, surrounded by windows glowing with golden light, keeping his watch over the train.

Then I reached the caboose's rear platform. The gleaming rails stretched away through the idyllic pastoral landscape, a pair of unswerving straight lines that vanished out of sight at the horizon, where the green grass and gentle streams met the prismatic sky. I despaired at the long distance we'd already traveled.

"It's so hard to let go," a voice said beside me. Maggie Fannon had appeared on the platform, looking fully restored and revitalized like the others, her red hair styled in what looked like some very labor-intensive looped braids. Her red dress fluttered in the warm wind, which was redolent with the scent of blooming flowers. I noticed a sound like chimes ringing in the background. They seemed to originate from the rippling colors in the sky above.

"I can't. I still have so much work to do," I said. I looked down at the polished ironwood railroad ties whisking away at high speed from beneath the train, nestled in spotless white gravel. The gravel, on closer inspection, actually appeared to be made of tens of thousand of white seashells, not one of them broken.

"If you choose to return, be careful," she said. "There are others trying to deceive you."

"I know," I said, and it felt like I understood exactly what she meant, though I couldn't put my finger on it.

"May I ask one favor?" She took my hand as if we were old friends.

"Of course."

"Be lenient with James McCoyle," she said, and I remembered she'd fallen for the train robber in the course of deceiving him. "His soul is tarnished, but not lost."

"I can do that." I stepped to the very edge of the platform, between the rails and looked downward. I took a deep breath, which made me aware that I hadn't actually been breathing at all. I didn't seem to need it.

Very reluctantly, I leaned out over the blur of the railroad ties, holding onto a railing with each hand.

Then, with an act of will, I released the railings and let myself fall, towards the pain and suffering waiting below.

Chapter Twenty-Five

The pain was everywhere. I gradually became aware that my battered, beaten, scalded body was being dragged over rough earth. Rocks. Gravel. Everything was dark.

My head struck a solid metal rail. Beefy, clammy fingers lifted my head and set it down on the strip of cold metal, as if I were meant to use it as a pillow.

In the distance, a light pierced the darkness. It swelled, growing closer. The steel rail beneath my head trembled and hummed.

Gradually, my aching, slow-moving brain put these pieces together and sorted out that I was lying on railroad tracks with a train roaring toward me through the night.

As soon as I tried to move, I discovered that coils of wire bound my hands and feet, the copper wire Michael had used to connect the old tracks with the new. Something as heavy as a bear, but with a less pleasant odor, pressed down on me from above, squishing me into place under its weight. Its breath reeked like rotten eggs.

Kroeller. He'd tied me up, and now he would hold me here until the oncoming train splattered me across the tracks.

"Please," I whispered. "Let me go."

I could feel his body jiggle on top of mine, and he panted and snorted, as if laughing under his breath. The headlamp of the locomotive swelled as it charged toward me. The engineer should have seen me by now, should have applied his brakes or at least blown his horn. Kroeller was somehow hiding me, making me hard to see.

"Come on," I urged. "I can't die like this. Not in a silent-movie cliché."

Kroeller had no response to that. He'd almost certainly never seen a movie in his life, and so had no idea that the mustache-twirling melodrama villain tying a girl to the train tracks had already been done to death. He probably thought he was being quite original by killing me this way.

"Ellie!" a voice shouted. Michael. The hero arriving just in time to save the girl, I hoped.

"Over here," I rasped out as loud as I could, which wasn't very loud at all. His footsteps rushed toward me, though.

"You have to get up!" he shouted.

"Oh, wow, I hadn't thought of that," I said. "Help me!"

His hands were already on me, trying to raise me from the rails. He let out a grunt.

"You're too heavy," he said, which I thought was a little less than chivalrous, but I didn't have time to snark at the moment. The train showed no signs of slowing as it rolled toward my face. The headlight lit the area around us like a football stadium on game night, but the engineer apparently saw nothing at all.

In that bright light, I saw Michael's face as he leaned over me. One eye was swollen shut and purple, and the cheek below it was bruised. I felt awful for him. Whatever he'd suffered was completely my fault. He could have been at home tonight, repairing one of his antique automaton clocks, or out playing tennis or basketball with his sister (they're both *very* aggressive about sports, which is a little hilarious but can also get old...). Instead, I'd asked him for a favor and he'd gotten his face bashed in for it. I tend to have that effect on people around me. It's why I don't have many friends. I usually don't ask them to help me with my work, of course, but sometimes evil things follow me home. And mostly people think I'm crazy if I tell them too much about what I do. I've tried being vague and pretending my PI work is all boring insurance-related stuff, but then they learn the truth and just think I'm crazy *and* a liar. You can't win.

The train bore down on me, the tracks shuddering hard beneath my head as the metal wheel, the one that was on its way to crush my skull, loomed larger and larger.

"Michael," I said. "My iPod."

Fortunately, he knew me well enough to understand. He found the device mounted on my belt next to the little portable speaker. I hoped they hadn't been broken by my adventures tonight.

The last song I'd queued up, "Oh Happy Day" performed by Aretha Franklin, blasted out from my waistline.

When weaponizing holy music, no matter from what tradition, it's always best to crop out the slow parts. Facing a horde of angry and murderous ghosts, you can't afford to wait for build-up or interludes. You have to skip right to the crescendos.

So it was a soaring choir of voices that blasted from the speaker, creating a cone of bright, energized sound that, hopefully, would weaken Kroeller's hold on me for a moment.

The weight vanished. Kroeller stood in the gravel between the northbound and southbound lines, glaring. Michael lifted me from the tracks and carried me back and away, getting us off to the side of the tracks just before the freight train reached me. An enormous gust of wind sent us staggering backward, but he kept his balance.

Michael lowered me to my feet, keeping an arm around my waist to support me. He said something as I looked up at him, but I had no hope of hearing over the train thundering past us a few feet away.

I touched his face, showing concern for his injury. He kissed my fingers, then he untied my hands and feet, carefully not to cut me with the copper wire.

Kroeller remained standing on the other side of the train—I glimpsed him in the gaps between cars and over the occasional empty flatbed. His hatred for me was plain on his face. I'd helped uncover his secrets, released his captives, left him with nothing.

Michael pointed away down the tracks. We could start toward his car, probably parked by the same Chet's Discount Grocery where I'd left the van the other night, and get ourselves a head start on Kroeller in case he decided to come after us. He was a wounded and angry predator now.

I shook my head. I wasn't sure how I'd get rid of Kroeller now, but running away and giving him time to recover wasn't going to help.

We stood our ground and waited as the train passed us by.

As it rolled away, Kroeller continued to stare at us, as if he wasn't completely sure what to do next, either.

"Let it go, Kroeller," I said. "You have no secrets left. You can move on. You don't belong here anymore."

Kroeller looked at me for a long moment...then his face twisted into a hoggish snarl, and he advanced, balling his hands into fists.

Michael edged in front of me, ready to take one on the chin for my honor. I drew my flashlight. It was all I had. The music blaring from my speaker wasn't stopping him now.

The moment Kroeller stepped onto the tracks in order to cross over them, a deep rumbling sounded from farther up the line.

Darkness spread toward us from the north, blotting out stars, trees, and earth, turning everything around it solid black. The ground trembled as the darkness rushed toward us like a low stormcloud, or the shadow of the moon across the land as it eclipses the sun.

The tracks on which Kroeller stood seemed to change in the moonlight. The rails appeared to me as if they were made of the long bones of a gigantic primordial creature, laid end to end and bolted together. The ties, too, resembled the ribs of some great animal sunken one after another in the railbed, where the gravel had turned to smoldering coal. Taken together, the rails and ties seemed like the backbone of some unimaginably huge beast, its flesh having long since been burned to ash by the long bed of coals in which it lay.

As the darkness fell over us, I had only a quick impression of an immense mass racing by, scooping up Kroeller in its jaws. There was iron and smoke, but also pebbled gray skin heavy with soot, a spider-like row of black eyes, and plates and horns evoking a Jurassic monster. I could not tell you the overall shape of the thing, only that it was huge, far bigger than the train that had nearly flattened me, casting everything around it into deep shadow.

I am glad I didn't get a closer look at it. The horror might have been too much for a mortal brain to handle.

Then the shadowy thing was away down the tracks, moving the wrong way, southward on a northbound line. The steel tracks in its wake looked normal again, as if the great bones had only been a nightmarish mirage.

Kroeller was gone.

"Did you see that?" I whispered.

"I saw him disappear," Michael said. "Where did he go?"

"I don't know, but the trip there looks like hell," I said. "What happened to you? You look hurt."

"There was the debris from the exploding gate." Michael pointed at his swollen-shut eye. "I'm pretty sure I got sucker-punched by an invisible man, too. I never saw him coming."

"I'm so sorry I dragged you into this." I hugged, leaning against him—but lightly, in case he had more injuries. "I won't do it again."

"Don't make promises you can't keep."

"I'll *try* not to do it again."

"You look pretty banged up yourself."

"I should've chosen a safer line of work," I said. "Like cage-fighting with rabid hyenas."

I heard footsteps in the woods as something approached at high speed. I drew my flashlight and turned to look.

Stacey emerged at the end of tracks, panting, having sprinted half a mile to catch up with me.

"Hey," she said, catching her breath. She looked at the destroyed gate and fence, then at Michael and me with all our new injuries. "What did I miss?"

Chapter Twenty-Six

I spent that night at Michael's place. I didn't want to go home and lie alone in the dark for the rest of the night. I don't like that under the best of circumstances—I'd much rather sleep in the day, because I've encountered far too many spirits who prefer to do their harassing at night. I managed to kiss him a little before passing out, his muscular arm wrapped around me like a barrier to shield against all the evils of the world. It was a nice illusion.

The next day, after one of my too-frequent medical visits to make sure I hadn't sustained anything that was likely to kill me or require immediate surgery, I headed over to the office to speak with Calvin. I'd given Stacey the day off since we didn't have another client waiting for our help at the moment, unfortunately.

I started by letting him know we'd wrapped up the case, though I held back just a couple of details that I didn't feel comfortable sharing with anyone, like my time on the happy train with the ghosts. I'd been unconscious and having a bizarre dream, I told myself.

Calvin didn't bring up Paranormal Systems, Inc. at all, which I took as a bad sign—surely if he'd decided to dismiss their offer, he wouldn't mind telling me. So I had to ask him about it.

"You're not really going to sell the agency, are you?" I asked.

"I've looked into them," he said, sighing. "If we don't sell, they'll open a competing office somewhere nearby. Maybe Atlanta or Charleston, maybe right here in Savannah."

"So you're just going to give up without a fight? That doesn't sound like you. What aren't you telling me, Calvin?"

He was silent for a long moment while I waited for his response.

"I've been talking to my daughter," he said.

"Oh." That was my great and carefully thought-out response. I looked at the pictures on his desk—a smiling gap-toothed girl of three or four on Santa's lap, then onstage competing in a spelling bee at about age ten. Graduating from high school. Draped in a wedding gown, marrying some guy in a tuxedo. I couldn't remember the last time Calvin had mentioned her to me. "That's...good news, right? How is she?"

"She's going to have a baby," Calvin said.

My mouth actually dropped open at that.

Calvin had already been divorced when I'd met him eleven years earlier, just after the pyrokinetic ghost Anton Clay burned my house down and killed my parents. His wife had left around the time Calvin became the go-to homicide detective on the Savannah police force for cases involving the supernatural. Calvin's related study of the occult and ghost lore, as well as some of the nasty spectral entities that followed him home, had repeatedly upset her. His daughter had been five years old at the time. That meant she was about twenty-three today. As far as I knew, she hadn't spoken to her father in years, until now.

"Congratulations," I remembered to say. "You're going to be a grandfather."

He nodded. "That must be why she's reaching out to me. She hasn't said it in so many words, but I think she's ready for me to be part of her life."

"Are you planning to...visit her?" I knew Lori lived in Florida, hundreds of miles away.

Calvin looked at me and didn't say anything.

"You're not thinking about moving there, though? Right?" I

asked. He'd mentioned it before.

"I could be near my grandchild," he said. "They don't know if it's a boy or girl yet."

There was no way for me to reply to that. It obviously didn't feel right to discourage him from being closer to his family. I wanted Calvin around and needed his guidance and advice, but it was hard to argue that I needed him more than a newborn baby would. Then there was the whole specter of working for PSI and having to teach crystal-gazing meditation and lead inexperienced ghost tourists into haunted old buildings for their amusement. I didn't even want to think about that. The idea of Calvin leaving was bad enough.

"I could also retire and turn the agency over to you," he said. "Then I'd be leaving you in a difficult situation, with a larger company moving into the area and taking away business."

"And you'd never get the big payday of selling the company," I said. "Just a monthly trickle from whatever cases we land while you're away."

"That's not my biggest concern," he said. "I may look useless, but I can find other work. My concern is you. Stacey, too, but mostly you." His smile was a little wry. "My own daughter grew up far away from me, kept away by her mother. You grew up here. You're like another daughter to me."

I don't want to get too sappy here, but my eyes did sting a little at that. When I was fifteen, Calvin was the only one who really understood what had happened to my parents. When I talked about the man I'd seen in the house who was immune to fire—a strange, handsome, psychotic man in a silk cravat and tails, who'd tried to stop me as my dog led me out to safety—most people would have shoved me at the nearest psychiatrist and told him to stuff me with meds.

Calvin, who'd encountered his share of ghosts during his career of investigating questionable deaths around the city, took me seriously. He didn't say much about it then, but later contacted me with his research. Clay had burned down a nearby antebellum plantation house in a twisted lovers' murder-suicide, and his ghost had burned down five more houses over the years, including mine.

I'd forcibly apprenticed myself to him when I was a college freshman. Over time, as he taught me the ghost trade, he'd become something of a substitute for my lost father. I supposed I stood for the daughter missing from his life. We'd never really talked about this openly, but the feelings were there. On both sides, I now understood, not just on mine.

"I don't want you to leave," I said. There was nothing mature or wise there, not even a consideration of what was best for him, just me and my emotions.

Calvin looked away and cleared his throat.

"When we spoke about this before, you said you didn't feel ready to take over by yourself," he said. "With Paranormal Systems, you could work with other experienced ghost hunters. You'd access to the latest methods and technology. You'd be safer than if you try to go it alone."

"I'd rather take over by myself than work for them," I said. "Let's remember we still have a couple hundred thousand dollars' worth of cash in the safe downstairs. I say we get in touch with some coin traders and start the bidding. Then you can still get an apartment in Florida and travel back and forth. A week here, a week there. You wouldn't have to run the agency day to day, but you'd still be involved. You'd still be here for me." I gave him a hopeful smile, hiding how sick and scared I was feeling inside.

"That money was at the center of a major haunting," he said. "Kroeller, that psychopath, killed thirteen people over it."

"Why did he suddenly go all mass-murdery, anyway?"

"We can't know for sure. Maybe it wasn't so sudden, and he left bodies out in the desert that we don't know about. Or he saw the robbery as his chance to run wild, since he'd arranged for others to take the blame. In any case, it's not just blood money, it's ghost money. The repercussions of taking it and using it for our own benefit could be extremely negative. How would you like Kroeller's ghost stalking you for the rest of your life?"

I was pretty sure Kroeller wouldn't return anytime soon, considering how his final departure had unfolded, but I'd held back on telling Calvin about that, especially since Michael hadn't seen the great monster barreling down the tracks at all. Besides, who knows how the universe works? I certainly didn't want to risk summoning Kroeller.

"I don't think I'd like it," I said.

"Even if that doesn't happen, it could bring bad luck. Sell the old cash, use the proceeds to go on a lavish tropical vacation...and then your plane crashes, or you contract an exotic new virus."

"Do you really believe that?"

"The money is spiritually tainted." He shrugged.

"There must be some way to lift the taint off the money."

Calvin steepled his fingers in front of his face, slowly tapping his index fingers together. Thinking. He spoke again after a minute.

"You might be right," he said. "But you'll have to take a road trip."

"If I didn't take road trips with Stacey, how would I learn all the intricate details of Jason Momoa's dating life?"

"I have no idea who that is," Calvin said.

"Should I have referenced Errol Flynn?"

"How old do you think I am?"

"Douglas Fairbanks?"

Calvin scowled, but he was smiling a little, too.

"So where do we go to launder cursed money?" I asked.

Chapter Twenty-Seven

We had to settle the question of what to do with the three bandit ghosts we'd trapped. Dangerous ghosts are typically taken to a certain remote and long-abandoned cemetery in the Appalachians, where they are buried in their traps. Should they eventually escape their traps, they'll find themselves under the authority of the dead Reverend Mordecai Blake and his ghostly flock, as well as imprisoned by the graveyard walls.

Nicholas Blake, the young English man from Paranormal Systems had the same surname as the Reverend Blake, a snake-handler who'd drawn a minor cult-like following in the mountains about a century earlier. I wondered if they were related somehow.

Taking Maggie's special plea into consideration, I insisted we release McCoyle at the "nice" cemetery over in the abandoned western town of Goodwell, where we let the less dangerous ghosts roam free among the wildflowers and massive oaks. Removed from their original haunts, they might be able to reflect on their lives, accept their situation, and move on. If not, at least they're trapped far away from the living.

We didn't know of McCoyle killing anyone until the night of his final robbery, and even then, he'd only shot the mass-murdering Kroeller, who'd died of the infected injury weeks later. We released the O'Reilly brothers along with him, since we had even less information about them, and I definitely didn't want to make an entire separate trip to Reverend Blake's graveyard if I could avoid it.

After disposing of those ghosts, Stacey and I made another road trip the following day, in my car. It wasn't nearly as far—just to Charleston, South Carolina, a drive that takes one to two hours, depending on how fast your car is and how many highway patrol officers are around.

We parked on Broad Street in downtown Charleston, lined with stately old federal and neoclassical buildings housing assorted money-jugglers—banks, insurance and investment companies, and so on—and the sorts of steakhouses and pubs where bankers and lawyers apparently like to eat lunch. It was nestled in a part of town reminiscent of downtown Savannah, streets filled with lovely old mansions and gardens. It was a fairly haunted area, too–I'd been in the nearby neighborhoods a few times on different cases.

"Look at that." Stacey pointed up at the triangular pediment of the building as we approached it. A huge golden eagle perched above the doors, glinting in the sun. "That ices the cake, doesn't it?"

"What do you mean?"

"The building already looks like some ancient temple," she said. "But putting a giant golden animal on the front really drives it home. I feel like we're supposed to sacrifice a chicken on the way inside or something."

"That's one of the top thirty weirdest things you've ever said, Stacey. Okay—the Bank of Charleston was founded in 1836. That's where all the stolen money was supposed to go. In 1926, it merged with the National Bank of South Carolina, which was later acquired by Wachovia, which was acquired by—"

"Wells Fargo." Stacey pointed right in front of us, to one of the black and gold signs with the company's name mounted on the exterior of the building. "I'm guessing."

"The point is that this isn't just the same building where the cash shipment was supposed to go, it's the same institution, in continuous operation," I said. "We're lucky it still exists, or we'd just have to burn the money. If this doesn't go well for us, we'll still have to burn it."

"That's too bad. Well, they're going to call us crazy, but I guess it's worth a try."

We opened one of the glass front doors and walked inside. I carried the cash in an old briefcase I'd borrowed from Calvin, since it seemed like a less obtrusive thing to bring into a bank than a musty old leather satchel.

The interior was posh, built in an age which nobody skimped on marble, crown molding and hardwood.

A young man in a cardigan and glasses that were a little big for his face approached, smiling and greeting us. "I'm Dennis. What can I do for you today?"

"I was hoping to speak to the bank manager," I said.

"I'm sure I can help you," he replied with a big smile, which seemed a little more aimed at Stacey than me. Typical male. "Come on over and have a seat in my office."

The office turned out to be one of a cluster of cubicles with high glass walls, right out on the main floor. I doubted we would be sitting there very long, but I let him pull the seats out for us anyway. Very gentlemanly. I don't know if that's standard Wells Fargo procedure or if it had more to do with Stacey's charming smile.

"Now, what I can do for y'all today?" Dennis asked, dropping into his chair across from us. "Are we opening an account?"

"We're private investigators," I said. "In a recent case, we came across some property that was stolen on its way here, to the Bank of Charleston, in 1902."

"Did you say 1982?" he asked.

"No. Would you like to see it?"

"All right." He looked uncomfortable, out of his element, which was probably handling complaints and selling loans.

I placed the briefcase on the table, unlatched it, and raised the lid, revealing stacks and stacks of national bank notes.

He gaped at it, adjusted his glasses, and gaped again, then frowned and furrowed his brow. I could see him going through the same thought process we had when we'd found it—surprise at the amount of cash, then confusion as we'd realized how strange the money actually looked, with unfamiliar faces and prominently displayed city names.

"I'm, uh." He adjusted his glasses again. "I'm going to have to get the manager."

"Thank you," I said, closing the briefcase again.

Soon we found ourselves in the office of the bank manager, a woman in her fifties with a close-cropped haircut that fell just shy of a flattop. She had a sharp, no-nonsense look about her, from her sensible shoes to her sensible earrings, but she gaped a little as Stacey and I unloaded piles of long-lost bank notes onto her desk.

"I've only seen these in textbooks," she said, a little bit of wonder in her voice as she lifted a stack of National Bank of Atlanta notes, turning them in her fingers. "You're sure these are real?"

"We've had them examined by a numismatist," I said. Grant had put us in touch with an expert. "Obviously, you'll want to do the same."

"And you said this deposit was from...when?"

"1902. I don't have any of the paperwork for it, but it was definitely coming to this bank."

"It's going to take some time to find those records." She was looking at us like she'd decided we were pulling some kind of scam.

"Also, it's less than half the original deposit," I said. "One of the thieves got away with the other half." Some had also been used as bandit bait and was subsequently buried along with the ghosts, but I didn't see any reason to get into that. "There's twenty-two thousand, one hundred dollars, including some five-dollar coins." I jingled a cloth bag tied tight with a drawstring. "All of it meant for the Bank of Charleston."

"So you happened to run across all of this," she said. "You took it to an expert. And then you decided to just bring it on over to us? It seems like the last thing most people would do in your situation. Assuming this money is genuine and you had a numismatist examine it, you must know what it's really worth."

"Yes," I said. "And I agree, most people would sell it themselves, or keep it, or do anything but return it to its rightful owners. Our problem is that this isn't just money that was lost or stolen. Fourteen people died over it in one of the deadliest train robberies in history."

The bank manager continued watching me, waiting to see if I had a point, or what I expected to gain from the situation.

"Now, we did recover this at some difficulty," I said. "And, as you've said, most people wouldn't have brought it here at all. And half the money's already lost to history. So, what we would like, in payment for our services, is a portion of the recovered sum. Ten percent is a common finder's fee."

She raised an eyebrow, as if she'd finally seen the point of our scam. "You want me to write you a check for two thousand dollars? In exchange for this?" She gestured at the stacks of bills, probably deciding they were fake.

"No, thank you, ma'am," I said. "We'd actually like ten percent of the same money we brought in. That would be this amount." I patted a few stacks of currency that we'd place a couple of inches away from the others. Our proposed cut, with a face value of twenty-two hundred dollars, the bills hand-picked for us by Grant's numismatist. "If you could just give us this part, you can keep all the rest and we'll be on our way."

I could see she was a little puzzled. Any rational person would be.

"So you want me to give you back this portion of the cash that you discovered and chose to bring us in the first place..." She placed her own hand on the indicated stacks of bills, and I felt a little thrill. Maybe she was going for it. "And then leave the rest of this for us to deal with?"

"Exactly, yes, thank you," I said. "We wouldn't feel right keeping all of it for ourselves. This way, we've returned the lost money where it belongs, and you're just giving some back as a reward."

She still look puzzled, but she slid the stacks back toward me across the desk, probably just curious to see what we would do next.

"Thanks so much!" I hopped to my feet, and so did Stacey. I gathered up our share of bills and dropped them back into the briefcase. Completing the money's journey to the bank, according to Calvin, was the best way to clear any cursed energy from it. I handed the bank manager copies of several very old newspaper articles about the train robbery. "I'm sorry we don't have more information, but this should help you sort things out. They'll give you a date to start with, anyway."

"Thank you..." The manager looked from the blocky print of a 1902 newspaper to the rows of money on her desk, as if dazed and completely unsure what to make of the situation. Still, she'd accepted the cash and given us a portion of it.

I offered her a handshake to seal the deal, and she accepted it.

"I hope the rest of your day is great," I told the manager, while nudging to Stacey to move on. "The weather's so nice today."

"Yes..." She stood there, looking perplexed, then grabbed the telephone on her desk as we left the room.

"I can't believe that worked," Stacey whispered, which brought a glance from an elderly security guard.

"It was a fair deal," I said. "Calvin said once we return the money to the bank, any bad juju is discharged. It's the bank's discretion what to do with it at that point."

"What do we do with our cut?"

"I'm leaving that up to Calvin," I said, but I already had plans for a sturdy new leather jacket to protect me from the biters and scratchers. There's a reason people used to make armor out of leather, but never out of denim.

With that, the case was finally closed. We drove home along the coastal highway, salt wind in our hair. I felt the first cold hint of the coming fall, and I shivered. I kept the windows open anyway, as if to insist it was still summer.

Chapter Twenty-Eight

Tom and Ember were somewhat distracted with the hospital and the birth of their first child, Brayden Kozlow. Stacey and I visited them at home a few days later. As we sat in the living room, the little newborn yawned and slept in his mother's arms, swaddled in one of those ubiquitous baby blankets striped with pink and blue. Both parents looked exhausted, Tom unshaven, Ember's hair more wild and tangled than I'd ever seen it.

I gave them a quick rundown of the case, along with a written report, some CDs with images, sounds, and video we'd picked up along the way, and (ahem) our invoice. We'd made plenty from the old currency, discreetly sold to a coin dealer for about thirty thousand dollars, and that would keep the lights on at the agency for a few months. We take on a lot of clients who can't pay much, stuck in their haunted houses precisely because of financial reasons. But Tom drove a seventy-thousand-dollar Lexus, and I figure anybody who can afford to spend seventy thousand bucks on a car can afford to pay his ghost-removal bill.

I quietly hoped the little windfall from this case would change

Calvin's mind about selling the agency. He did give me more than enough of a bonus to buy a new jacket. Ember also gave me a box of pralines and mixed chocolates, so I was getting bonuses all over the place.

After some mutual recovery, Michael and I finally had our date —plantains and crab cakes by the ocean, followed by an actual long, starlit walk on the beach. Some things are cliché because they're true.

He said the guys at the firehouse had seen his black eye and accused him of having an abusive girlfriend. I promised myself not to ask for his help on future cases. It wasn't like he dragged me to fires and car accidents.

We talked about everything but ghosts. Our lost parents. His sister Melissa's carefully played ascent to captain of the soccer team. Which Muppet would win in a fight, Animal or Cookie Monster. I was strongly in the Cookie Monster camp, because when he wants something, he's relentless.

I did not talk about the strange otherwordly glimpses I'd seen, not to him or to anyone. The train rolling through the endless green landscape, under a sky made of color and music. The hellish monster that had finally snapped Kroeller in its jaws and taken him southward on rails made of bone. Nobody had seen these things but me, so the logical explanation was that they'd only happened in my mind.

Some part of me wanted to believe, though. It was tempting to believe that a little of the veil had been lifted, that I'd been given a glimpse of the strange inner workings of the soul and the cosmos. Or, as the man says, maybe it was just an undigested bit of beef, a blot of mustard, or a fragment of underdone potato.

Looking out on the visible universe high above the ocean, I thought it might be nicer to believe.

THE END

From the author

Thanks for continuing the story of Ellie and her mission to rid the world of unfriendly ghosts! I continue to enjoy writing them, so I'm glad to hear such a positive response from readers so far. If you're enjoying the series, I hope you'll consider taking time to recommend the books to someone who might like them or to rate it or review it at your favorite ebook retailer.

The fifth book should be out in August or September 2015! Sign up for my newsletter (link available at my website) to hear about new Ellie Jordan titles as soon as they come out. You'll immediately get a free ebook of short stories just for signing up.

If you'd like to get in touch me, here are my links:

Website (www.jlbryanbooks.com)
Facebook (J. L. Bryan's Books)
Twitter (@jlbryanbooks)
Email (info@jlbryanbooks.com)

Thanks for reading!

Made in the USA
Lexington, KY
20 October 2016